SEPARATE WORLDS, RISING SHADOWS

Terence S. McNamara

Inspiring Publishers
P.O. Box 159, Calwell, ACT Australia 2905
Email: publishaspg@gmail.com
http://www.inspiringpublishers.com

A catalogue record for this book is available from the National Library of Australia

National Library of Australia The Prepublication Data Service

Author: Terence S. McNamara
Title: Separate Worlds, Rising Shadows
Genre: Science Fiction

Paperback ISBN: 978-1-923449-24-4
Hardcover ISBN: 978-1-923449-52-7
eBook ISBN: 978-1-923449-25-1

DEDICATION:

To my work colleagues that allow me the time to write and
the encouragement to persist.

CHAPTER ONE

The Visitors

Tiberius Xander was tinkering in his workshop, housed within a large warehouse that sat on thirty acres of industrial land just outside Dallas, Texas. The old warehouse, the size of a football field, had forty-foot-high ceilings with a gantry crane running the entire length of the building. It was a cathedral of lost industrial endeavour—once a metal fabrication shop, now stripped bare to the concrete floors, abandoned like much of American manufacturing. Tiberius liked to look up at the rafters, imagining the history of the building and the revenants of the workers who had once laboured there.

Inside that building, Tiberius had constructed three sheds: an office, a small workshop, and a well-resourced computer room. Each shed was no more than ten feet high and approximately one hundred and fifty square feet, covered inside and out with whiteboards and plugboards filled with scribbles, ideas, and incomplete mathematical equations. The land had been left to him by his father and contained eight warehouses of various sizes spread across the property—only one of which was rented. The rental income was sufficient to cover maintenance expenses and rates for the entire property.

Tiberius was sixty-seven years old and had recently sold his highly successful investment consulting business for over eight million dollars. With both time to tinker and the money to do so, he immersed himself in projects of personal interest. His doctorate in mathematics, obtained in his twenties, had keenly informed the investment strategies he had sold to clients over the years. He had always worked hard, and that, in part, was why his marriage had failed ten years earlier; he now lived alone.

His daughter believed she had the right to blame him for the marriage breakdown, despite the time and effort he had invested in his family. Consequently, they had not spoken in several years. His son, having been caught up in one of Tiberius's more adventurous but ultimately failed business ventures, was also largely estranged. Tiberius had spent nearly thirty years in that marriage, devoting enormous time, money, and emotional resources to it and his family. He sometimes felt he had exhausted his entire reservoir of emotional energy fulfilling his parental responsibilities and enduring a loveless relationship with his wife for the final decade of their marriage. Extricating himself from that situation had been particularly draining.

In more reflective moments, he believed he had married too young—before he had fully understood himself, let alone the qualities he might seek in a partner. He considered himself an excellent father who had diligently raised his two children, both of whom had wanted for nothing. They were now successful in their respective careers, largely due to the education and support he had provided. Yet, he had nothing to show for it. He hadn't seen his four grandchildren in over six years.

The marriage breakdown had plunged him into deep depression, and his children's estrangement had only worsened his mental state. His son had disrespectfully berated him over the two hundred thousand dollars lost in the failed business venture—an investment Tiberius had suggested. Upon selling his company, Tiberius repaid the money, though he was under no obligation to do so; his son had been an adult when he made the investment. Even so, the repayment had not repaired their relationship.

His daughter's judgemental attitude was equally painful. She had sided with her mother, holding Tiberius solely responsible for the marriage's demise without ever hearing his side of the story. Tiberius believed the details of his marriage were a private matter between him and his ex-wife, and he refused to discuss them with his daughter.

In recent years, he had recovered his mental stability. Emerging from depression, he found himself more interested in product development than financial markets—perhaps drawn to the tangible nature of creation. He felt driven once more, believing his sixty-seven-year-old brain was sharper than ever. He had freed himself from the distractions that preoccupied younger men: the maintenance of a romantic relationships, the pursuit of sex, the accumulation of memorabilia tied to inconsequential events, and the constant chase for ego-driven gratification. Liberated from these burdens, he could now devote himself entirely to his new vocation.

That day, he was hunched over a lathe, fashioning a template for a product design he had dreamt up. The lathe was situated outside the workshop shed but still within the general warehouse area when two men walked in through the large open roller door.

"Can I help you, gentlemen?"

They were well-dressed, tall, and thin—both completely bald, with large dark eyes and an olive complexion. They were almost identical.

"It is us who can help you, Tiberius," one said casually, with an air of unexpected familiarity.

"We know each other?" Tiberius asked, pulling off his gloves and goggles.

"No, we know you, but you haven't had the pleasure. My name is Standart, and this is my colleague, Endurnard."

"Out-of-towners, judging by those names."

The two men exchanged glances before one of them responded, "Sure, out of town."

"So, how can you help me?"

"We noticed that you have many of the relevant pieces on your whiteboards over there but have yet to connect the dots on most of the key concepts."

"Pieces of what? You've been looking at my whiteboards?"

"We have done much research on you—personal research," one said. The other added, "Perhaps we could sit down and explain."

"I think you'd better. I have a shotgun to hand if you have anything weird in mind." Tiberius wanted them to know he had access to a weapon, as all good Texans do, but strangely, he did not feel threatened.

"Violence won't be required." One of them gestured towards the office, expecting they would sit there to discuss the matter. Tiberius complied.

"It might surprise you to know that we know a lot about you, Tiberius… and your work."

They all sat down in unison.

"Is that so? And why would that be?" Tiberius pulled a hanky from his pocket and wiped his glasses clean to get a better look at these men.

"We have decided it's time, and we needed a suitable person to participate in something of a mutual bargain—a project, if you will. We picked you."

"What project?"

"To move the technology of this planet forward. You went to the moon sixty years ago, and other than some advances in computing, you've done little since."

Tiberius had no response, other than puzzlement over why they said *you* and not *we*.

"We want to offer you a leg up, so to speak. By now, this species should have fully grasped ways to manage gravitational forces instead of using those ridiculously expensive and dirty rocket ships and motor cars. You should be conversant in shielding technology as it pertains to security and environmental management, and you should be better versed in nuclear fusion… and you shouldn't still be using those needles and scalpels."

The two looked at each other and grimaced in disgust.

"Most concerning is that we fear you will extinct yourself by annihilating the planet," Standart added, "before you get a grip on the technology needed to avoid such outcomes."

Tiberius was baffled, confused, and beginning to believe that these two were either pranksters or delusional.

"You see, technology *is* in fact the answer. You started to believe that at the beginning of the nineteenth century but abandoned the idea when you saw the potentially devastating effects of industrialisation and the pollution it generated. Then came your near-lethal dalliance with nuclear weapons. So, you started to believe that technology might be the enemy rather than the saviour. That belief became widespread, and combined with petty political squabbling, has left you intellectually stunted as a species."

"You continue to talk endlessly about clean air and climate change but do nothing—adding only an endless stream of verbiage coming from millions of climate *experts* who absorb enormous resources *researching it* and flying around the world in pollution-spewing aircraft to discuss it. Then, they proceed to do absolutely nothing technologically to fix it. You are only adding hot air to an already gaseous situation."

"Was that an attempt at humour?" Endurnard asked, his tone filled with apparent disdain.

"I can't disagree with what you're saying," Tiberius responded. "But to put a fine point on it—who the hell are you, and what are you doing in my office?"

"That is why we picked you, Tiberius. Of course, you agree—we knew you would. You not only have the brain capacity, even though most of it is unused, but you have also imagined many of the solutions about which we speak—some of which you have even made progress on in this very workshop, despite your handicaps. None of what we can teach you will be a surprise to you. That is what makes you unique. And believe me, we have looked at many candidates."

"It is, in fact, extremely important that what we impart to you is not a shock to your system—that you can rationalise the information as simply a progression in your currently embryonic understanding of such matters."

"Immensely important," Standart added. "To you, much of what we can show you already exists in your head, and has for many years—you just don't know how to convert it into reality. You are, in your own right, a genius, Tiberius, albeit unrecognised by your colleagues—or indeed, even by yourself."

"For us, that is also an important moral issue. We are not giving you anything you haven't already invented, at least in concept. You just need some help with the maths, and given the urgency, we thought we'd assist."

"Look, I think you should leave. Thanks for all the compliments and the offer to help, but I can take it from here. Perhaps you guys should go speak to Marvel Comics or something."

"This is too important to fob off."

"Sure—if it were real."

"It is real."

"I don't believe you. I think you need to leave and go get some counselling."

Tiberius stood. The visitors left as requested.

Tiberius woke suddenly from a sound sleep, sitting up in bed and exclaiming, "What the fuck!"

"We need more time," one of the two shadowy figures in his bedroom said.

Tiberius couldn't make them out—his vision was blurry. He hurriedly tried to get out of bed, but before he could react, he was quickly put back to sleep.

"Are you sure we don't want him to know what we are doing?" Standart asked.

"No, it would possibly send him mad. Aliens? Information downloads directly into his brain? He would never believe it, nor would he be able to rationalise it."

"Really? He's a bright guy. I would have thought we needed his consent to do this."

"We got his consent this afternoon."

"We got his agreement regarding our views on the state of the planet this afternoon—not an approval for this intervention."

"Look, no other species is aware of this planet... yet," Endurnard pressed with urgency. "We need to help them now, or they won't be ready for first contact. Besides, they are killing the planet. The need is urgent, Standart."

"Sure, some of the other developed planets, if they find Earth, may not be as helpful as we intend to be."

"Especially the Tracalonians."

"There's a scary thought. Time for this species to wake up, get moving, and stop sitting on their hands—technologically speaking."

"Stop spending time and money on bombs and bullshit, you mean."

"Very colourful," Standart critiqued.

"Thank you."

The visitors proceeded to discuss what they proposed to provide to Tiberius and the conditions under which they would offer it. They had him hooked up to a memory management and information download device.

The information they were in the process of downloading included full knowledge of how to manage gravitational forces— the systems and mechanics that would allow vehicles and machinery to eliminate or manipulate gravity for on-planet and inter-planetary travel, as well as other industrial applications.

"How far along do we take him? All the way up to schematics for this stuff?"

"Not a hundred percent sure. We can't just hand it to him—he won't be able to reconcile how he got there so quickly."

"But we have to give him enough to ensure he can fully realise these concepts"

"Indeed. You know our last two attempts at this led to very little. The Council isn't going to give us another go after this one."

"So, we should err on the side of too much information rather than too little. This species has been wallowing for decades."

"But we can't destroy this guy's mind."

"They are already sending messages into space. If an aggressive species hears them, they'll be helpless."

"Yeah, they're sending invitations out into open space without knowing who's coming to dinner."

"They're inquisitive."

"Or stupid."

"I'd be more worried about what they're doing to this planet rather than what someone else might do to them."

"Alright. We'll give him the specifics of fusion and gravity management, but no prototypes or designs."

"And shielding."

"And a memory of how he got there with those concepts."

"Agreed."

"We'll take him to the point of inventing those three systems."

"We'll have to give him cell regeneration just to protect our investment here."

"Agreed."

In the end, they decided to include the means, methods, and technology behind the use of protective electromagnetic shields—capable of application at a personal level, as well as for enveloping buildings or spacecraft to provide security and prevent unwanted intrusion.

They also transferred knowledge on nuclear fusion using helium-3 and how it could be scaled for both land-based and mobile power generation. This form of nuclear power was highly efficient, producing virtually no waste, no radiation, and no risk of reactor explosion.

Additionally, they provided advancements in next-level battery storage technology and, most significantly, equipment that could manipulate the genetic makeup of adult human cells—eliminating toxins and rejuvenating the body at a cellular level.

The visitors ensured that Tiberius had a clear pathway to developing these technologies, supplying him with all the fundamentals necessary to guide him down the correct path. They knew that Tiberius lived a solitary life—no one had visited him in his workshop for years—so the sudden emergence of advanced materials and prototypes would go largely unnoticed. However, he urgently needed to upgrade his security.

Among the most important gifts was the cell manipulation chamber—a device that, if regularly used, would revert and stabilise Tiberius's chronological age back to 35 years. Over several months, his body's age, appearance, and physical condition would gradually improve until he reached the desired youthful state.

Tiberius would be free to explain his transformation truthfully—he had simply been experimenting with cell manipulation and had used it on himself. The visitors saw this as protecting their investment—Tiberius needed to remain youthful and healthy for many years to execute the plans they had set in motion. Alongside his regenerative health, they provided him with a personal protection device to safeguard him well into the distant future.

There was so much more they could offer, yet they had deliberately chosen not to reveal everything. They wanted to see what Tiberius would do with the knowledge he had been given.

One notable exclusion was faster-than-light (FTL) space travel. The visitors believed Earth would be better off "poking around in this part of the galaxy for a while" until they matured as a species. Early exposure to certain regions of the galaxy and certain species could prove highly detrimental to human long-term survival.

So, warp drive, interstellar propulsion, and other higher-level advancements would have to come from Tiberius's own discoveries.

Even so, they believed that what they had provided today would break the Earth's technological stalemate.

They foresaw that Tiberius's work, once published, would inspire other scientists across the planet to adopt his findings, accelerating human progress in what they viewed as more productive and meaningful directions.

Of course, much of what they had shared had potential military applications.

This was a fundamental concern.

To prevent any misuse of the technology, they implanted a deep-seated psychological directive into Tiberius's subconscious: none of these advancements were to be used for military purposes. Furthermore, they gave him the means to ensure that restriction remained unbroken.

The visitors had also devised an agenda for Tiberius to follow once they were finished with him.

The first step would be the publication of mathematical solutions to two of the great unsolved mathematical puzzles. This would establish Tiberius as the preeminent mathematician on the planet, granting him the credibility and attention needed when he later published his technological findings and sought funding to build them. The visitors knew that he was already partway to solving these two problems, so a sudden burst of inspiration would not seem unusual to him.

After that, he would file patents and publish designs for his fusion reactor, given the planet's urgent need for clean energy.

Next would come the gravitational management system (GMS).

He would first apply the technology to cars, in the beginning cannibalising existing electric vehicles and replacing their drive system with the GMS, which both levitated the car and propelled it, through the manipulation of gravitational force, in any direction. The GMS could both cancel out the effect of gravity on any object as well as manipulate the gravitational force to push or pull it in any direction.

The system was highly energy-efficient, expending minimal electrical power, since friction from wheels on road surfaces was eliminated.

The transition to GMS-driven transport was critical, as fossil fuel-driven vehicles were causing catastrophic pollution.

Additionally, the GMS had applications beyond transportation. It could be integrated into spacecraft to generate artificial gravity. Inside a ship, the GMS could simulate Earth's gravity at sea level, providing a comfortable and familiar environment for its occupants.

Tiberius had been on the right track with his gravity management system for years before the visitors arrived.

This was one of the reasons they had chosen him.

He had correctly conceptualised a GMS that involved a series of pipes running through the underside of a metal alloy plate forming the base of a vehicle.

The vehicle's structure would then be built on top of this plate—whether it was a small car or a massive space station.

His own design featured an electromagnetic liquid, pumped through these pipes, that would generate a field capable of cancelling or manipulating gravity.

It was the constituents of that liquid where Tiberius had gotten stuck, but the rest of the design was pretty much as the visitors were about to give him. Tiberius had hypothesised that the speed at which the liquid was pumped through the pipes would determine the strength of the repulsive forces that acted against gravity. He had designed a series of louvres within the pipes that modified the direction in which the fluid would flow, impacting the action of the anti-gravity resistance. When the louvres were pointed directly down, the plate would rise directly upwards. Depending on the speed at which the fluid was passing through the pipes, the plate would simply hover when the flowrate was slow or move upwards at varying speeds as the speed of the moving liquid increased, making the control of the craft's ascent available to a pilot on demand.

The maximum speed at which the plate could push away from the gravitation source, Tiberius theorised, was unlimited—perhaps all the way up to light speed, if the craft was given enough time to build momentum. If the louvres were facing in another direction, the craft would move accordingly, much like the blades of a helicopter control both the upward and directional movement of the aircraft.

The gravity management system would also work in reverse. The plate could be used to pull objects towards it if the flow of the liquid was reversed, generating gravity-like forces directed downwards towards the plate. This would be ideal for managing the gravity inside a ship operating in an otherwise weightless environment. Tiberius envisaged, therefore, that a spacecraft would have two plates—one to manage flight and propulsion, and another, laid on top of the first plate, to regulate the gravity within the craft.

He also correctly theorised that plates installed in the walls of the craft could, if programmed appropriately, manage the force of inertia imparted to the occupants or objects within the craft. As inertia pushed them backwards when the craft accelerated, or forced them forwards when it decelerated—even if it stopped suddenly—the appropriate gravitational force could be generated by the wall plating to counteract the inertial forces. This would ensure that the occupants remained unaffected by inertia, staying in place. As a result, they would have no sensation of the craft accelerating, decelerating, or turning and would be entirely insulated from the forces acting upon the ship.

The visitors decided that the patents lodged for the GMS would be incomplete. Several key elements of the design, particularly the formula for the electromagnetic fluid running through the system, would be omitted from the patents and exist only in Tiberius's head, ensuring they could not be stolen or replicated. The final formulation and manufacture of the liquid material used in the GMS would be left solely to Tiberius—perhaps to be produced at the site he already owned in Dallas.

Similarly, the design of nuclear fusion reactors had become an urgent matter, aiming to replace the old nuclear reactors based on fission. Traditional nuclear power plants generate radiation, and their nuclear waste, though minimal, presents a significant disposal challenge. Fusion, a form of nuclear energy generated when lightweight atoms are forced together and fused, as opposed to being split in a traditional reactor, is the process that fuels every star's core, releasing an enormous amount of energy. Earth's researchers had been striving for years to harness fusion and reproduce it in a controlled manner. Successfully doing so would provide the world with a safe, sustainable, environmentally responsible, and abundant energy source.

In fusion reactors, light atomic nuclei are compressed under intense pressure and heat to form heavier ones, releasing energy in the process. Tiberius had theorised that Helium-3 would be a superior fuel choice compared to deuterium and tritium—both heavy isotopes of hydrogen—that most Earth scientists were working with at the time in proposed fusion reactors. One key reason for his choice of Helium-3 was his awareness that massive deposits of that material had been left by the sun on the surface of the moon, extractable through surface mining alone.

For fusion to be viable, the process must be optimised to generate more energy than it consumes. Helium-3 offered a better solution to this challenge. If a sufficiently large and sustainable energy profit could be achieved, fusion could be used to safely generate electricity on a commercial scale, without the nuclear fuel waste or radiation issues associated with fission. For decades, the scientific community had pursued nuclear fusion, but Tiberius had already, in concept at least, proposed the design of an experimental reactor that might one day demonstrate the commercial viability of fusion power. The visitors provided him with information that perfected that design.

The visitors had also devolved the system that controlled GMS-driven vehicles in flight. It was entirely inappropriate to expect the average person to be capable of safely piloting such a vehicle, regardless of how it was powered. As a result, the driver was to be completely removed from the equation. The system ensured that no vehicle could collide with another vehicle or object while in motion. Once airborne, the vehicles would autonomously calculate safe pathways to their destinations while avoiding obstacles.

It was envisaged that as thousands of commuter vehicles moved through the air simultaneously, they would naturally form efficient transit channels—aggregating into formations similar to birds in flight or the way bats navigate. The same principle would apply to space travel. The system was given a name: *The HIVE*. Certain critical elements of the system would be patented, while others would be kept secret.

The burden was that Tiberius would be on his own after the visit. Once the information was provided, the visitors had decided that they would not return; the outcomes of this intervention would be left to the human species. Tiberius alone would bear the responsibility of carrying it forward and dealing with all the consequences that ensued.

Tiberius was unsettled the next evening, having awoken that morning with a massive headache. He fiddled with a notepad and pencil, seemingly compelled to write out parts of the math solutions he'd been working on since university, as if struck by a sudden burst of inspiration—though in truth, unbeknown to him, the insight had been provided by the visitors. He felt an inexplicable urge to complete and later publish solutions to two of the eight great mathematical problems on the planet. The visitors believed that by publishing these results, he would establish himself as the pre-eminent mathematician of his time. As a result, his subsequent inventions would be more readily believed and taken seriously when the time came to seek collaboration and funding for their development.

He became obsessed with the idea that Earth had fallen dangerously behind in technological advancement—another fine legacy of our politically obsessed and corrupt leaders who, he mused aloud, had hindered human progress. As a species, we had developed intelligence but were refusing to use it, largely because it had become almost universally accepted that humanity was a blight on the planet rather than its potential curator.

The phone rang.

"Grandpa?"

"Elizabeth, is that you?"

"Yes."

"Does your father know you're calling me?"

"Grandpa, please, I'm ten. I have my own phone now."

"Where did you get my number?"

"I copied it from Daddy's phone."

"Won't he be angry if he knows you called?"

"That's his problem. It's silly and mean that he doesn't call you."

From the mouths of babes, Tiberius thought.

"It's lovely to hear your voice."

"I miss you too—soooo much. What you doin'?"

"Well… puzzling over a problem. A serious problem."

"Can I help?"

"You already have, darlin'."

"I have a problem too that I've been worrying about."

"Really?"

"My teacher at school says that California will be underwater within a few years because of global warming. I'm not that good a swimmer, Grandad."

"Your teacher is wrong to alarm you like that. Some teachers can't help bringing their own political views into the classroom."

"So, she's wrong?"

"We need to clean up the atmosphere and stop dumping rubbish into it, for sure. But it is fixable—certainly before the outcome she mentioned."

"She said three years."

"That's just stupid. In fact, I'm working on something right now that might fix it."

"That's good, Granddad. Can I call you whenever I feel like it—for an update and a hello?"

"I'll be counting the days."

"Love you, talk soon."

"Love you too, baby. Bye."

CHAPTER TWO

The Road Ahead

The subsequent ten years had been a difficult journey for Tiberius, fraught with funding, staffing, supply, and security issues. Yet, he had persevered through those challenges and was now building his first two rudimentary space platforms using his GMS technology. The stations were constructed with a two-kilometre diameter GMS plate, topped with a dome made of a special alloy glass supported by hexagonal titanium alloy beams. They would be protected externally by Tiberius's first-generation electromagnetic invisible shielding. One dome was set to be deployed in the Mare Imbrium basin to mine Helium-3 on the moon, while the other would be placed in Earth's orbit, about a quarter of the way to the moon. It was Tiberius's intention to expand the orbiting station by daisy-chaining several globes into a self-sustaining habitat, which would serve as a research facility, a Helium-3 processing centre, and an administrative hub for sales and communications.

Tiberius had converted his property in Dallas to accommodate the construction of the domes. Due to the sheer scale of the required construction docks—capable of building two-kilometre diameter GMS base plates and their associated dome structures—he had also acquired several adjoining properties. There was no need to assemble them in orbit; once complete, the GMS plates would lift the domes off the planet and transport them to their intended destinations.

Six of the Dallas warehouses had been adapted for the manufacture of the GMS vehicle drives and production of the GMS liquid that flowed through the plate piping to facilitate gravity management. Each of these buildings, along with all construction docks, was secured by Tiberius's first-generation electromagnetic shielding nets that covered the whole site, ensuring complete control over access. Seven additional globes were under construction on-site, and Tiberius was searching for another large property to expand production to even larger globes.

The efficiency of construction had been greatly enhanced by the use of GMS-powered equipment. Scaffolding was no longer required—both people and materials could be effortlessly moved into position using gravity-defying equipment. GMS-powered platforms could be locked in place at specific GPS coordinates, remaining steady as construction platforms wherever required. Materials and personnel could move swiftly and efficiently between tasks. The need for massive cranes to lift heavy materials had been eliminated, as GMS carriers could do the job more quickly and efficiently.

But construction was not the only industry benefitting from GMS technology. Cars, buses, and trucks powered by GMS engines were now being produced by traditional car manufacturers using engines supplied by Tiberius. Other equipment, such as window-cleaning and painting platforms, parcel delivery drones linked to the HIVE, boats, and long-haul aircraft, had also been revolutionised. The traditional airline industry had almost abandoned jet-powered passenger planes in favour of GMS-powered alternatives. However, Tiberius refused to allow the military to utilise GMS for fighter aircraft or any other military applications.

One unexpected consequence of GMS technology was its impact on long-haul travel. Car manufacturers had begun offering larger, long-distance flight-capable versions of their GMS vehicles aimed at the private user, equipped with increased battery storage and onboard toilet facilities—essentially airborne campervans. These vehicles were creating logistical challenges for border control agencies and international flight authorities, as the distinction between cars and aircraft blurred.

Tiberius now employed over five thousand workers at his Dallas site, including traditional building contractors, shipwrights, boilermakers, carpenters, and plumbers. The structures built atop the GMS globes followed conventional construction methods, as the gravity inside each globe was regulated by additional GMS gravity-generating plates layered over the GMS propulsion plates. This ensured that, regardless of whether a globe was in space, on the moon, or on Mars, its internal gravity would remain identical to that of Earth. Consequently, buildings were constructed with bricks, mortar, steel, and all standard utilities—including gas stoves and electronic appliances—just as they would be on Earth.

Each globe was equipped with a fusion reactor for electricity generation, as well as hydrogen-based gas supply for appliances. The danger of compressed hydrogen had been avoided by using a large electrolysis plant that generated the hydrogen, converting it from water, in real time as demand required, there was almost as much water produced per volume of hydrogen burned which assisted water recycling in the station. Water was both recycled and stored, with regular deliveries sourced initially from Earth. However, Tiberius planned to extract water from Ganymede, one of Jupiter's moons, which held the largest volume of water in the solar system. He had commissioned the construction of special-purpose tankers that, using GMS technology, could complete the 628-million-kilometre journey to Ganymede in under five hours.

The orbiting station would feature a park, residential buildings, and research facilities, all built in traditional architectural styles. These buildings were not structural components of the station but were instead housed within the dome. The orbiting station was designed to operate in tandem with the lunar surface globe, which housed mining equipment and personnel. Both globes were scheduled to commence operations simultaneously.

Following the successful licensing of many of his innovative products, Tiberius had become the richest man on the planet. The long-awaited dream of the flying car had finally been realised, with all major car manufacturers now licensing his GMS drives. GMS engines had begun to replace traditional petrol and electric engines in all surface-based vehicles. Meanwhile, the HIVE software, a critical component of his Moving Object Control System, had been universally adopted in most countries to regulate airborne vehicular traffic. Recently expanded to international flight control, it was now being rolled out across all major metropolitan areas.

Initially, car manufacturers had simply retrofitted existing vehicle designs with GMS drive systems replacing combustion or electric engines. Most now incorporated Tiberius's new battery platforms, marking the dawn of a new era in transportation.

The negotiations with car manufacturers had been long and arduous. Most wanted to build the engines themselves, and all were pressuring government regulators to loosen design constraints on the vehicles. Numerous stylish versions of GMS cars had begun appearing on the market, featuring no wheels at all, no driving, steering, or braking components, and many incorporating voice-generated commands and responses. However, the Jetson-style bubble cars were not part of this new generation of vehicle designs—travelling in a glass bubble was incompatible with internal climate control and exposed occupants to intrusive sun rays.

Many of the new designs were constrained in size by the garage space available in typical homes. House designs were now being influenced by the need for larger garages to accommodate the growing popularity of oversized GMS vehicles, which were not only used for touring but also international travel. Since vehicle size was no longer dictated by petrol consumption, manufacturers had greater design freedom. The traditional layout of a car—centred around a driver seated at the front—was now obsolete, as self-driving technology had fundamentally changed both the internal and external structure of vehicles.

Some of the more expensive models featured GMS inertia-control wall plating, meaning the interior could be arranged in a circular layout, as occupants were unaffected by sudden movements.

To date, the new flying cars had a flawless operational record. Their onboard control systems, combined with the HIVE network, ensured that accidents were virtually non-existent. The cars could not fall from the sky due to the GMS, nor could they collide with other vehicles or objects thanks to their advanced navigation systems. Stackable car parks had begun appearing at office buildings—once occupants exited their vehicles, the cars would automatically park themselves in designated stacking areas and could be summoned back on demand.

One of the key advantages of GMS vehicles was their lower production cost. Tiberius was able to sell the GMS engines at a lower price than traditional combustion or electric engines. Unlike conventional vehicles, GMS-powered cars did not require transmissions, wheels, suspensions or brake assemblies, significantly reducing manufacturing expenses. It was expected that within ten years, traditional petrol and electric vehicles would no longer be sold—or even permitted for use— except in designated areas for combustion engine enthusiasts. Much of the millions of acres of roads on Earth could then be repurposed for more productive uses.

With zero vehicular carbon emissions and the gradual replacement of coal-fired power plants with Tiberius's new fusion reactors, some agronomists had begun warning of a potential shortage of carbon dioxide in the atmosphere—an element essential for sustaining plant life.

Tiberius had only licensed the GMS for use in cars, heavy lifting and construction equipment, planes and orbital shuttles—eliminating the use of heavily polluting rockets. However, he had not yet authorised the production of the large plates used for his space platforms. Enforcing his licensing restrictions was straightforward, as the production of the GMS engine liquid remained a closely guarded secret, with all manufacturing confined to Tiberius's Dallas facility.

All Tiberius's properties were protected by his new electromagnetic security shielding, preventing any unauthorised intrusion—including attempted intrusions by overzealous government authorities seeking to confiscate his technology under the guise of national security. To date, all such attempts had failed.

Tiberius had assembled an aggressive legal team to protect his patent rights. Additionally, through various financial channels, he had secured the political support of numerous elected officials in every country where his vehicles and equipment were sold—including, notably, the President of the United States and his family, who benefited from substantial *campaign funding* and other financial backing from Tiberius's companies.

However, the most significant factor keeping national security hawks at bay was the fact that much of the key technological knowledge remained exclusively in Tiberius's head. These critical details were not part of any registered patents and were therefore unobtainable, even if government agencies attempted to confiscate the equipment used to produce GMS drives or security shielding technology.

Tiberius had also modified the initial design of the rejuvenation chamber provided to him by the visitors, developing several specialised variants. One version targeted and eliminated toxins in the body, another destroyed viruses and bacteria, and yet another eradicated cancerous cells. Due to the non-invasive and highly effective nature of these treatments, health clinics using Tiberius's medical technology were opening at an unprecedented rate around the world.

Additionally, he had designed a rejuvenation chamber for cosmetic purposes, particularly for skin repair, anti-ageing treatments, and fat reduction. His Health and Cosmetics Division had quickly become one of his most profitable ventures.

Tiberius himself had adopted the habit of regularly using his personal full-body rejuvenation chamber—though, for now, it was not available for sale to the general public. He had customised his own unit to include the ability to impart muscle memory to his cells. As an experiment, he had used it to teach himself the piano—and had successfully done so in a single session in his rejuvenation tank.

He had not released the full-body rejuvenation chambers to the public due to his concerns over who would gain access to them. Tiberius had no interest in granting many of the prominent arseholes who ruled the planet the privilege of eternal life.

Tiberius had forged several strategic alliances in the field of commercial space technology, including partnerships with NASA, SpaceX, and other international space consortiums. The use of rocketry had been almost entirely phased out among participating members in favour of faster, cheaper, larger, and cleaner GMS-powered craft—most of which utilised the new fusion technology for power generation.

The increasing demand for Helium-3, required by these fusion power stations, had accelerated Tiberius's near-term targets for establishing mining bases on Earth's moon. Helium-3 was scarce on Earth, but vast quantities had accumulated on the moon's surface over millennia, deposited by the sun in the absence of an atmosphere to impede its accretion. These deposits were accessible via surface mining alone, making lunar extraction both practical and lucrative.

These technological advancements, combined with the mathematical proofs Tiberius had published shortly after his encounter with the visitors—an event erased from his memory—had earned him two Noble Prize awards in physics and mathematics. It was only the fourth time in history that any scientist had won two awards, and the first time they had been awarded simultaneously.

Tonight, Tiberius was in attendance at the Konserthuset Stockholm to accept these prestigious honours. His plus one for the evening was his now twenty-year-old granddaughter, Elizabeth.

NOBEL PRIZE SPEECH. Tiberius begins politely in Swedish:

Mina damer och herrar, ärade gäster, det är med stor stolthet och ödmjukhet som jag står här för att ta emot dessa Proze. [A smattering of applause for his effort to begin in Swedish].

Switching to English, he continues:

As a species, we have stagnated technologically since our first moon landing. We became frightened by the power of the atomic bomb, and earlier in that century, we had begun to see industrialisation as the enemy of the Earth rather than its saviour. Instead of mastering nature, we withdrew from technological progress, paralysed by fear rather than inspired to curate and refine the world around us.

Within ten years, my companies will have fully self-sufficient bio-domes orbiting this planet—environments free from deadly viruses, harmful bacteria, and creatures that pose a threat to human life. These domes will be entirely self-sustaining human habitats, teaching us how to maintain and manage extraterrestrial life, while giving us the courage and knowledge to better govern our own planet.

We need to control nature, not fear it. Ignoring this reality is to our own peril.

In the spirit of the Nobel Prize and in honour of Alfred Nobel's vision—conceived by the inventor of dynamite—I give this commitment to the Nobel Prize Committee and to all of you here tonight:

None of the technology developed by my companies will ever be used for military purposes.

[A standing ovation erupts as he makes this commitment. He waits for the applause to subside before continuing.]

Let us all move forward together, free from the fear of climate catastrophe, and instead embrace the vast possibilities that our intelligence and endeavours can unlock for our species.

CHAPTER THREE

Then It Rained

The view was mesmerising from the covered balcony outside Tiberius's two-storey apartment on the fifth floor of the block of units he occupied on Tellurium One—his new orbiting space station, circling Earth about a quarter of the way to the moon.

Ten years after his Noble speech, Tiberius and his granddaughter, Elizabeth, were enjoying the breathtaking sight of the vast blue planet below, half fading into darkness before them. The station was being manoeuvred into Earth's shadow to observe a ten-hour night, causing the yellow-grey moon to become more prominent as the station rotated. The moon appeared like a massive searchlight; its brightness mitigated only by the cratered terrain visible on its surface. Below, Earth was half-lit by sunlight, while the encroaching darkness revealed the glow of city lights. The main street of the station extending from their apartment stretched three kilometres towards the edge of the globe, and from their vantage point, it created the optical illusion that the road continued all the way down to Earth.

The apartment's balcony overlooked the low-rise streetscape that ran through the Primary Globe, the main section of the station. This vast globe, with its glass-alloy dome, sat atop the three-kilometre diameter GMS plate that formed the station's foundation. The station resembled a massive snow globe, with its transparent alloy panels— each measuring one hundred square metres—secured by titanium structural beams. The entire structure was protected externally by Tiberius's Mark IV transparent force field, capable of withstanding everything from nuclear blasts to solar flare radiation and meteorite impacts.

Internally the station's gravity management system maintained an Earth-like gravitational pull at sea level, just as it did on the now fully operational lunar and Martian bases. The Main Street was lined with apartments on one side, with cross streets branching off to create a city-grid layout. The buildings gradually decreased in height as the cross streets neared the globe's edge. At street level, the apartment blocks housed a variety of shops, nightclubs, and bars.

Opposite the residential area was a large semi-circular park, filled with edible plants freely available to residents. The park served as both an amenity and a gathering place, offering space for walks, picnics, and recreation. Towards its far end, near the exit to the next globe, stood a mall containing grocery stores and retail shops.

Produce was abundant and affordable on Tellurium One, grown both in the park and in two dedicated agricultural globes within the station's expanding chain of habitats. A vintage trolley car, running on aesthetic-purpose rails, served as the primary mode of transport, connecting all five globes currently in operation.

The Primary Globe housed not only residences and essential amenities but also a large tourist hotel and spa, located adjacent to the park. The station's environment was permanently maintained at 22°C (72°F), except during Christmas, when the atmospheric controls generated snowfall between Christmas Eve and New Year's Day, transforming Tellurium One into an actual snow globe.

To ease the transition for new arrivals, the station adhered to Earth's calendar and time measurement protocols. The diverse architectural styles, inspired largely by nineteenth-century European towns, enhanced the station's visual appeal, lending it the atmosphere of a quaint village.

Standard apartments were provided rent-free to station workers, though those willing to pay for an upgrade—beyond what their rank entitled them to—could access larger, more luxurious homes. However, all residences were generously sized.

The balcony where Elizabeth and Tiberius sat was covered but not enclosed or screened. There was no need for insect screens—the station was entirely curated, meaning flies, mosquitoes, fleas, bed bugs, and other pests simply did not exist. The only insects present were bees, housed in the farm globes for agricultural purposes. Similarly, there were no snakes, spiders, or rodents lurking in the shrubbery or hiding in buildings.

The age-old fear of disrupting the *balance of nature* had proven unwarranted. The station's ecosystem was fully controlled and managed—not dictated by unpredictable natural forces but optimised for human habitation. The billions of dollars spent on environmental research back on Earth had often failed to acknowledge that nature itself was a fluid system, one that could be refined and curated for better living conditions.

As Tiberius often remarked, "Mother Nature is simply a comedian."

The ten years Tiberius had referenced in his Noble Prize speech had passed quickly and productively, though not without difficulties and frustrating setbacks. Nearly twenty years had passed since the visitors' arrival—the catalyst that had set Tiberius's journey into motion.

Despite the challenges, the quality and importance of the technology had ensured his continued success. More recently, progress had accelerated into a period of immense momentum. Commentators described this era as a new technological revolution, one sparked—like so many others before it—by the genius of a single person.

Yet, Tiberius himself saw it only as a beginning. There was no time to sit back and enjoy the fruits of success—not when there was still so much more to accomplish.

At precisely eight o'clock, as it did every evening, the rain began to fall—cleansing the streets and promoting plant growth.

The rain, combined with the approaching nightfall, transformed the streetscape into something reminiscent of a Film Noir scene. The glow of Earth's cities, visible through the transparent dome, cast an ethereal shimmer over the urban landscape.

Unlike traditional space stations, Tellurium One did not spin to generate gravity. Instead, it rotated slowly along its central axis, providing a shifting perspective of Earth, the moon, and the remnants of old orbiting satellites—including the now-abandoned International Space Station.

Tiberius and Elizabeth sat under cover, sheltered from the rain. A small hydrogen gas fireplace with imitation wooden logs glowed warmly beside them, creating a homely, intimate atmosphere.

The gentle sound of rain tapping against the roof made their conversation relaxed and reflective.

"So… it does rain in space," Elizabeth said, now nearly thirty years of age.

"Every day."

"My God, Grandad, look at what you've created."

"I had some help. This ring of globes won't be completed until later this year. We're adding another farm globe and a second research and processing centre. We'll also be enclosing the waste, materials, and water-processing facility—along with power utilities and electrolysis plant—into its own two-kilometre-wide globe. We'll repurpose one of the first globes we built for that service hub. There it is, hanging there, waiting to be hooked up and equipped. Once complete, the full circle will be formed. We'd just need to add some boosters, and we could take her anywhere in the solar system… or beyond. But she'll be staying on station here permanently."

James, Tiberius's personal valet, arrived with a scotch and cigar for him and a cold glass of pinot grigio for Elizabeth.

"Can I have one of those, please, James?"

"What, a cigar?" Tiberius asked.

"Yes."

"You'll make yourself sick."

Elizabeth shot Tiberius the look of a spoilt child.

"James, do we have something very mild for my grandchild? Probably the ones you smoke—you know, the pussy brand."

"Very good, sir."

"I can't say no to you. If you start feeling queasy, just put it out. Not everything's a competition."

"You two are close."

"James? Sure. A long time—nearly as long as I've been at this, starting back in Dallas."

Elizabeth swirled her wine thoughtfully. "Along the lines of not saying no… I want to come work for you. I submitted my doctoral thesis for review a couple of years back. I'm now Doctor Elizabeth Xander, if you please. I've been stuck in a dead-end research job ever since."

Tiberius raised an eyebrow. "Goodness, sweetheart. Congratulations! I'm surprised you didn't mention your doctorate earlier—I would have come to the ceremony. But I don't know about you working for me. I really value our time together. In some ways, you're my second chance at a family. I wouldn't want to mess that up."

"I don't know what that shit is all about between you and dad—or my aunt, for that matter—but you all need to grow up."

Tiberius sighed. "I fear it's too late for that. Any relationship with them now would be based on what I've become, rather than the father I so diligently tried to be for them both. It would hard not to see any affection from them now as sycophancy because…"

"You're the most powerful person on the planet."

"Something like that. Except I'm not, you know… on the planet right now."

She laughed. "I don't understand why you three don't talk, and I don't want to get in the middle of it."

"Best you don't. Your father is something of a dick sometimes, but I don't want to be judgemental like he and his sister."

"Dare I ask?"

"Well, both of my children seem to believe they have the right to judge me for the mistakes I've made. And I have made a lot of mistakes—anyone who doesn't sleepwalk through life does. But your aunt, she even thinks she has the right to run a commentary on my marriage to your grandmother. Marriage is not a spectator sport, my dear. No one truly knows what happens inside one except the two people trying to survive it. I won't break any confidences talking to them about my relationship with my ex-wife, not like she did with our kids. They got the full, unabridged, one-sided story from her. One of my great fears for them is that karma has a way of coming back around in matters like these."

"What does that mean?"

"If they give me the cold shoulder, they should be careful tempting fate when it comes to how their own kids treat them—no matter how pure and blameless they think they are."

Elizabeth smirked. "So how do you know I'm not just sucking up to you for your money?"

Tiberius grinned. "Well… three reasons. First, unlike your dad, I don't think you care much about money. Second, you started connecting with me when I was just some old guy farting around in a shed in Dallas…"

"Honestly, I had no idea what the hell you were doing in that shed."

"Neither did I, for the most part. I've never thanked you for you staying in contact, that phone call I got from you when you were ten, turned things around for me. It was clear from what you said about drowning in California and all the bullshit being put forward in schools that I'd better get my arse into gear. It was the very next morning that I sat down with a new sense of urgency looking at the two mathematical problems I'd been working on for years. I had belted out most of the solutions by the end of the week."

"I'm glad I could help. And the third reason?"

"It's too mushy."

"Awww, Grandad, mushy? Really? How sweet."

"So, what would you do."

"You mean working for you? Something very important, of course." She smiled.

"What's your doctorate in?"

"Environmental physics."

"Sounds useful. You'd want to get paid, right?"

"Fuck off. Of course." More laughter.

Tiberius took a sip of his scotch. "I'm planning to amalgamate Mars, the moon, and this station—along with all of our non-terra stations—into an independent federation. It'll include any colonies we establish in near-star systems once we start the launches next year. The Federation of Non-Earth Planets and Orbiting Stations. FNEPOS." He paused. "Strictly hush-hush, of course. The name is a work in progress."

"I sincerely hope so."

"Probably just the Federation of Free Planets, the FFP. I will declare it to be a sovereign entity—an independent nation—when the time is right. Maybe after we get to the Centauri system."

Elizabeth frowned. "Can you even do that? Declare it an independent nation?"

"Who the hell could stop me? I'm going to structure it as you would a public company, where directors are selected on merit. Absolutely no politicians. Proper safeguards, full transparency. No corrupt elections, no bureaucratic nonsense. And it'll be built with mechanisms to protect the rights of the citizen-shareholders."

Elizabeth raised her glass. "*No taxation without representation.*"

"Quite right. But there's no taxation—except for some sales tax on certain items. Each citizen will hold shares. The production from the bases, this station, and the others soon to come—along with my intellectual property licensing, including my medical division—are already highly profitable."

"I'll bet it is. So… I'd be President, then."

"You didn't want to start in the filing room or something?"

"Ah… no. But there must be something in there for me?"

"We have eighteen globes under construction at the moment in Dallas, plus more in the new Australian complex. All of them are at least twice the size of this one. Six of those will be daisy-chained into an interstellar craft, aimed at a mission to the Centauri System in the middle of next year. It's a binary star system, so there will be a lot of work to do there. We plan to launch at least one starship every few months after that, gradually increasing to one a month. The ship's gravity drive will be augmented by a large fusion propulsion system, which will take it up to nearly half the speed of light. That means they should reach Alpha Centauri in just over eight and a half years—nearly ten years Earth time."

"So… not a starship, like Star Trek?"

"No need. The globes create a complete living and working environment, made possible by gravity management and fully shielded from random asteroids or debris. There is no air resistance in space, so the ships don't have to be pointy or enclosed with a surrounding hull. Everyone on board may as well enjoy the view of the stars as they travel. More importantly, the globes can be placed on any planet we decide to colonise. The artificial lighting will make the glass look blue in the daytime and when switched off at night it will be the same as the stars in the night sky on Earth, except the stars would be moving more quickly. The closer we can make the environment identical to a clean natural Earth environment, the less impact there will be on the mental and physical wellbeing of the inhabitants of the craft as they travel. We might need to enclose a ship with a hull if we crack faster-than-light travel—but that's a bridge we'll cross when we get there."

"You don't stand still for long, do you"

"A lot to do, sweetheart."

"You're not working on that warp speed shit?"

"Not as easy as it looks. Other Earth nations are trying. I think I would rather have us potter around in the nearby galaxy for a while."

"Why?"

"Aliens."

"You think we're not alone?"

"Of course we're not alone. But we're definitely not ready to poke that bear. Besides, the inter-stellar globes will have all the amenities. Life onboard will be great—an eight-year trip will be a walk in the park, literally. I'm thinking of adding a golf course and a country club globe to the next one. We also need to build up our star maps before we start flipping around faster than the speed of light. There's no GPS in space."

"Tell me more about these aliens you're worried about."

"They're out there, for sure. And when I say 'out there,' I mean probably way out there. They could potentially be helpful—or they could be the worst possible thing we ever encounter. Carl Sagan used to say that the biggest factor in whether we ever meet alien life is whether they annihilated themselves before we found them. Civilisations might come into existence, develop, then destroy themselves or their planets before we ever reach them. God knows we nearly did—and that story isn't over yet. First, we nearly burned ourselves down through mismanaged industrialisation. Then came the nuclear threat. And back in the late 20th and early 21st century, biological warfare was a big concern. China used to make a sport of letting some virus loose on the West every ten years or so while feigning innocence.

Even today, viruses are still a global threat—but not so much now, thanks to our medical scanning chambers where they are available. The scanners just need to decode the genetic makeup of any new virus or bacteria, issue a software update, have people step through the scanner—bang, fixed. Of course, historically it's possible the virus outbreaks from China were accidental. Maybe just poor hygiene. But let's look at the pattern: H2N1 in 1958, H2N2 in 1969, h5N1 in 1997, Sars in 2003, bird flu in 2006, swine flu in 2009 and covid in 2019. Accidental? Maybe. But how many times do you need to be struck by the same bolt of lightning from the same source before you say *what the fuck*? How China escaped scrutiny is a testament to bullshit international politics—and to their strategic funding of certain global organisations. China's financial grip on the World Health Organisation made sure no serious questions were ever asked. Compare that to the number of global disease outbreaks caused by the United States: zero—unless you count HIV, though many argue that originated in Africa. Now, America, on the other hand... they've bombed the living crap out of a few places."

"So, how do your scanners fix the virus problem?"

"The scanners identify the intruding pathogen's DNA, then kill the viruses or bacteria in the living human tissue—without harming the body's natural antibodies."

"The pharmaceutical companies must love you."

"I've been careful. I license the scanners to them, as long as they adhere to pricing guidelines for their use. I didn't want to destroy the industry, but I was more than happy to put an end to their rapacious marketing of often useless drugs. Every starship will have the latest scanners onboard. No infections—same here on Tellurium One."

"So, you think we're not going to wipe ourselves out?"

"Well, thanks to a lot of determined people, maybe not. Less likely now that we're leaving this planet. But yeah, all of that happened in three hundred thousand years, so the results aren't in yet. We evolved, infected, or killed in wars hundreds of millions of people, nearly nuked ourselves out of existence, then came close to poisoning the planet to the point it was unliveable; and we did all of that without having any lifeboats. The three hundred thousand years of human existence on the planet is a blink of the eye in cosmic terms, the first two hundred and ninety thousand years of that timeframe we were just wandering around picking berries and killing the fauna."

"But if the aliens are out there, do you think we may not want to meet them?"

"Arguably, if they made it past the self-annihilation phase, they should be enlightened. But what if they made it past that phase by waging war on nearby similarly advanced planets instead of waging it on themselves? They might have won those wars and developed into some kind of super-warrior species."

"A Klingon."

"Yeah. That's why I don't think we should be gallivanting around the galaxy until we are a little more sure-footed."

"Won't your shielding system protect us?"

"Against anything we know of, sure."

"You can't set up a planet-wide shield?"

"Working on it. It may actually be the final step in a complete climate management system, as it would also protect against—or even regulate—solar radiation. It would also solve the asteroid problem, especially if we accidentally send one hurtling toward Earth while mining the asteroid belt. But, as always, I think regional politics will get in the way of that good idea."

"So, do you think warp speed is possible?"

"Yes."

"But you haven't cracked it yet?"

There was no response.

"You have, you old goat, and you're just not telling anyone."

"Not quite, but yeah… I think so. I'm hoping to have an operational model before the interstellar missions reach their destinations—within the next three to four years. If we do, then we can catch up with them and retrofit the long-chain globe starships with warp drive. And, by the way, I'm not that old."

"Eighty-seven by my count."

"Chronologically, sure. But thirty-five physically—and I intend to stay that way."

"So why haven't you unleashed that technology on the world?"

"Well, largely, I have. The medical division has released cell manipulation technology to treat cancer, burns, all types of infections, and trauma injuries. A hugely profitable division by the way, particularly the cosmetic clinics."

"But not the whole-body fountain-of-youth thing that you use on yourself."

"No."

"Why."

"I'm testing it on myself."

"For how long?"

"So far, nineteen-plus years."

"And you think it's not ready?"

"Well… frankly, it is definitely ready. But who do you sell it to?"

"Everyone will want it."

"Then what. You know how many people there are on that planet below us? Probably three times as many as appropriate for a rock that size. And you know how many rich dickheads would buy it? Then what do we get? Dickheads who live forever."

"You could be selective."

"Then I'll just get a whole lot of rich people hating me because I won't give it to them because I think they're dickheads."

"I thought we were trying not to be judgmental."

"Funny. But let's be honest—I would feel compelled to be selective, and I don't want to put myself in that position."

"It's a reset, isn't it. Once you do it, you start aging again?"

"Yes."

"So, they wouldn't live forever."

"I guess."

"How often do you do it?"

"About every three months or so. It clears out all the toxins as well as renews the cells."

"The toxins from the cigars and the booze."

"Now who's being judgmental."

"You look pretty ripped, so it replaces muscle?"

"Sure. Removes fat, reshapes the muscles into any size you want. Better still if you also exercise… but what's the point."

"So, you can reshape anything?"

"Within your existing genetic makeup. It can't introduce new genes."

"So, you've given yourself a bigger dick, right? I'm sure someone in your heritage had a big dick."

Tiberius looked at her disgusted.

"So… you have!"

"I remember a time when ladies didn't make comments like that, or swear."

"I'm sure you remember steam engines too. Women have come a long way to assert what they can and can't do or say."

"But you still call them women."

"Only because every other name they came up with was stupid."

"You got that right."

"You'd let me use it—the machine, I mean?"

"Yes… of course… when the time comes."

Changing the subject, he said, "I've got a meeting at Apollo Base on Mars tomorrow morning at 10:30 AM. Want to come? You're on holiday, right?"

"Sure. What time do we leave?"

"We'd need to get away by about 8:15 AM. I'll get Mrs Mac to pack us breakfast."

"Two hours? I thought you had it down quicker than that."

"My personal boat doesn't have a booster—just the gravity drive. Given where Mars is in its orbit right now, it will take us about an hour and a half. You OK to stay there over-night? I'll show you around."

"Sounds good. What's there now?"

"Well, the processing plant is in full swing now that Morpheus Base is stationed near the asteroid belt. The new asteroid capture ships are working well—they're huge. They catch the asteroids, break them up internally, and then ship the rubble back for processing at Apollo."

"Surely some of those asteroids are too big to handle."

"Yeah, we're just cherry-picking for now—until we figure out how to safely break up the big ones in situ without, you know, sending one hurtling toward Earth."

"That would be bad for business."

"And several million Earthlings. So, we're proceeding carefully. But they'll figure it out."

"So, how many of these dome thingies do you have operational at the moment."

"Dome thingies, really. There are five here now in this chain, with four more to link up in a couple of months. Six at Imbrium Base in the Mare Imbrium basin and two more in the Mare Nectaris Sea."

"Those are both moon bases?"

"Yeah—mostly mining Helium-3, rare earths, silver. The mining is all surface-based, so we've designed scrapers that do the job nicely. Kicks up a fair bit of dust, though. With low gravity, we need to come up with better dust control before the moon starts looking like a giant cotton ball. We also get large quantities of ilmenite from the scrapings—it's a fantastically useful mineral. Contains iron, titanium, and oxygen—all of which we use ourselves. We don't sell any of it."

"And what's next?"

"We're talking about adding a third moon base near the original landing spot in the Sea of Tranquillity—as a tourist hotel. We'd offer tours to the Apollo 11 landing site, maybe a golf course. You can fit an entire golf course and resort inside one of the new ten-kilometre-diameter globes we're building in Australia right now."

"What's that little one sticking out near the exit to this globe?

"Yeah, it's not that little when you get inside it—about the size of a football stadium, which, by the way, it is. It's the sports stadium for this station. It's out on its own because the grandstands have gravity, but the playing area can be weightless. They use it for weightless football… and quidditch."

"The Harry Potter quidditch?"

"Yep. The broomsticks they ride have a micro-gravity management engine beneath the seat. It's great to watch. We had J. K. Rowling up here for the first game of the season a couple of months back. I'm told they're getting pretty good at it—there are four teams on the station, part-time amateurs at the moment, but I understand there is talk of expanding it to Earth and taking it professional."

"You'll have to take me to a game. So, what do we have on Mars?"

"Eight five-kilometre-diameter globes currently—three of them processing asteroid materials. We're just putting down a ten-kilometre housing dome, much like the one you see below us here, only bigger, the beginnings of a new city to house the workers. We're going to call it Copernicus City. The planet engineers have come up with a way to build a huge twenty-plus-kilometre dome *in situ* to cover and reinforce the water storage damn for Apollo and Copernicus. They are going to build the cover to fit in with the natural contours of the canyon in which the water storage currently sits and then sink some GMS plating into the lake to take care of the gravity issues. There is already a fair bit of water there, which we shipped in, but we lose a lot of it because of the cosmic winds and the weak Martian gravity. So covering it will serve a practical purpose, of protecting the water, but also provide something of a playground for the citizens. It will end up being the size of a large lake, and under the glass people will be able to use the area without protective clothing. We plan to open it up to water sports and picnic areas, increase the amenity for the residence. Again, a couple of tourism globes are coming, probably adjacent to the lake. Also, the new station just arrived orbiting Ganymede, the largest moon of Jupiter. There's a shitload of pure water on that moon, much more than on Earth. Titan has a lot of water as well, we're about to put a station on the surface there to assess mining opportunities. That is a very interesting moon. We'll certainly never have to depend on water from Earth no matter how large we grow."

"Quite the empire."

"You mean Federation. Which reminds me, we have a soiree at my L.A. home on Saturday evening, lots of important people, some who only think that they are important, but they're coming anyway. Some of them work for our media company."

"Why the hell did you buy that company? Their news coverage is so biased."

"That was one of the reasons we bought it—to provide fact-based, unbiased reporting, particularly about what we are doing up here. There's a lot of bullshit in the media trying to demonise us to justify breaking our patents. We'll use the film division to make real space movies and corporate recruiting videos and some of their television intellectual property rights are useful when we chose names for certain things."

"What things?"

"Star Trek-type things. Warp-drive, for example—that's a Star Trek phrase. Did you bring any formal wear?"

"No."

Tiberius pressed the intercom and James reappears.

"James, where are Buck and Joanna?"

"On your bed, sir. Asleep."

"Damn cats think they own the place. Don't they know Elizabeth is here."

"I'm sure they do, sir. They just don't give a shit."

"How old are the cat's now, Grandad?"

"Twenty-three. I put them through the cell regeneration equipment about eight years ago. They're probably due again now."

"It works on cats?"

"On any living being. It just needs to be calibrated properly."

"What do they do when you're not here?"

"Mrs Mac takes care of them. James is usually with me, but she doesn't tolerate their eccentricities the way I do, and they resent her for it."

"I would have picked you as a dog person, Grandad."

"Dogs love you even if you're mean to them. Cats have free will; dogs just follow. You have to earn a relationship with a cat. James, get Marsha from the costume department at the studio to pick out a few formal wear choices for Elizabeth, please. Have them delivered to the Hollywood house by Saturday morning. Elizabeth will give you her sizes before we leave in the morning. And get one of the hair and makeup girls from the studio to be at the house Saturday afternoon too, please."

"Why, Grandad? Hair and makeup? I didn't know you were that vain."

"It's for you, stupid." More laughter. "One more thing before bedtime."

"Being?"

"I have a gift for you."

Tiberius pulled out a small box from underneath his chair and opened it.

"It's a gold bracelet. A large one. Similar to yours."

"Sorry I couldn't make it any smaller."

It was gold in colour, covered in what looked like computer circuitry underneath gold plating with a two-and-a-half-inch rounded protrusion running up the arm like an antenna.

"I will need to explain this to you, because once you put it on, I'm the only one who can remove it."

"Sounds ominous."

"It's the second of its kind. Mine is the first."

Tiberius rolled up his sleeve, revealing an identical gold amulet on his wrist.

Tiberius pressed the intercom again.

"James, bring out a baseball bat, will you?"

James appeared on the balcony, carrying a bat. Tiberius stood.

"You will need to decide for yourself whether you want to wear it. But first, this is what it does. James, if you will."

James stepped closer with the bat.

"Allow me to say, sir, this is my favourite job."

"Get on with it."

At that, James struck Tiberius several times, eventually breaking the bat over his head. Tiberius didn't move, flinch, or show any sign of injury.

Elizabeth jumped up in shock.

"It's a personal shielding device. Nothing can get through it. If James tried to grab me, he would be repulsed. James?"

"I don't like this bit, sir."

"Grow a pair. Go on, try and grab me around the neck."

James reluctantly reached for Tiberius—and was instantly thrown backwards, landing on the ground.

"It's similar to the outer shielding on our space suits—only ten times more powerful. And the protection on the suits is only active outside the habitats. I want you to wear it—for your personal protection. You can't be grabbed, shot, stabbed, or hit."

"Grandad… of course. It would be my privilege."

She held out her arm.

"You can't take it off, you understand."

"Sure. Does it make me a superhero?"

Tiberius laughed.

"It's makes you safe." He held it out. "Alright?"

She nodded; Tiberius put the amulet on her wrist.

"Should I go get your cape, sir?" James quipped.

"Fuck off, James. And take what's left of that bat with you before I trip on it and actually hurt myself."

James rolled his eyes, as if to say, *You can't hurt yourself.*

"You can still be intimate with someone—it senses your mood. But if you want them to stop touching you, it will push them back. It's self-charging. I'll explain how one day. And for Christ's sake, don't hit anyone—you will definitely hurt them. It won't let you eat or breathe anything harmful either. It has a built-in scanning function."

"Whiskey and cigars excepted, I assume."

"Yes, except those."

"Jesus, Gramps, what else do you have up your sleeve?"

"Just one of these. Our little secret, okay? A shared bond."

To Elizabeth's surprise, the meeting at Apollo Station the next morning was a full Board meeting. All twelve of the Department Heads were in attendance: Finance, Procurement, Product Development and Construction, Technical Maintenance, Flight Control, Mining and Minerals Processing, Media, Sales and Marketing, Medical, Tourism, Security and Personnel, and the Domestic Services.

Tiberius kicked things off without pleasantries.

"Ladies and gentlemen, this is my granddaughter, Elizabeth. She'll be sitting in. I'm bringing her on as a management intern. I've sent her resume to each of your inboxes for your review—you'll find that Dr. Elizabeth Xander is extremely well qualified. She'll be spending a couple of weeks with each of you over the coming months before taking up a yet-to-be-determined management post. Please give her the courtesy of showing her your operation and sharing with her your frank and open views about your operation. She has full security clearance. She won't be auditing your work, so she won't be reporting back to me. This is purely for training purposes. I'd also like you to meet Major General Fitzgerald Burke—former U.S. Air Force General with a distinguished career. We're lucky to have him. He'll be heading up the Academy. General, welcome aboard."

There was a short round of applause.

"Jim."

The Finance VP, Jim Chambers, took up a briefing of the financial status of the company and its near-term projections. Each Department Head followed, giving a concise update before the meeting opened to key decisions.

Tiberius: "General Burke, have we started recruitment?"

Burke: "Yes, we have social media ads running plus some well-placed billboards. The response, may I say, has been overwhelming."

Tiberius: "Good news. And the construction of the Academy globe."

Burke: "Almost complete, we'll have it in orbit by the end of next month."

Tiberius: "I've decided we're going to attach it to Tellurium One to make the environment for our cadets more diverse."

Burke: "Good deal."

Tiberius: "I want all key flight operations in the interstellar fleet scheduled for next June to be staffed by Academy graduates. Will the first graduate class be ready for deployment on the Centauri mission?"

Burke: "The first intake was selected from already well-trained military personnel, so I can make that commitment, yes, within that timeframe."

Tiberius: "They must have spent at least two weeks on one of the outposts to ensure that they can deal with life under the glass."

Burke: "Noted."

Tiberius: "You'll have to finalise your uniform designs."

Burke: "Well underway, sir."

Tiberius: "I assume you have the relevant creative resources to complete that job."

Burke: "We have three design houses working on it."

Tiberius: "Feel free to use the Star Trek uniforms. We own that franchise, not because of childhood nostalgia but because we need the dreamers not the schemers as recruits. Besides, they are recognisable and, like it or not, those uniforms stand for something positive. Use the ones from the recent movies, not the original series. My granddaughter thinks my purchase of the franchise was hubris, but it actually was about the equipment, designs, recruitment aids, and nomenclature. I'd like it if you brought the final designs to our next Board meeting for approval, if that is OK."

Burke: "All good. Are we on schedule for the interstellar mission to Centauri?"

Julia Davies, Flight Director, takes up the briefing: "Yes, all moving along as planned. We have missions scheduled for Proxima Centauri A in June and after that, in order of launch, to Barnard in August, then probably bi-monthly launches to Lalande 21185, another Centauri launch to Centauri B, Sirius, Ross 154 and Ross 128. The Ross ships will be launched at the same time and travel together most of the way. They will also be extra-long chain star ships because of the length of time it's going to take to get to Ross, approximately sixteen years, onboard elapsed time. On current estimates, we'll have all ships away within the next eighteen months."

Tiberius: "Julia, I want full plans to evacuate the ships tabled at the next Board meeting. With the protective shielding, there is little or nothing that can go wrong with the ship's hull integrity, and all systems have triple redundancy plus spare parts along with the engineers to use them on board. I'm thinking more of the evacuation of a disgruntled or mentally impaired crew member. They will have the relevant medical resources to deal with any health issues but if we have to remove someone we need to be prepared."

Julia: "Noted."

Tiberius: "I am struggling with the timing to declare the independence of our Federation. I was originally thinking of doing that after we reach the Centauri System, but I can see advantage in doing it now. But there are exposures, of course, particularly regarding how our current commercial collaborators and clients, or more specifically their governments, might react. Can I have your written submissions on the matter by Monday, please. The Australian shipyard?"

Fred James, the Product Development and Construction Director, responded: "All thirty-two globe construction bays have been fitted out and are commencing work and four are well advanced on constructing the globes for the Barnard mission. We have no problem fitting all bays into the sixteen hundred square kilometre site. No issues with staffing, great locale in South-East Queensland, great weather. Everything is ahead of schedule."

Elizabeth: "Mr Chairman, have you considered working with NASA on their Helical near-light-speed engine?"

Tiberius: "Nice to hear from you, Elizabeth. Frankly, I have concerns about matter distortion at near light speed. Too many unknowns, so we'll tread lightly and go with our fusion boosters for now; they will get us to half-light speed which won't expose the ships to any matter distortion effects. I think there is a bigger future in space manipulation technology, bending space not the ship, warp technology to use the Star Trek wording."

Tiberius looked at Elizabeth as if to say *see I told you so* regarding the use of Star Trek references.

Tiberius continued: "Bending space is far more attractive than bending the ships and the people in them. Bend space, not people."

There was a ripple of light laughter around the room.

Tiberius: "For our new intern's benefit—because we are bending space to shorten the journey, we don't have to worry about what happens to matter at near-light speed. The Helical drive relies on matter changing its nature for it to work—theoretically, at least. Let's see what they come up with. If there's nothing else…"

The meeting was closed.

On Saturday evening, at Tiberius's estate in the Bird Streets of the Hollywood Hills, the party was in full swing.

Tiberius had purchased two neighbouring mansions, demolished them, and rebuilt one grand estate, complete with a landing pad for his personal boat.

Flight zone approvals for the use of his craft were easily obtained from the California government, thanks to the leverage his company held—after all, Tiberius's companies controlled both gravity-managed vehicles production and the fusion energy reactors, which the State had adopted to supplement its renewable energy investments.

Elizabeth, fashionably late, was embracing her right—a privilege of both women and men alike—to be a princess for the night.

As she walked toward Tiberius, heads turned in admiration. She was fully anticipating compliments from her grandfather.

"Quite a crowd, Grandad. I think I see a few of my favourite movie stars." She scanned the room. "Is it still OK to call you Grandad in mixed company?"

"Being your grandfather is my greatest claim to fame, so yes. Wait until you see the entertainment." Then in a conspiratorial whisper— "Alicia Keys. Always thought she was the most beautiful woman on the planet."

"Past tense?"

"Until you, of course."

Marsha sidled up beside them.

"What do you think?"

"Marsha, great choice of dress."

"It was easy. She could have been a model."

"Why don't you introduce Elizabeth around? I have a quick introduction to make."

Tiberius stepped onto the small stage—just one step up from the large open-plan lounge room floor—and took a seat at the piano.

He began playing and singing the first few bars of "When You Wish Upon a Star."

His rich, familiar voice carried through the room, and as he finished, he kept playing—softly, as background music for his little speech.

The applause was generous.

"Our expedition to the Centauri System leaves June 12th".

The room erupted into applause.

Still playing, he continued:

"We'll be having a send-off for the crew at the sports stadium on Tellurium the weekend before. You're all invited."

More applause and whistles.

"One of the tasks of that mission was to deliver a wish—my wish— directly upon that particular star. But as it turns out, they won't need to make that request—because that wish has already been granted. She is here tonight."

He stopped playing and stood.

"Ladies and gentlemen—one of the most beautiful and talented women on this planet… Ms Alicia Keys."

The applause was deafening.

Later that evening at 1:30 AM, Tiberius was seated on the balcony, enjoying a cigar and a twenty-five-year-old single malt with James. Both men had their feet up on the balcony rail, taking in the spectacular view of Los Angeles, glittering below.

Tiberius was a stickler for convention, so illegal substances were strictly forbidden on the premises.

As a result, many Hollywood elites had already slipped away, likely reconvening in less restrictive environments after fulfilling their obligations to the boss.

Sycophants, all.

But a smaller group of about twenty remained in the lounge room, exchanging stories, drinking, laughing, Alicia was fiddling on the piano, an adoring cluster of friends leaning against it, sipping champagne from Tiberius's private cellar.

Elizabeth was utterly enthralled. That, to Tiberius, signalled a successful evening.

Then, Cheryl Bennet appeared on the balcony.

She carried a half-full bottle of champagne by its neck—no glass.

Both men stood.

She was petite—as all actresses tended to be, owing to their need to appear proportionate against short-statured male leads.

Long blonde hair.

Thirty-five-ish.

Mini-skirted.

Beautiful.

And slightly plastered.

Tiberius had to catch his breath.

He knew her face—one of his favourite crime drama procedurals.

But her name escaped him.

Tracy? Holli?

"Ms Bennet," James piped up. "May I get you an ice bucket and a glass?"

"Well, yes, thank you."

"Please, have my seat."

James disappeared on his errand. Yes, that's it—Bennet. Tiberius thought to himself, what's her first name?

"Nice of you to join us, Ms Bennet." Tiberius sat down next to her.

"Cheryl, please."

"Of course, Cheryl, big fan. Love your work," and all the rest of the Hollywood bullshit Tiberius thought to himself.

"I thought I'd come out and meet the big man himself. I thought you'd be older."

"I am older. Did you bring your husband?" Tiberius said, scanning the crowd behind her, assessing the field of play, looking for anyone straining their necks to see what Cheryl was doing. There was no one.

"I'm between relationship disasters at the moment. You?"

"Ancient history, I'm afraid."

James arrived back with a bucket of ice and a champagne flute, taking charge of Ms Bennet's drink before leaving them to it and attending to the other guests.

"So, you can sing as well. That rendition to introduce Ms Keys was exceptional. You always wished you'd meet her. Really?"

"Too corny?"

"It was sweet. And accompanying yourself on the piano, well done. You have a nice touch. Are you trained?"

"You have no idea. I have a machine that implants that stuff. The singing voice is mine, sadly. I used to be a choir boy."

She laughed. "I'll have to borrow your machine."

"Sure."

"What else does your machine do?"

"Manipulates my cellular makeup. Keeps me young."

"Now you'll have to give me a go of that, I'm getting too old for this game."

"Nonsense, you took my breath away."

"There's a song in there somewhere. Did you give yourself a bigger dick whilst you were at it with this machine?"

What is it with women these days? Tiberius thought. He played along.

"Of course."

"Not too big, I hope, because my bit is only little."

She had Tiberius's full attention.

"Because you think that those parts might meet up at some point?"

She looked at him sensually.

Tiberius jumped straight in, leaning forward in his chair towards her. "Maybe you would want to come to the weightless football match this Saturday on Tellurium."

"Sounds insane, but I'm not much of a football fan."

"Well, I know a little Italian restaurant," he said, sitting back. "Great food, right on the beach."

"Where?"

"On the Amalfi Coast. I know the owner."

"Italy? We're going to catch a flight for our first date?"

"First date. That sounds good, yes—first date." He gestured toward the boat. "The boat you see over there can get us there, door-to-door, in about twelve minutes. Say Friday."

He shouted to James. "JAMES!"

James responded from just within earshot in the lounge room.

"Call Antonio at Tre Gali in the morning, will you? Please, and book us a table on the beach at his restaurant for Friday, say 9:30 their time."

"Certainly, sir." That was quick, James thought.

"I'll have James pick you up at noon—time difference and so forth."

She hesitated for affect, then jokingly said, "OK. Any duty free?"

"James will organise anything you need." Tiberius felt the need to set the ground rules. "You know I stay out of all casting decisions in my media company."

"Are you suggesting that is why I'm sitting here?"

Tiberius looked carefully at her. "Certainly not."

She seemed placated, but she was an actress. She knew he was being disingenuous, though. If Tiberius Xander said jump to any casting director in his portfolio of media assets, it would only be a question of *on who?*

James wandered back out on the balcony as Cheryl left to rejoin the party.

"You know that's one of the top investigative journalists from our rival network, right?"

"Really? I thought she was an actress."

"I'm sure she is, but she's moved on, apparently."

"Should I cancel?"

"I'd let her investigate your brains out."

"Noted. I think I can stay on top of her."

"Of course you can, sir."

"Enough *double entendres*?"

"Please."

At breakfast the next morning—late morning—things were moving slowly in the kitchen as Elizabeth and James were trying to keep out of each other's way to get to the coffee machine when Tiberius came bounding in wearing just a towel and swimmers after his morning swim.

"Pair of sleepy heads."

"Jesus, Grandad, you're built like a brick shithouse."

"Not a current-day bodybuilder's physique, thankfully. Those guys look like they're going to burst. Their tiny, pea-sized heads would just pop right off. I modelled it on an old-school bodybuilder, Frank Zane—I'm not as big though, three-time Mr. Olympia back when you could recognise bodybuilders as human beings."

"Still, Grandad, my god."

"What are you doing this morning, sweetheart? I want to get back to Tellurium."

"I'll come with. Give me a chance to get dressed—and by that, I mean get my head screwed on."

"Thirty minutes—out at the boat. And you?"

"I have cleaning up to do."

"You mean supervise. And by supervise, I mean give the job to someone and go back to bed."

"Whatever."

CHAPTER FOUR

From Russia with Love

"They seem to be just drifting."

"Try and hail them. It looks Russian—use the translator."

Tom Burke, the Flight Control Officer on duty in the control room on Tellurium, rank of Captain, was giving orders to Jenifer Watson, the loading dock supervisor over the communicator. Burke was in the Control Room watching an apparently disabled Russian craft drift slowly towards the Station. He presses the communicator to the loading bay again.

"Get a shuttle out there with a grapple. We may need to bring them into the dock."

"Hailing unknown Russian vessel. What is your status?"

[In Russian] "We've lost all power, running low on life support. Please assist urgently."

Tom called to the technician at the back of the Control Room. "Put a scan over them, will you, please, Bill. Let's see what we've got."

"Only two occupants," the scanner operator responded. "The ship is completely powered down. Yielding high readings of plutonium, Captain."

"Yea, that's a fission-powered craft. You can tell by the shape of their booster nozzles. Troglodytes." Now, to the shuttle pilot on the communicator: "Hook them up, Hennessy, and bring them into Bay Twelve. I'll lower its shields."

"Yes, Captain."

Just as the craft cleared the loading bay doors, it exploded into a massive fireball.

"Cut the loading array loose. Let it drift clear of the Station," Burke ordered with urgency. "Initiate all fire control mechanisms in the loading bays. Open all the loading bay doors—let it vent into space."

They all stood and watched in disbelief.

"How many staff are in that loading bay array?"

"Thirteen. All with suits—not that I think they would help."

"Bring in all shuttles operating in free space. Bring the super-heavy loaders in from the Moon and Mars bases to assist in any rescue and to protect the station if needed."

"The Martian loaders are over an hour away, Captain."

"That's why I want them called in now. Do it," Burke said, a little peeved with the operator. "Deploy the two large loaders from the Moon base halfway between us and the Earth. Scan for further Russian launches."

To the station pilot, Sheila Frederickson, he instructed, "Take us out to a higher Earth orbit. We'll collect what's left of the loading bay when we know what's happening."

Tiberius and Elizabeth saw the explosion as they approached the Station, returning from LA. Tiberius had his own docking port replicator attached to his station home. He docked, then he and Elizabeth went directly to the Control Room. There, they were met there with a high sense of urgency from the crew, but the activity seemed controlled and purposeful.

"Brief me," Tiberius barked at Tom Burke.

"A distress call from a disabled Russian craft. We towed it into Bay Twelve. We had to lower the shields in the loading bay to bring it in. It detonated as soon as it was inside. The rest of the Station's shielding protected us from the blast. No damage to the Station except for the loading bay array, which has been decimated. I released it into free space while we assess the damage."

"Nuclear explosion?"

"Yes."

"Personnel?"

"Thirteen missing… presumed dead. Two in the Russian craft—definitely dead."

"An accident?"

"The timing was too convenient, in my opinion."

"Let's get the facts, Captain. We'll save the conjecture for later."

"More incoming missiles, Captain."

"There are some facts for you, Mr President. Intercept them with the loaders. Just ram them—the shields will protect the loaders. Where are the super heavy loaders from Apollo base?"

"Fifty-five minutes out."

"Direct the super-heavies to the source of those launches. I want both loaders to sit right on top of the Russian launch sites. Are the loaders carrying any material?"

"About one hundred thousand tonnes of meteorite rubble, Captain."

"Tell them to give all of that to the Russians."

"Yes, Sir."

"Give me a line to the super heavy loader pilots."

Now, speaking directly to both super-heavy loader pilots, he ordered: "Bury their launch sites, then use the ships to crush everything you can't bury. Comms, send a warning to those missile launch sites. Tell them that there will be nothing but rubble there within the hour—they had best evacuate."

"Tom." Tiberius called Tom Burke over, now quietly. "Once the loaders are finished at the launch sites, send them to the other Russian missile sites and disable those sites as well. Get their location from the Russian military database—IT will be able to hack in and get you the locations. Have them locate their nuclear-capable submarine and surface fleet, and send the super-heavy carriers to go get them one at a time and relocate them to the Siberian wasteland, crew and all. Use the mining bots from the superheavy carriers to relieve them of their nuclear warheads before you dump the ships.

"Have the carriers arrange the ships when they dump them in a manner that spells out 'FUCK YOU' in Russian when seen from the air.

"Send one of the small bulk carriers to the Kremlin now—have them wait on station there, ten feet above the structure, until further instructions. I'll be in my office. Get me a casualty update from the loading bays as soon as you can, Captain.

"And give them something more to think about—suggest they need to evacuate the Kremlin as well… but await my orders. Comms," Tiberius spoke directly to the comms officer, "inform the American Chief of Staff and NATO top brass that within ten days, Russia will no longer be much of a nuclear power. They forfeited their right to own such weapons when they fired them at us."

Then to Burke, he added, "What they do with that information is up to them."

"Yes, Sir," Burke replied. "Regarding the survivors—I don't think anyone could have survived that blast in the loading bays. Thirteen dock hands. They were all in exo-suits, but that was a hell of a blast. The shuttle pilot, Buch Hennessy, is a friend of mine. He survived it because his shuttle shields were up. The shuttle just got blown out into space on the other side of the docking complex. He's still out there, assisting in the recovery."

"Get him back in and into sick bay. He must have been knocked around—at the very least, traumatised. Arrange for him to be replaced. And broadcast an *all-clear* to the Station to alleviate any concerns but get all hands on deck to assist with the recovery. We're in no danger now that we are aware of the threat."

"Yes, Sir. Mr President… it was my fault. I should never have brought them into the dock."

"Tom, humanitarian assistance is one of our founding principles. Besides, nobody told us we had a war on our hands. We'll have a close look at all of this in due course, but you can't blame yourself. Put your focus on the recovery of those hurt or killed."

"Thank you, Sir." Then under his breath as Tiberius left: "Screw humanitarian—what I'd give to have a few missiles of my own right now."

Two weeks later, Tiberius had brought together the full Board to discuss the Russian attack. They had rambled on for an hour, discussing the minutiae of what happened, with most Members bemoaning the lack of offensive weapons available to the Federation—particularly father and son, General Fitzgerald Burke, the head of the Federation Academy, and Captain Tom Burke, the officer in charge in the control room on Tellurium during the attack.

Tiberius: "I'm not prepared to entertain the acquisition of offensive weapons. Let's move on."

Tom Burke: "We confiscated four thousand three hundred and fifty-two nuclear warheads, some of which don't work, but we can harvest the fissionable material. We also got nearly fifteen hundred conventionally powered missiles that carried those warheads. If we wanted to start an arsenal, now would be a good time."

Jim Chambers: "What the hell do you do with four thousand warheads?"

Tom Burke: "Blow shit up."

Tiberius: "Sounds productive."

Markena Abara, the Technical Director, chimed in: "I had no idea that the heavy carriers could be used in that way."

General Burke: "They harvest asteroids whole—twice the size of even the biggest Russian surface ships. They hit the Russian ships with an electro-magnetic pulse, which rendered them dark, then picked them up like a dead fish floating in a pond. We use the electromagnetic pulse generator to remove the static electricity from the asteroids before we grab them. Once hit by the pulse, the subs had no option but to surface—if they didn't, we just went and got them anyway. No one onboard got hurt from the pulse, but there were a few cuts and bruises resulting from us moving the ships. The mining-bots easily extracted the warheads and missiles, and with their shielding, there was nothing the Russian sailors could do to stop them. They could only watch. Serves them right for using twentieth-century technology."

Georgina Devante, the Director of Mining: "We could use the nukes to break up the big ones in the asteroid belt."

Tiberius: "Subject at hand, please. But yes, that is probably where they'll end up. We'll store them in a secure, safe environment in the meantime."

Devante: "Titan. On the other side of the moon, away from the current facilities, in their own globe."

Tiberius: "Good enough. Get it done. We have satisfactorily proven—to both us and them—that there is nothing they can do to hurt us."

Tom Burke: "Except blow up our cargo bay module."

Tiberius: "Thanks for the update, Captain. I want you to give us a set of recommendation that will prevent that from happening again without giving up on our commitment to assist stricken vessels."

Jack Dwyer, Security and Personnel Director: "But you know this means they will all be afraid of us now—all of them, Earth's nations, I mean. We'll have some of the smaller non-nuclear countries cheering us on because they are sick of living under the yoke of the current power structure of Russia, the USA, China, and Europe. But the Yanks don't like being afraid, nor do the Chinese. We'll need to up the security at the construction sites, particularly in Dallas, and we need to think through how this is all going to pan out."

Tiberius: "That's why we're here, Jack. Make the relevant security changes happen. General Burke, do you have any sense of what the hell they thought they would achieve?"

General Burke: "Clearly, they had no idea of how effective our shields are and how huge those materials tankers are when you see them up close. And they got a good close look at them, I assure you. They also saw—when fully shielded—how effective those tankers can be in forward defence, as can our shielded smaller craft and mining bots. To answer your question, the Russians would have seen the acquisition of the station as an important strategic and economic asset. And allow me to agree with Jack that the other superpowers will now view us with increased nervousness. There was evidence at the Russian main shuttle launch site that they had around sixty fully armed elite soldiers ready to launch if they succeeded in breaching the Tellurium's defences with the missile attack. Your well-known attitude to non-aggression, Tiberius, could have been interpreted by them as a lack of readiness— or capability—on our part to hold off even a modest attempt to board us by force."

Tiberius: "What happened to that shuttle carrying those Russian soldiers?"

General Burke: "The bulk carrier pilot kept nudging it while it stood on their launch pad until they evacuated. And once they had, he squashed it like a bug—along with the rest of their launch facilities."

Constrained laughter—relief rather than amusement.

Tiberius: "Do we have any idea of the Russian death toll?"

General Burke: "Best estimate is eighteen, based on the news broadcasts—including the two in the vessel that they blew up in our launch bay. The rest were mainly accidents as they evacuated their launch sites in a hurry but a handful got caught under the rubble. We warned them; they failed to act quickly enough."

The mood in the room became more sombre.

Tom Burke: "They started it."

General Burke: "There will be a rebalancing of the power structures on the planet arising from these events. It will take the Russians years to recover an effective offensive nuclear capability—that is, if the Americans and the Chinese let them do it. They won't be able to lift those ships out of Siberia, so they'll have to disassemble them and rebuild them in their shipyards."

Devonte Jones, Sales Director: "We sell them the gravity drive assemblies for the car manufacture, but none of the big stuff that they could use to lift those ships—and none of the shielding technology, which they haven't been able to reverse-engineer. We could further hurt the Russians economically if that is what this Board wants. We sell them various medical equipment and systems as well, and they are big users of some of the materials Georgina pulls out of those asteroids."

Tiberius: "Well, that all ends today. All trade with them is suspended, effective immediately."

That ruling from Tiberius met with general applause.

Tiberius: "Do we purchase anything from them?"

Jim Chambers, Finance Director: "Nothing of note… caviar."

Tiberius: "Not a fan of caviar in any case."

Nervous laughter.

Jim Chambers: "I think cutting trade and diplomatic ties with the Russians might give anyone else pause to act against us."

General Burke: "At least overtly. I want our IT people to stay inside the Russian intel systems to see what they have in mind to do next."

Tiberius: "Agreed."

Tom Burke: "And the Americans and the Chinese? NATO?"

General Burke: "I had a report from my source at the Pentagon just before this meeting. They said their top brass were in a meeting at the White House where they discussed a mood swing towards attempting to acquire our technology—particularly as it relates to gravity management and spaceship construction—by force, if necessary. They felt what happened to the Russians makes it imperative that the USA has access to that technology."

Tiberius: "Good luck with that. You could see that one coming even without the Russian attack. It makes taking our production facilities off-planet all the more urgent. General, can we get inside the US military IT systems without being detected to see what they are planning, if anything?"

General Burke: "Yes, we're already there and they haven't seen us so far. They'll be pissed as hell if they find us in there, though."

Tiberius: "Well, don't let them find us. General, I want you to provide a full report for this Board regarding our security arrangements and your recommendations to improve them. Julia, I want you to move Tellurium into a closer lunar orbit immediately. Fred, wind up our Texas and Australian construction operations and move them to Mars. Give me a timeline for doing it ASAP."

Fred James, Construction Director: "That's a hell of an investment to turn our back on."

Tiberius: "I don't expect you to do it overnight, but we need to face facts. The planet below us is morally and politically corrupt—and they're dangerous. I think we need to leave them to it."

Fred: "We'll need to expand Copernicus City to house the Martian workforce."

Tiberius: "Does that sound like a problem to anyone in this room? Offer the Martian jobs to the current workers in Dallas and Australia first. Jim, I want generous layoff packages for those who choose not to come. The rest of you—get your heads together and your arses into gear. I want a plan that gets us totally off-planet within twelve months without disrupting our interstellar launch schedules or our commercial sales. That's it. You've all got a lot of work to do. Tom, can you stay behind, please? You too, General."

Now in the anteroom—Tiberius, Tom, and General Burke.

Tiberius opened the conversation.

"Tom, we need to establish a self-defence force—both ground and air. I've discussed this with your father, and we want you to head it up."

"I'd… I'd be honoured."

"A promotion, of course, to Colonel," the General added. "Later, Brigadier General once the Defence Force gets large enough to warrant the rank—perhaps after that, Major General like your old man."

The proud father went over and shook Tom's hand. "Well done, son."

"I don't know what to say."

"It is, in fact, a steaming pile of dogshit," Tiberius elaborated, "with a lot of work to do to make something of it, but I will give you the resources. That world below us is a violent one. Any visiting alien species would view it with great trepidation. That's one of the reasons we need to distance ourselves from them. And that's also why none of our ships will ever carry offensive weapons—we wouldn't want to provoke a war with an alien species that almost certainly has superior technology. But we need to be ready—for our alien friends, as well as for Earthlings when the time comes for them to have another go at us. I don't think the Americans, or the Chinese for that matter, are going to give up on us any time soon. You're in?"

"Yes. Absolutely."

"General, you're going to have to ramp up your recruitment. Give Tom your best recruits—provided they have the right attitude and training. In your advertisements, push the non-offensive angle—the enlightened advancement of humanity and so forth. That is what we are on about here—Star Trek without the photon torpedoes."

"Done."

"Earth's political systems are largely corrupt. Churchill said that democracy was the worst form of government—except for all the rest. The first part is right, second—maybe not. Manipulated election results and officials on the take make democracy just as bad as the rest. In a democracy, it's not who votes—it's who counts the votes. Dangerously, the American military industrial complex might now want to paint us as the next bad guys—to ramp up military spending supposedly in order to defeat us, or keep up with us—or, as they would put it, to protect America against us. They control enough *duly elected* officials in Washington to do it. Hell, even Eisenhower warned the American people about those guys. I'll put our media people on the task of getting the right message out there, but one of the problems you are going to have to deal with is the optics of us building a defence force here—even though it's now, after the Russian attack, obviously warranted."

"I'll get the relevant advice and come back to the Board with a plan to build the Force." Tom said, then added, "I could use some photon torpedos, though."

"I'll see what I can do with our shield technology. But make it happen—without any guns, bombs, or torpedoes, please, gentlemen."

Elizabeth was waiting in the lounge outside the conference room.

"You waiting for your grandad?" Tom had noticed her as he passed down the hall. "I think he's done."

"No, you."

"Me?" Tom stopped and went over to talk to her.

"In case you hadn't noticed, you're drop dead gorgeous and have been through a few difficult days of late. I thought I'd buy you dinner."

"Look Ms…"

"Elizabeth, please."

"Elizabeth, I appreciate the sentiment, but I've just been given a shitload of work to do and…"

"I thought he was going to ask you to set up the Defence Force. He thinks a lot of you. A man's gotta eat, though, right?"

Tom hesitated.

"That little Italian place off Main, on 4th Street. Say, 8:30?"

"Sure, but make it 9:30. I must at least look like I'm taking my new job seriously."

At dinner that night.

"So, Colonel Burke."

"You heard."

"It's been broadcast Federation-wide. Nobody missed it. You're going to be on the late news on Earth tonight—stressing that the new Defence Force is defensive, of course."

"Of course. It's important that any Earth nation thinking of following the Russian example knows we are not sitting on our hands up here—and that they be reminded we have the massive intellect of your grandfather behind our efforts not to get hit again."

"My grandad owns movie studios. You could become a movie star. Who's going to play you in the movie? Henry Cavill?"

"Too old, but certainly good looking enough."

"Do you see yourself as good-looking? Because you are, you know."

"I still have trouble with the forthrightness of women these days. Thank you, but I think all that stuff is superfluous."

"What about beauty in a woman?"

"Beauty doesn't define a woman, if that is what you mean. With all your grandad's beauty treatment clinics anyone can be good looking, even an ageing movie star. Not that Mr Cavill needs any help."

"Have you been in a long-term relationship, Colonel?"

"Tom, please. Had a couple of goes. Too in love with my career, I'm afraid. Not met the right girl… and so on."

"So, you're looking for the right girl?"

"Yes. A girl, a woman, a lover, a friend, a mentor. I haven't found those in one person."

"Have you exhausted your search?"

"No, but I am exhausted. Let's eat."

CHAPTER FIVE

Centauri One and The Endeavour

It had been a difficult four years following the Russian assault. Initial unease about Tiberius's withdrawal of manufacturing facilities for his space platforms and interstellar craft to off-world locations had been replaced with international acceptance—even given his declaration of an independent state, the Federation of Free Planets (FFP). That acceptance had been engendered by both Tiberius's control of a substantial media conglomerate, which continued to put forward the FFP's point of view, and by the underlying massive demand for his medical, energy, and automotive products—access to which no nation wanted to attenuate. Alienating the new Federation made no economic sense for any nation. No one really wanted to upset that applecart; otherwise, it would be back to ground-based transport, scalpel-and-needle medicine, and fission- or coal-based energy.

The Federation had successfully removed all space-globe production facilities from Earth, reestablishing them on Mars and closing the Dallas and Australian manufacturing sites. Tiberius still manufactured their medical and automotive products in various Earth-bound locations but also had similar production facilities on Mars. There had been no further attempts to launch aggressive actions against Federation bases—largely due to the technological inadequacies of any Earth nation to mount such attempts and the near impossibility of breaching Tiberius's protective shielding. That technology still being a well-guarded secret.

Nothing had been done by the USA, China, or NATO to invade Russia now that they had very few nuclear deterrents. Russia was left to its own devises to progress toward a non-nuclear future, though it was floundering economically in the absence of trade with the Federation. Nonetheless, large government-funded efforts were underway by all nations to reverse-engineer Tiberius's Gravity Management System (GMS) and shielding technology. To date, however, all efforts had failed to overcome Tiberius's intellectual property protection mechanisms and the secrecy surrounding the core technology.

A city of over one million people had grown up next the Martian Apollo Base. Tiberius had called it Copernicus City, servicing material production facilities that processed rubble mined by the Federation's operations in the asteroid belt, as well as the now massive space-globe production facilities. These facilities were mostly housed under eight large protective globes near the Martian equator in the Valles Marineris Basin. New globe assembly, however, was done in the open Martian atmosphere because of the size of that endeavour, with workers wearing protective suits—the lower Mars gravity assisting productivity.

The quality of life in Copernicus was attractive: fresh air, good schools, no crime, low rental costs, excellent amenities, including three golf courses, each with their own well-resourced country club. The city also had a lake beach—the lake supplied fresh water and was stocked with trout, making water sports a popular pastime. A yacht club had been built on its periphery. The demand for jobs from Earthlings looking to move to the FFP far exceeded the availability of places, with the prospect of migration made even more attractive by the absence of income tax.

The Federation had launched several interstellar expeditions, all well progressed, using non-light-speed craft—globes daisy-chained into lengthy aggregations aimed at colonising any suitable planetary object in the target systems. The FFP had also colonised Titan, Saturn's most commercial promising moon, which had also shown signs of an indigenous ecosystem. Titan was now part of the Federation, as was Ganymede, Jupiter's largest moon and home to the largest reserves of clean water in the solar system. Both worlds were able to supply the Federation's water requirements well into the distant future.

With GMS compartmentalised production techniques, they could build globes quickly and economically, and plans were in place to launch a further six daisy-chained interstellar ships within the next twelve months.

Elizabeth and Tom Burke had been dancing around an on-again, off-again relationship with their diverse careers pulling them in different directions. It was not over, but it was on hold. Elizabeth lived alone in a penthouse apartment in Copernicus and held a senior position as head of the city's Council, effectively Mayor of the thriving, fast-growing metropolis. A new ten-kilometre-diameter globe, almost complete, was slated for domestic housing.

Tom, on the other hand, lived wherever his job took him.

Their most recent split had been caused by Tom's prolonged absences—and a rumoured dalliance with a very attractive African-American, now African-Martian, lieutenant, a pilot in the new Defence Force frontline fighters. The romance, according to Tom, was untrue, but the woman—like Elizabeth—was undeniably beautiful. It didn't help that her mother had named her after her favourite actress, Zoe Saldana, to whom she bore a remarkable likeness. In the social media-driven world of closely watched relationships, accusations alone were proof positive, even if unsubstantiated.

Tiberius had perfected space-manipulating travel, warp travel— and had put aside his concerns of attracting unwelcome alien attention. He had built faster-than-light (FTL) spaceships—four craft in total. On this day, he had travelled aboard one such vessel to catch up with Centauri One, the first of the previously launched, large daisy-chained-globe craft heading towards Alpha Centauri. The ship was just over four years from its destination at current speed.

Tiberius's new flagship warp-capable craft was named Enterprise, and he was unapologetic about the Star Trek reference—because he owned the franchise. He understood the implications that the name would have on recruitment interest in his new Defence Forces, with the waiting list for General Burke's Academy now extending five years into the future.

The new warp-capable craft looked nothing like its Star Trek namesake. It was needle-shaped, designed to meet the rigorous requirements of generating a warp bubble, and it accommodated fewer than eight crew members—but it boasted a large cargo bay.

On this day, at Tiberius's request, the ship was captained by General Tom Burke, with his co-pilot, Zoe Jefferson—yes, that Zoe, known to her friends as Zoe Zee or simply Zee.

They had just boarded Centauri One and were greeted by its captain, Maureen Burgess, in the loading dock, where Enterprise had been accommodated. The three shook hands, exchanging pleasantries.

Tiberius had brought with them two small warp-capable shuttle craft to station on Centauri One. The shuttles carried a two-person crew with a small cargo bay, and they had brought the fitment tools to maintain them and a senior mechanic to train the relevant staff resident on the star ship on how to do that maintenance. The shuttles were to be used for forward star mapping, the road ahead was still unknown, and to facilitate return visits to Mars for emergency supplies and communications purposes. Tiberius had discovered that the prospect of *sub-space communications* as proposed in the Star Trek franchise was not possible, so any communications had up to this point taken months or even years to be sent and received. Now with the warp shuttles, the communications could be physically delivered in a matter of minutes back to Apollo Base and then responses returned to the star ship within the same time frame. Tiberius had not yet engineered a method of enveloping an entire daisy-chained star ship the size of Centauri One into a warp bubble so it would have to, for the moment, make its way to Alpha Centauri at sub-light speed. But he had hopes of being able to retrofit his entire globe-based starship fleet with warp capability within the next year, certainly prior to their arrival at their designated destinations.

At dinner that night, Captain Burgess was explaining to Tiberius, Tom, and Zee that the journey to date had been relatively uneventful.

Burgess: "The shielding has proven to be entirely effective against even the larger asteroids we have encountered."

Tom: "In any case, we've brought an upgrade for your shields with us, Mark V. Sorry, Boss, I didn't mean to steal your thunder."

Tiberius: "Boss… really? And the psychological wellbeing of the crew, Captain?"

Burgess: "They all undergo quarterly assessments. Generally, emotional stability, even happiness, is prevalent, some boredom. Importantly, no signs of dysphoria. Productivity is high."

Tiberius: "Good leadership, no doubt. I don't want the crew to know that we will probably get them to Alpha Centauri three years early once we figure out how to envelope this ship in a warp bubble. Best leave expectations where they are, especially given that peace reigns here in the New World."

Burgess: "Noted."

Zee: "So, what happens when we can move these massive ships faster than the speed of light?"

Tom: "We populate the near galaxy, dear."

Zee: "Don't call me dear. With whom?"

Tiberius: "We have lengthy waiting lists to enter our migration program or to join Tom's Defence Force. The problem will only be vetting the candidates. No ratbags or dickheads."

Burgess: "Is that in the employment manual?"

Laughter.

Tiberius: "You bet it is. It also says only 'nice' and 'positively minded' people."

Burgess: "How do you determine that?"

Tiberius: "Ask your head phycologist. It is most certainly possible, to a high degree of accuracy. There is deep-seated dissatisfaction on Earth with the corruption prevalent in all governments, so people just want to leave because, seemingly, they can't change it. Politicians or dictators alike are lining their pockets whilst they talk, distractingly, about matters irrelevant to the wellbeing of the general populace with no free press anywhere on the planet to call them to account, other than our own wholly owned media networks. But they have, sad to say, become a voice in the wilderness."

Tom: "We could fill a hundred of these ships tomorrow if we had the equipment."

Burgess: "I'm keen to have a go of your new warp shuttles. I'd like a trip back to Apollo myself to catch up with some friends, make some noise."

Zee: "Yea, it's got some great party spots now."

Tiberius: "Use the shuttles as you see fit, Captain. You'll be required to do a communications run at least daily to Apollo from now on in any case, including private emails. Perhaps you could fit one of the shuttles with an extra dozen seats in the cargo bay and do round trips for the staff, as passengers. Take them one day, bring them back a week later in another mail run."

Burgess: "I think that would prove popular. It would eliminate the unavoidable sense of isolation."

Tiberius: "You could up it to two or even three a day if it proves popular. The comms would benefit. It only took us twelve minutes to get here. There is a daily 100-seat sub-light shuttle from Apollo to our Dallas Space Port if they want to visit Earth; forty-five minutes on average."

Tom: "Seven minutes to here from Apollo if you take out all the preflight crap, which we are only doing because the ships are new."

Tiberius: "Pre-flight crap… really? I want the other shuttle dedicated to mapping full time. I don't want to be sending warp-capable craft of any size hurtling off into unchartered space."

Burgess: "Yes, sir. Any side effects from your trip here at warp?"

Tom: "None. The craft itself isn't actually moving that fast, it's space that's moving. So, no side effects. In any case, these shuttles have wall-mounted GMS to manage the inertial forces on the passengers and cargo inside the craft. You don't need it in a juggernaut like Centauri One, but it is handy in the smaller craft. You don't get any feeling of speed or directional change."

Zee: "I can vouch for that."

Burgess: "On a different matter, if you don't mind me asking, I always wanted to know why you didn't attempt to reconstitute the Martian atmosphere."

Tiberius: "There has to date been no need. The domes work fine and have the same gravity as Earth because of the GMS foundation on which they sit. Besides, Mars lost most of its atmosphere for a reason—it has no magnetic field like Earth, it lost it billions of years ago. Earth has this massive molten iron core that is revolving, creating powerful magnetic fields that protect the planet from solar wind and, in part, radiation. It also meant that Earth retained its atmosphere. The Martian core is relatively stable and much smaller. The original atmosphere, which did in fact form, just blew away in the cosmic winds. If we were going to build a new atmosphere, we would first need to figure out how to reproduce a planetary magnetic field or alternatively shield the whole planet. If we figured out how to recreate an Earth-type magnetic field around the planet, or duplicate one artificially with global shielding, it would probably regenerate its own atmosphere over time, but you would still be left with the problems associated with lower gravity. We are doing some work on it, but it's not a priority at the moment. The motivation to do it would be to watch the planet heal itself, rather than to live outside the globes because of the gravity differential, like a huge environmental experiment, if you will. The results from doing that may be useful down the track as we populate the near galaxy. It is probably something we may consider for one of your Centauri planets, perhaps even all the planets that we decide to populate. The absence or presence of a suitable magnetic field is probably going to be the most important impediment to the generation of life out in the open on any particular planet."

Burgess: "So, the requirements for a stable, life-sustaining planet are, as we all know, quite complex and unique."

Tiberius: "Not with the domes they're not."

Zee: "You've just added another dimension to our quest for interplanetary life—that is, we will create it. Planetary regeneration. Would we seed the planets once they were protected by our shielding?"

Tiberius: "Possibly. Maybe. I think we would just watch with interest within our bio-domes. Some planets may already have rudimentary life to varying degrees, but it would be fascinating to see what develops if the planet was fully shielded, climate-controlled, and had a stable atmosphere. Is Mother Nature a universal force, or is she unique to each planet? Understanding the evolutionary process would be hugely beneficial."

Zee: "And what if life is not so rudimentary when we get there?"

Tiberius: "Let's find out. If there are nascent beings, we will work with them—to help. We're not going to hide. That Star Trek *Prime Directive*—insisting you can't contact any intelligent but undeveloped life forms—is one of the biggest pieces of bullshit I've ever heard. If we can help, we will. Did humans go to the Sudan and happily stay out of it whilst the indigenous people died of starvation? No. We will guide. If they want us gone, we'll leave. More likely than not they would join the Federation and benefit from a relationship with us."

Zee: "So, if we left, we'd just leave them to their own devices. Take the shielding?"

Tiberius: "Leave the shielding, and monitor. If they develop orbital flight, we'd have to talk to them about the shielding—hence the need to monitor. I expect that situation to be rare or even non-existent."

Burgess: "So, just amoeba then? Basic life?"

Tiberius: "I have no idea—neither do you—what life would be there when we get there or what would develop once we provide protection for the planet. What we do know is that the more planets we shield, the more that will develop independent life. We don't yet know how to provide planet-wide shielding, but I want us to lead that destiny, whether we are there to watch and enjoy it or not."

Tom: "Speaking of supposed nascent life—changing the subject back to Earth, the one with the magnetic fields, and all the dickhead politicians—where's Earth headed, politically and socially?"

Tiberius: "You've earnt the right to call me Tiberius, Tom—at least socially. But not Boss, please. If it was up to me, I would run Earth like we do here, as a public company. In that vein, I would appoint administrators to most of the countries, especially the USA. Its leaders seem to be morally corrupt, and the country is financially bankrupt."

Zee: "Harsh."

Tom: "Accurate, though. But in the absence of ethical and efficient administration, what's going to happen? And if it were possible to install an Administrator, where do you find them? What's stopping them from just lining their pockets? How's that different from a military coup?"

Tiberius: "Propriety and transparency."

Tom: "So, where do you get the Administrators?"

Tiberius: "Potentially off-world, or domestically—if the right people with the right training can be found."

Tom: "What does that mean?"

Tiberius: "They would need the proper education and training and with the appropriate level of oversight they could well clean things up, improve the quality of life, and lower government wastage."

Zee: "So… one of our people, then?"

Tiberius: "Perhaps. They may come from sources as yet unknown."

Tom: "Aliens?"

Tiberius: "Sure, why not—if they are the right type of aliens, with the right skills. What do you think an invading alien species would do when they encountered a fundamentally corrupt, inefficient, ineffective system of government on a planet they *discovered*? And I use the word *discovered* in the same way the original Earth colonial powers did. I'm sure the indigenous of those regions didn't feel *undiscovered*. They certainly wouldn't let Earthlings sit at the adult table with their current history of corruption and violence, of which all nations are guilty. The European colonial powers never let the indigenous into the adult dining room—except as waiters. They would do one of two things: wipe the humans out and start again or replace the existing governmental arrangements with one that works but leave the indigenous in place. Either way, they would redirect the productive abilities of the indigenous people to ensure that they, the aliens, profited from that encounter, often much like the original colonists in Earth's history. I know that sounds overbearing, even violent, and it may not end well, but God knows the Earth colonial powers always acted out of self-interest. And in the end—in some instances, at least—that benefited the indigenous long-term, even if dislocation and violence was part of that process."

Burgess: "It will all come down to money then, in any alien encounter."

Tiberius: "It will come down to productive outcomes. When they meet us—that is, the Federation—and they will meet us probably before they get to Earth, we need to have a lot to offer without the pain, cost, or loss of resources that would come from a violent exchange. It will, of course, always come down to cost versus benefit—for them, and us for. We will want a friendly exchange, not a shit fight. If they can't improve on the way we administer ourselves, because we are doing a great job of that all by ourselves, they will leave us to our own devices and just trade with us, especially if we are not armed to the teeth and have a history of non-violence."

Tom: "Aliens… really?"

Tiberius: "Get used to the idea, my boy. We won't need to find them—they will find us, especially once they see us fliting around in warp-capable vehicles. Hopefully not for a while yet. In the meantime, we need to distance ourselves—literally—from those dickheads running Earth."

Burgess: "Unless the aliens are a bunch of warmongering arseholes."

Tiberius: "If that were so, they would have probably wiped themselves out. But you're right—it's highly unlikely that we would do well against a race of Klingons."

After the meeting, as everyone was leaving the dining room for their quarters, Zee approached Tiberius.

"Fancy a drink?"

Tiberius was a bit taken aback. "Sure, why not? I'm still a bit hyper since my first warp trip—I could use something to take the edge off."

At the bar, Zee and Tiberius.

"I thought you and Tom were… well, I thought he'd be here with you."

"He's in love with your granddaughter."

"He's got a funny way of showing it."

"He's also in love with you, and his job. It's a conflict really."

"Yes, I can see that."

"Don't you get lonely, Tiberius?" Zee was straight to the point; she hadn't dragged him down to the bar for social pleasantries. She had something in mind. She always had a plan—whether for work or pleasure. "The point being, there is no one in the Federation who isn't subordinate to you. So how can you ever meet someone—socially, I mean—if you wanted to date, without breaking any rules."

"Unknown. You are assuming I do want to *date* someone."

"What happened to that actress you were involved with?"

"You mean journalist. That wasn't dating—she was just digging up a story. After some push and shove, if you know what I mean, I wasn't that interested in her either." Tiberius paused, reassessing his openness. "That's blunter than I intended to be. Maybe warp travel exposes your soul."

"One can only hope. I think people are less and less interested in bullshit the older they get."

"And I'm pretty old, right?"

"Not that you'd notice."

"You're right, though. I have no time for, or interest in, the bullshit people feed each other in relationships, or any other type of interaction for that matter."

Zee wasn't really listening—just taking a good look at him, up close for the first time.

"I have a lot of trouble seeing you as a grandfather. How old are you now?"

"Ninety."

"You look thirty."

"I am thirty…five, physically."

"Elizabeth says you're built like a brick shithouse. She's seen you in your pool at your LA house."

"I keep in shape."

"With or without exercise?"

"Without."

"When are you going to release that fountain of youth thing you use?"

"Never. Well, bits and pieces of it have already been released through the medical clinics, they have similar tanks, just not a complete set of cell manipulation treatments like mine. As if you need it. You're gorgeous… and more than capable. A rare combination. Tom says you're our best pilot."

"Captain Burgess and Captain Jarvice from the Denderah might have something to say about that. Plus, have you ever seen Tom fly one of those new fighters? Whoa."

"You mean Defence Force Space-Capable Craft, not fighters."

"DFSCCs, sure. The new FFP MARKIIs are something else. Retrofit those babies with warp capability and it won't matter who we run into out here."

"You flew fighter jets on Earth, didn't you?"

"Yea, I graduated to the new Gen-8 hyper sonics in the US Air Force just when Tom's dad recruited me to the FFP's defence forces."

"Impressive. You don't look old enough."

"Thirty-two. I work out, but I actually exercise, no technological assistance."

"So, you're old-fashioned as well? Aren't the Gen-8s fully AI-controlled?"

"They ended up AI-assisted. Experience with the fully AI driven Gen-7s didn't go so well. They wanted human hands back on the stick."

"But AI is prevalent in other military equipment."

"To varying degrees, yes. Right through to the public service as well, as you probably know. Even in the last three presidential elections, the voting machinery was AI-*assisted*."

"You sound sceptical."

"Those elections in the US were all won by the same party. They don't have to illegally stuff ballot boxes anymore or dig up dead people to vote."

"I get your drift."

"Not that it matters out here."

Now on their third drink, Zee decides to be blunt.

"I say we take this back to your quarters and move things along."

"My God, I might be thirty-ish physically, but my social mindset is still ninety years old. Look, there is a certain part of me that thinks that is a very good idea—out of politeness, I won't mention which part—but we have both been drinking."

Tiberius was, however, quite taken with her and thought for a minute.

"I'd like to call you, though—once I've had the chance to rationalise any potential relationship."

"Very sensible, of course. Serious, but sensible. I think I can deal with that—as long as it's not a hard no. I suppose you can get my number if you need it."

"Time for bed."

"That's the spirit."

He saw she was joking. "Barkeep, what do I owe you?"

"On the house, Mr President."

A few days later, Tiberius was back at his large, mostly empty home in Copernicus City—apart from James, the two now-Martian cats, and Mrs Mac.

All four Martian citizens—cats and dogs were non-voting but otherwise fully constituted citizens.

Tellurium One was still in Earth orbit, mostly acting as a trading post with Earth, as well as a materials packaging hub. It remained a vital link, with the Federation still having substantial mining and tourist interests on the Moon, along with a large number of trading partners on Earth.

Tiberius's apartment on Tellurium One had since been allocated to the Director of Earth Sales and Distribution, Marchia Burnley—a highly capable administrator, originally from Barbados.

But Tiberius's thoughts kept circling back to Zee. After all, she was a difficult woman to resist.

He decided to call her, and they ended up setting dinner plans at one of Copernicus's swankier restaurants for Friday night.

Zee was based out of Apollo, so a dinner date in Copernicus wasn't difficult to arrange.

At the restaurant.

"The chef here used to run one of the best restaurants in New York," Tiberius said. "He says he got mugged regularly—regardless of the precautions he took, so we scored him as a migrant. Have you been here before?"

"No."

"You're in for a real treat."

"New York used to be such a beautiful place to visit, or live. They've lost a lot of their top businesspeople because the politicians have let the place go to shit."

"All made worse by the fact that it is entirely possible to maintain order in any city. Copernicus is a great example. The politicians in New York just had other priorities."

"Like getting paid off."

"Yeah, I presume, or progressing their careers within a morally corrupt political party. Both are full-time jobs, it seems. If you're dealing with crooks every day, you need to spend time keeping an eye on them to ensure you get your cut. And if you're cutting deals with your fellow politicians about your next move up the ladder, then you need to be on the phone a lot. New York taught us many things about running urban environments—you just take what they did and do the opposite."

"You look well—even happy," Zee said, changing the subject, giving Tiberius the once-over. "What made you call me?"

"Happy? Yes. Because I'm here with a beautiful woman and expecting a great meal. So, why wouldn't I be happy. As for the phone call, I love what I do, Zee. And Elizabeth has been such a positive force in my life, but I thought it might be good to, eventually… theoretically, have a partner in crime, so I don't mind the occasional foray into the real world to test that theory."

"So, you after an accomplice or… a sex partner?"

"I still haven't got used of how forthright women are these days. Both I guess, or maybe just a friend. Does the age difference worry you?"

"I'm nearly thirty five myself," Zee skated past that issue, thinking there was none, especially given the way Tiberius looked—"so as I see it we're pretty much the same age. More significantly than age differences, I suspect you would find it difficult to find someone intellectually compatible regardless of their age because you're… you."

"I'm not looking for someone to help me with the maths. In fact, lately I wasn't looking for someone at all—until you asked."

"Bullshit. You must have women hitting on you all the time."

"Not so much."

"That's because you're misanthropic."

"That's an interesting adjective. I'm not egotistical, if that's what you mean."

"I meant aloof, untouchable."

"I don't mean to be—I'm just busy."

"When's the last time you took a couple of days off?"

"The Eisenhower administration."

"I know you're not that old. I've got some leave due—a couple of hundred days, I think. It's Friday. Let's both take the weekend off and see where this goes."

"That sounds pretty… good. What happened to *let's take this back to your cabin?*"

"Disappointed? In for a big night, were you?"

No response.

Zee continues. "This—us, I mean—might be serious. Not sure, too early to say. But I'm happy to go down that path and see where it leads."

On the lake that Saturday morning, without intimacy the night before, just an exceptional meal and a meandering soul-searching walk back to Zee's condo, sharing thoughts elsewhere unrevealed.

They were in a boat that Tiberius had rebuilt—an old-fashioned, petrol-powered wooden speedboat, modelled after the Italian Comitti runabouts, the ones so popular on Lake Como in the 1920s.

The lake, the city's main water storage facility, had been repurposed for sporting and fishing, all safely ensconced under a twenty-kilometre-diameter globe.

They were belting along at the boat's top speed, water spraying everywhere from the bow and stern, heading towards the yacht club, where they intended to take refreshments and cucumber sandwiches.

Their laughter was gregarious as the boat bounced roughly over the waves—but their glee was drowned out by the roar of the massive onboard Evinrude engine.

At the dock.

"That was fun," Zee said, her body still vibrating as Tiberius held her hand to help her onto the wharf outside the club. "You're such the gentleman," she continued, referring to the unnecessary assistance she'd been offered, and happily taken, to help her out of the boat.

The dockhand, left to tie up the craft, watched them curiously, wondering if that was indeed the President—whom he knew always travelled without security.

There was no need for ostentatious displays such as guards or attendants, according to Tiberius.

And given the state of law and order on the planet—and Tiberius's eidetic memory—there was simply no need for note-takers or security personnel either.

They both made their way up to the club's dining room, where they were seated by the front windows, overlooking the large freshwater lake, which Tiberius had indulgently named Ziva National Park and Lake after a lost love from his teenage years.

"Ah! What a blast."

He fell into his chair, his pulse still elevated from the ride. "I regret that I extincted petrol engines—they can be such fun. My ears are still ringing, though."

Zee laughed and waved the waiter over and ordered for them both without consultation.

"Wherever did you get it… and the petrol?"

"My engineering shop rebuilt it from an old wreck we found at a place near Lake Tahoe, Nevada. The seller asserted that it was the exact one from *The Godfather* movie. I thought that was bullshit though, but I bought it anyway. You can get petroleum and oil here from specialist outlets, for hobby enthusiasts. It's not widely distributed on Mars, a tribute I guess to the near elimination of fossil fuel usage on this planet."

"I'm so glad we're doing this, Tiberius," Zee said as she leaned across the table and rubbed the top of his hand softly, genuinely. "It's so… old-fashioned. It's like you're courting me."

"I am. And enjoying it."

"So far."

"Indeed."

"Everybody is pretending not to look at us, but they are, of course."

"They're looking at you, Zee. That chiffon dress and scarf makes you look like a movie star."

She unwrapped the scarf and put it on the back of her chair.

"They're looking at their President and wondering if they can get an autograph."

"I'm busy… well… too enthralled with my present company to sign autographs. You're a beautiful woman, Zee, and I'm saying *woman* in the traditional early twentieth century movie star kind of way, if that is OK to say. I mean it as a compliment."

"I'm happy to be put in the same class as Grace Kelly, Hepburn, even Lillian Gish, if you wanted to go back before the talkies".

"Film buff?"

"God, yes."

"Do you have a favourite?"

"Robert Mitchum, Out of the Past," Zee said without hesitation.

"Ah yes—Jane Greer carrying her shoes as she walks along the beach with Mitchum. Sooo sexy."

"She was so small standing next to him." They took a moment to explore the aesthetic of that movie in each other's eyes. "So, you're a romantic?"

"God, yes." Tiberius deliberately mimicked Zee's enthusiasm for movies.

"Do you think a relationship like ours can survive in this century?"

"Having second thoughts, Zee?"

"Not yet."

"I have no idea about relationships. You're asking the wrong guy. I was married once. I married very young, to the wrong woman, a rebound from someone I was smitten with as a teenager."

"Ah, the mysterious, and now famous, Ziva."

"The very same. My marriage quickly became all about responsibility and role play, certainly not romance."

"So, I'll have to lead the way."

"Yes, ma'am. Where to from here?"

"You got a pool?"

"Sure."

"Then it's to your place—I want to judge for myself whether you are indeed *built like a brick shithouse,* as Elizabeth said. Just research, you understand." Then, to the waiter—"Check, please."

The cucumber sandwiches would have to wait.

Zee was still at Tiberius's place that Sunday morning, after spending the night. It had been a very long night, something of a renewal for Tiberius. As usual, he was up early, having just finished his morning swim, towelling himself off as he found Zee fumbling with the coffee maker in the kitchen, blurry-eyed and somewhat spent.

"Leave it," Tiberius said. "I have brunch organised at Anna-Lee's Bistro."

"But I'm on holidays," Zee complained as she wandered over for a kiss, thinking more likely a lazy day on the couch watching old movies would be more appropriate to her mood. "Yeah, that's right, brick shithouse," she said under her breath as she turned back to the task of acquiring a coffee. Tiberius, only wearing his swimmers, was scrounging on the lounge looking for the jeans and T-shirt he'd worn downstairs.

"Come on, throw something on and I'll introduce you to the beast."

"I thought I met him last night." Tiberius had already disappeared into the garage, carrying his clothes.

Zee caught up a few minutes later, wearing a very short, single-piece red A-frame dress and sneakers—her date night carry bag always prepared.

From the skintight outline of the dress, she'd clearly forgotten to bring clean underwear. No makeup, which she rarely wore, it wasn't needed.

"It's a 1970 Plymouth Barracuda with a 7.2-litre monster powerplant capable of 390 horsepower… meet Betsie." Tiberius pulled off the car's dust cover elaborately, then stood up straight, one hand outstretched, presenting the vehicle like a motor show host.

After discarding the cover, he held open the passenger-side door.

He had a huge smile on his face, the look of a proud parent.

"My God, Tee, she's beautiful. Where on Earth can you drive it?"

They had jointly decided on *Tee* as her pet name for Tiberius, playfully, last night even though Tiberius thought Tee and Zee was trite he welcomed the lack of formality between them.

"Well, there's still lots of places *on Earth* where you can drive such a thing—but here, there's only a few kilometres of road available under the globe for petrol car enthusiasts. You wouldn't want to be driving this beast in Martian gravity—God knows where you'd end up. It might be interesting to find out, though." Tiberius laughed. "But it wouldn't aspirate in the Martian atmosphere. Though, I could fix that—feed it the right air."

Tiberius realised he was getting lost in beloved technicalities, so he cleared his throat and returned to the subject at hand.

"It's hard to get a license to own one. But as luck would have it, the one such stretch of usable road finishes right at my front door."

"Of course, it does."

"Jump in."

Tiberius started the car and looked over at her, seeking approval of the sound—like a teenager showing off his car for the first time.

Zee just laughed gregariously, accepting her role as girlfriend.

Her head fell back onto the headrest as Tiberius took off.

During the ride.

"Elizabeth will be there. We try and get brunch on Sunday when we're both in town."

Zee, nervously, uncertain—"Do you think that's a good idea… that I come along?"

"Sure. I hate creeping around… pretending."

"But… we, we just…"

"Met, yes, I remember. And I'm not going to forget that anytime soon."

"I mean it's early days… surely, too early to…"

Tiberius pulled over and turned to face her to accentuate the importance of what he was about to say, the noise of the engine still burbling. "I want her to know about you. Sure, we might not be very far along, but it was a damn good start, I can hardly walk. I for one am looking for something longer term if you're amenable. Look, she's the only family I have, and I want her to know if anything important is happening in my life."

"You think I'm important?"

"After last night, I know that you are. Besides, she's involved with Tom. She thinks you are involved with Tom. We need to shut that rumour down. OK? Or am I dropping you back at the house?"

Zee thought carefully. "Full steam ahead, Captain."

At the restaurant.

"Zee, what are you doing here?" Elizabeth had gone over, seeing them arrive to give her grandfather a welcome hug and a kiss on the cheek.

"She's with me."

"What do you mean *with*. Work with or with with?"

"With with."

"I thought you were seeing Tom."

"That was never true. I admire him as a pilot and we are friends, but that's all it's ever been."

"Oh." There was momentary silence as Elizebth processed that information and they all found their seating. "So, you're not seeing Tom, but you are seeing my grandfather?"

"First bit's true, second bit, it's early days but I hope it's true," Zee confirmed.

"Grandad, you dog."

"It's all good, Lizzie?"

"If you're happy, then sure—all good. Zee, you'd better let the old fart down easy when you're done with him."

"No plans to do that just yet. He's a big boy." Zee couldn't resist an inappropriate grin, given the unintended double meaning of that remark.

"Before we get started on brunch, I'm off to see the starship *Endeavour*, one of the ships headed for the Ross system, in the morning. She's huge—twelve globes. We built her that big because of the anticipated length of the trip—but now with our warp craft, that's going to change. We can catch up to her in about twelve minutes in my shuttle. Zee's going to drive.

"I am?"

"Want to come for a looksee, Lizzie?"

Tiberius awoke the next morning to the noise of Zee rummaging around, putting on her uniform.

They had stopped at Zee's place on the way back from brunch to "pick up a few things".

Tiberius had a massive headache.

He sat up in bed, feet on the floor, rubbing his head in circles, quietly groaning. Zee noticed.

"You OK?" She came over, sat next to him, and rubbed his back.

"Bad dream. Not the first time. Guys in my bedroom poking me with needles. I always wake up with a headache after one of those dreams."

"Probably just stress, we're off to a distant starship this morning."

"No, I don't get stressed. That dream seems so real. It'll wear off—it always does."

"How often does this happen?"

"Often enough. It's OK. I'm just not used to having amazing sex, I guess. Hopefully you'll give me time to catch up." Tiberius patted her leg, then used it to help himself up, shuffling towards the bathroom.

"Do you want to skip *Endeavour* and go see a doctor instead?"

"No," Tiberius yelled through the bathroom door, now closed.

Zee thought that was a bit abrupt but decided to talk to him about it later after his head cleared.

Now in the shuttle, travelling at greater-than-light speed towards *Endeavour*'s position currently part way to the Ross System.

"You had me a bit worried there this morning," Zee said as she flicked the autopilot on and turned around to resume that morning's conversation with Tiberius. "When was the last time you put yourself through that tank of yours? Do you think you need to have a go in it?"

Elizabeth, who had decided to come with them, looked concerned. "Why, what happened this morning?"

"I'll get some time in the tank when we get back. It was just a headache, for God's sake."

Neither girl was convinced—but just then, the shuttle dropped out of warp and brought the *Endeavour* into full view.

"Right on the button, Zee. Those new star maps seem to be accurate."

"With the right pilot, sure." Zee called the comms director on *Endeavour*. "This is Federation One requesting loading bay allocation."

"Loading Bay 4, Federation One. Here are your shield access codes."

"Roger that, *Endeavour*."

Zee turned control of the craft over to the loading bay supervisor who brought it about to align it with the loading bay access portal. Zee turned back to continue her conversation with Tiberius—but he beat her to the punch, changing the subject.

"You know, I initially thought I'd have to break these long sequence starships up into individual globes to get them into a hyperspace bubble. But then I figured that we can place a connective web of relays along all sides of the ship to transmit the warp enclosure from the space displacement engine and that meant we could do the whole ship all at once. Those Star Trek writers would feel a little silly if they could see this massive beauty go into warp. Why fly around in a tin can when you can, quite literally, take the world with you, or a sizable chunk of it anyway. Needs a shitload of energy, though, to create the bubble. We're going to have to give each starship an extra fusion reactor to get it done."

"Won't everything get squashed up as it goes to light speed?" Elizabeth asked.

"No, no," Zee responded. "The ship doesn't actually change speed. The space around it gets compressed to create and manipulate a warp bubble, making the distance the ship travels shorter. Same speed, less distance, you get there quicker. Well, it does pick up speed a little as it dispels decompressed space behind it, like riding a wave. The pilot has to make allowances for that as it comes out of warp."

"It will take a crew of thirty people about four weeks to install the bubble disbursement antennae on a ship as big as this one." Tiberius was once again getting lost in the technicalities. "The most difficult part is to coordinate the timing of establishing the bubble so that the whole ship goes into compressed space at the same time. Otherwise, you'd break the ship up as the parts went to warp at different times. It's easy with a small craft but enclosing this beautiful thing brought some serious technical issues."

The shuttle set down gently inside Bay 4.

"Welcome Federation One. The captain is on her way down."

CHAPTER SIX

The Final Straw

"I want you to meet my parents." It was two months after Tiberius and Zee had visited *Endeavour*. "It means a trip to LA. It's my mother's birthday. They intend to migrate to one of the outer systems once we're settled there. They'd love to meet you to discuss it. Will you have time this weekend for dinner?"

Tiberius was in the bathroom shaving, and Zee was tidying the bed. "I don't know, that sounds serious. I'm not sure I'm ready for…"

Zee was suddenly alongside him putting her hands around his throat, squeezing gently. "I'm not quite used to your sense of humour yet, but you had better be joking."

Tiberius turned to face her, still with half a face full of shaving cream. "I'm in love with you, Zee; I'd step in front of a bullet for you. Meeting the parents doesn't sound that hard."

"That's the first time you said that, Tee. I love you too, baby." They kissed, and Zee got shaving cream all over her left cheek. Neither cared. As she pulled away to get a towel, she added, "Not that taking bullet for me means much to you with that shielding you wear. Where's mine?"

"You spoiled the surprise. It's on the bed stand in the wrapped box. Number three of three."

"I wondered what that was. It was too big a box for an engagement ring."

"Now you are getting ahead of me."

"Just joking." She wasn't, not really, but it was too soon.

Tiberius, Zee, Zee's parents, Elizabeth (who Tiberius and Zee had brought with them), and Tom (who had flown up from Dallas) had all just finished dinner.

"So, *Endeavour* is on station in the Ross System now." The warp inducers had been fully installed just over a week before. "We're looking to put down six of her twelve globes onto a highly suitable area on the third planet to start a colony there next week. It was previously referred to as Ross 128B—inspiring name though that is—we're going to call it Novum Principium, 'New Beginning.' The locals have already shortened it to Principium."

Congratulations ran around the table.

"Zee tells me you guys want to settle on one of the outer systems. Perhaps Principium is the place. We are about to complete another dozen large globes to send there. They'll be in place within two months. It will be quite the township at that point."

"The atmosphere is not usable?" Zee's mother, Miriam, asked, screwing up her nose.

"No, but it does have one, and it's fairly benign—not much storm activity," Zee answered. "The star it orbits is a red dwarf, but it, too, is stable and provides a similar luminosity to Earth's sun. The gravity is stronger by a third, but it's within our equipment tolerances, so we'll be able to mine and build freely out in the open, including large water storage areas. The atmosphere and the gravity will hold the water in place without needing a globe to cover the water supply like on Mars. But we might put the water storage under a globe anyway to improve the amenity for the citizens."

"Look at you, Zee, quite the engineer," Tom said, teasing her.

Tiberius took over. "The bulldozers are already working on the planet's surface. The colony will be on a large flat rise just below the equator, overlooking a shallow valley with what appears to be a contiguous base of non-porous rock. That will become the water storage lake—massive, ten times the size of Lake Ziva. We'll be ferrying in water from Ganymede, the largest moon of Jupiter, using our new warp-capable super tankers. Fortunately, there are no bugs or contaminants in the atmosphere there—completely sterile, no indigenous life forms at all. But there's about to be: us. We're pretty certain the water will remain liquid year-round. It's a great addition to the Federation.

"Elizabeth, I want you to consider leaving Copernicus and taking over there. The colony is going to need administration and guidance, and with your experience, you'd be perfect." Tiberius left her to ponder that unexpected suggestion without pressing for an answer. "Tom already has his marching orders to set up a defence and police base there, so you two can get some time together, if that's what you want." He changed the subject quickly, pretending that wasn't an important personal issue for both Elizabeth and Tom. "You know, we had over one hundred thousand 'Fedorites' born in the Federation last year—not on Earth."

"So, Granddad, you think Tom and I should add to that tally? Is that what you're saying?" There was no laughter, only general discomfort around the table, so Zee's father, Jack, stepped in.

"Is that what you're calling them now, Fedorites?"

"It's what they are calling themselves," Tiberius responded with some pride.

"Will you ever occupy that planet without the globes?" Miriam asked.

"The planet is larger than Earth, and the atmosphere is correspondingly larger, but at the moment it's unsuitable for our species. It is possible to consider terraforming it to make it similar to Earth's atmosphere. The unfixable problem is the gravity—outside the globes it's 1.3 times Earth's. That's not intolerable for a human, and it's within our imagination that at least part of the colony could gradually adjust their globes' gravity settings over several generations to breed a human derivative capable of coping with the higher gravity. One would imagine them to be shorter but still human.

"I do worry a little about allowing a different species to develop, though—if you'd even call them a different species. Given humans' intolerance over the years towards humans with different characteristics, like skin colour, it could lead to social divides. Would they tolerate each other, or is it just another formula for conflict—terranes versus globe dwellers? Or have I seen too many science-fiction movies? The newly adapted humans could easily tolerate Earth gravity, but not so much the other way around, except for short periods. Whether that would create unwanted friction between the two is unknown.

"But I can certainly see that development happening, given the incentive to explore the whole planet without lugging a shell on your back or wearing an eco-suit. It might be the case sometime, somewhere, as we become the pre-eminent species in this part of the galaxy."

"You believe that antagonism and racism is a genetic imperative in humans then?" Tom asked.

A group of unkempt patrons wondered over to the table uninvited, offering a timely unsought answer to Tom's question.

"You guys think you're so smart, taking production jobs off-planet," a very large, unshaven, half-drunk man said as he and a few of his friends moved in. "Well, me and some other concerned citizens here might have something we want to say about that." There was one big mouth and six backup dancers.

Tiberius looked at Tom and put out his hands, palms up, to say— without words—I rest my case regarding whether antagonism was a human imperative. He found himself in exactly the right mood to have a *discussion* with these gentlemen and stood quickly to face the lead goon, stepping into his personal space. Tom stood on the opposite side of the table, behind Tiberius, so Tiberius didn't see him get up. Tom took his Earth-made Rolex off and put it in his pocket, signalling to their new, unwanted friends that he was ready for some exercise. He was very proud of that watch, a gift from his father back when watches were used to tell the time, and he didn't want it to get busted. The goon saw him do it. Tom was a big, fit guy, and that night he was wearing his Defence Force uniform, having come straight from Defence Station Burke in Dallas to the restaurant, so he looked formidable. The goon's facial expression became a little less cocky as he assessed the dimensions of both Tiberius and Tom.

The women fidgeted; Zee went to stand up, but Tiberius saw her and put out his hand to stop her. He leaned over towards Zee and slowly, deliberately, made sure she saw him turn off his personal defence shielding. A horrified look came over the faces of both Zee and Elizabeth.

"I think you're about ten guys short, arsehole," the goon said bombastically, "not counting the women, of course."

"I'll take my chances," Tiberius replied, turning back to face the goon. "You, however, are shit out of luck."

With that remark, the first goon took a swing at Tiberius but found himself flat on his backside, shaking his head after a lightning-quick straight left from Tiberius, who then used the seated goon's head to balance himself as he bent and kicked the next goon in the head. Spinning around without hesitation, he tripped another with a leg sweep, sending them both to the ground, one hitting his head on the floor and knocking himself out. Returning to his feet after the leg sweep, Tiberius spun to meet the next opponent with an elbow to the face, hit with sufficient force to break his teeth and render him unconscious. That gave the goon next to him pause, as he hesitated, clearly weighing his options but Tiberius decided the matter for him and struck him with a straight right, instantly knocking him to the ground—breaking his own right hand in the process. By now, Tom had made his way around the table and stepped into the middle of the fight; however, all but two of the troublemakers were already on the floor, groaning. Tom finished off the last guy standing and another who was trying to regain his feet. The seventh man made himself scarce. Tom looked back at Tiberius in surprise—bar fights were usually quick, Tom thought, but that must have been a record. Tiberius was shaking his right hand and laughing.

"This planet is truly fucked with specimens like this walking around. No wonder they can't get a job."

"Or fight worth a damn," Tom chimed in.

Zee, now standing and angry, grabbed Tiberius by the arm and pulled him around to face her. "You put your shielding back on right this minute," she told him sternly.

"Yes, ma'am," he complied. "But God, I really needed that. It totally cleared my head, put things into perspective," Tiberius added as he went over and shook Tom's hand—wincing with pain having forgotten he'd just broken his right hand. "Thanks for the assist, General. I wondered why that guy's mood changed; he must have seen you stand up."

"Miserable planet. We'd all be better off rid of it," Tom replied.

"Perhaps more imminently, we should find somewhere else to have an after-dinner drink. I suspect we're not welcome here anymore," Elizabeth suggested met with general agreement.

The after-dinner drinks didn't last long. Tiberius was in pain, and the otherwise splendid mood of the evening had been spoilt. On the way home, back to Copernicus in the shuttle…

"I didn't know you had martial arts training, Tee. I didn't think you needed it with your personal shielding thingy."

"I don't need it, but yes… training." Tiberius left out the fact that it was provided by his cell rejuvenation machine. "Not so old, eh."

"Wait, if you did that for my benefit, then I'm going to be very upset with you. I'm in love with your spirit and intellect, not some inner arsehole full of macho bullshit."

"In love?" Elizabeth said quietly. She was in the shuttle with them. Tom had returned to Dallas; he and Elizabeth were not yet reconciled but both were thinking seriously about it, especially now that the rumours about Tom and Zee had been put to rest.

"That fight was not for you, no. It was for me," Tiberius said. "I think I'm feeling guilty about my decision to leave Earth entirely behind us. I was originally planning to save it, not abandon it. That fight clarified things for me. Being presented with Earth's *finest* was the example I needed to prove, beyond a reasonable doubt, that it's one fucked-up, violent society beyond any hope of redemption by mortal man… or woman."

"You two are in love?" Elizabeth wanted to return to the exchange of affection between them, seeking clarification.

"Yes," came the chorus from Tiberius and Zee together. Neither Zee nor Tiberius was entirely satisfied with how the conversation about the fight had ended, and they continued staring at each other sternly.

"So… you're going to be my grandmother or something?" Elizabeth continued.

"Let's not get ahead of ourselves," Tiberius responded—a sentiment not entirely shared by Zee. Elizabeth noticed. "Besides, I don't think it works that way… step-granddaughter?" Tiberius offered, then, seeing an opportunity to take a dig at Zee, added, "Who's the old grannie now?"

"So, the fight was macho bullshit. You… arsehole. You could have got hurt—well, more hurt. You're too important to get hurt."

"Arsehole, eh?"

"You're going straight into that tank of yours as soon as we get home. That hand is broken for sure. Maybe you can do a brain reset whilst you're at it."

"Maybe we should get you a brain reset." It wasn't much of a comeback, but it was all Tiberius could muster.

"Listen, Macho Boy, turn that shield off again now and we can go right here. Whilst we're at it, how dare you exclude me from that fight. I can kick both your arses."

"I notice you're wearing the amulet," Elizabeth chimed in calmly, trying to turn the discussion to more important matters.

Tiberius, feeling guilty about not telling Elizabeth that he's given Zee an amulet—their amulet—spoke apologetically. "I was going to tell you, Lizzy, before I gave it to her, but Macho Girl here mucked things up the other morning."

"It's pretty handy," Elizabeth responded, now to Zee. "There used to be only two of them."

"I assume you were the second," Zee said warmly.

"Yeah." Elizabeth pulled up her sleeve to show Zee amulet number two. "Saved my arse on more than one occasion."

"Pretty handy for sure… IF YOU USE THEM." She was back to pointing her finger at Tiberius in admonishment, looking to continue the fight.

"Not as good as an engagement ring, I suspect, but more practical," Elizabeth offered, hoping to add perspective and defuse matters.

Zee's mood changed, and she sat back in the pilot's chair, feeling that she was right but also tired of arguing. Tiberius also sat, quietly letting out a whingeing groan and rocking back and forth; it had been a long time since he was last physically hurt.

"Shut up, Tiberius, or I'll punch you where it really hurts," Zee warned, wanting the last word. "You brought this on yourself."

Two and a half months later, all eighteen globes were in situ and functioning on Principium, with eight more on the way. A further ten were under construction on-planet about thirty-five kilometres south of the main settlement. That new globe cluster was going to form a second township. *Endeavour* had left Principium and was in orbit around a second previously unknown planet in the system supervising exploration and research there. Elizabeth was now Mayor and permanently station in Principium. The city's growth had been remarkably quick, probably because of its distance from Earth, Tiberius thought. The new colony had captured the imagination of Earthlings looking to make a fresh start and join Tiberius's adventure into unknown reaches; Principium was as far out as one could currently go.

Tom was also spending a fair bit of time there, getting its defence and police station up to standard. Despite the many disappointments that came with exploring new worlds, Tiberius remained excited about the Ross System, and he felt that Principium was now the jewel in the Federation's crown. At just over eleven light years from Earth, it was the Federation's outlier, the colony furthest into the galaxy that had been established by humans. But with his new mastery of warp travel, his dreams of exploring further into the galaxy were taking root.

Exploration of the Barnard System had proven to be uninteresting: the star's luminosity was inadequate, and the only orbiting planet was both too large to sustain a colony due to its massive gravity and too geologically barren to provide any incentive to try. The Federation's visiting starship, *Barnard One*, had been redeployed to the Centauri system to join *Centauri One* and *Rigil One*; all three starships were now orbiting Proxima Centauri-B.

Lalande 21185b had also proved to be a waste of time. It turned out to be a rocky super-Earth with a very hot surface temperature, the size of 2.69 Earth masses. It was found to be uninhabitable as it would need a Bond Albedo of ~0.9 to have temperatures of around 10°C. Having the same greenhouse effect as Earth would make temperatures intermittently soar by 27°C. The Lalande starship had been redirected back to the Ross 154 System, only to find that there were no planets orbiting that young star.

Meanwhile, the starship *Denderah*, named after the Isis-Hathor Egyptian temple that worshiped the god Sirius-Sothis, was in orbit around Sirius B and was about to take a closer look at a small previously unnoticed planetoid that they had discovered orbiting the binary star system's centre of gravity. Little hope was held as to its liveability, but the captain's interest was piqued when the scans they had made of the planetoid were not being returned. The mineral makeup of Bessel, the name that they had given this small planet after Friedrich Wilhelm Bessel, who first identified the Sirius System optically in 1844, was somehow absorbing the scanning broadcasts.

This little planet had been through quite a tumultuous upbringing during its relatively short life. Initially, Sirius B was a massive sun that had consumed most of its hydrogen fuel and shrunk to become a red giant before shedding its outer layers of hydrogen and collapsing into its current state as a white dwarf—its last metamorphosis having occurred around one hundred and twenty million years ago. Bessel bore the brunt of all those transformations, undergoing multiple changes during Sirius B's turbulent life. That process left an intriguing mineral footprint on the planetoid. Bessel was about the size of Earth's moon, and hopes had been raised by Captain Deborah Travice of *Denderah*— the same Captain Travice Zee had once praised as a better pilot than herself—that new mineral types might exist on its surface. Bessel was now sufficiently cool to allow a first-hand examination, which Travice intended to expedite.

Back in Copernicus on Mars, they had built a new twenty-kilometre-wide globe just south of the city at the southern end of Lake Ziva dedicated entirely to an entertainment district with hotels, amusements including a Ferris wheel, restaurants and parks. At the centre of the district was the massive new Martian National Opera Theatre, which had already become a highly regarded tourist attraction. It was a hugely impressive structure, a polyhedral embedding the classical Fricke-Klein regular map of genus 5 in ordinary three-dimensional space. It stood on one of its many flat surfaces and to look at it standing there, it seemed impossible that it could stay upright.

It was part of the new wave of architectural designs made possible by the gravity management systems used in the Federation. The building was imposing, authentic, and distinctly Martian. It represented a farewell to Earth-based architectural designs and signalled that a new culture had begun in the Federation for human artistic expression. Many prominent Earth architects had found their way to Copernicus and, more recently, to Elysium, the new colony on Proxima Centauri B, and as far out as Principium to explore the architectural opportunities provided there—all of whom enthusiastically embraced the Federation's use of the new scientific realities.

The Opera House was thirty-five "traditionally sized" storeys high, reaching almost to the very top of the globe. It was a statement that the Federation had arrived as a cultural force. Each of the eight theatres had their own gravity management platform, as did all the open areas with the non-supporting external structure built specifically for visual appeal. Importantly, for the growing architectural community, funding was available from the Federation for an increasing number of commissions for public works. The Opera House was just the first of these to be completed but there were many more in planning and development. A new Museum of Art was under construction in Elysium, and efforts were underway to acquire works of art and sculpture from Earth to fill it. There were American dollars in abundance, thanks to the lopsided trade from the Federation to Earth with little coming back the other way. This made such purchases possible—including the recent acquisition of two smaller public museums in Europe to relocate their entire inventories to the new Museum of Art. The Federation had agents at every major art auction on Earth. Ambitions were high, with Tiberius looking to create a new repository of interplanetary art. Artists were encouraged to migrate from Earth, supported by stipends that enabled them to work full time on their art. In the New World, the total population of the Federation had grown to over fifty million, and the money for these artistic endeavours was provided by Tiberius to help foster social cohesion.

On this evening, there was a formal gathering at the Opera House to welcome the Dutch Opera Company, which would be performing *The Marriage of Figaro* in the massive main theatre on the top floor. It was black tie and ballgowns and the invitees had gathered in the main foyer, which was resplendent in its height and marble columns, design themes deliberately selected to contrast with the otherwise modern shaping of the walls and ceiling, the images on which were heroically intwined to illude to the history of the Federation's colonisation of the planet. Those environs embellished the formality of the evening. The guests were being served champagne as Tiberius and Zee arrived to meet up with Elizabeth and Tom who had come earlier, all the way from Principium.

"My God, Lizzie, you look amazing," Tiberius greeted his granddaughter with a kiss. Tom was a little breathless at the sight of Zee in a full-length, tight-fitting formal dress—glimmering, low-cut, and split to the hip—that left nothing to the imagination. Her gorgeous figure and caramel skin were on full display. Elizabeth noticed Tom struggling to breathe. Zee was holding Tiberius's arm with both hands, but she couldn't resist looking at Tom's eyes, intrigued by his reaction.

"Grandad, you look very sharp. You'll have to give Tom the name of your tailor."

The waiters arrived with their champagne, along with a bevy of photographers who began buzzing around for pictures of what had become the Federation's very own "royal family," until Tiberius waved them off—an instruction that they dutifully followed.

"We should go in before someone comes over and wants to talk shop." Tiberius and Tom walked ahead, leading the way. "I've never seen this opera before. You?"

"No."

"I have the recordings," Tiberius added, "so I know how it turns out."

"You speak Italian."

"I am a little surprised you know that it's in Italian. My compliments. Yes, I do speak Italian."

"So how does it turn out?"

"Two words," Tiberius whispered, "double wedding."

"How appropriate."

"What does that mean?"

"I will brief you in full at intermission."

At intermission, in the foyer, the crowd had become loud with the champagne having taken full effect and the performance of the opera thus far having been compelling, even exhilarating. Tiberius and his guests were standing in a circle, sipping champagne, when Tom pulled back a couple of paces and dropped to one knee. He took a ring box from his breast pocket and waited to get Elizabeth's full attention.

"Oh, no," Elizabeth said involuntarily, taking two steps back. The nearby crowd gradually went quiet and gathered closer, noticing the unfolding drama.

"Elizabeth Jade Xander, will you marry me?"

Elizabeth was totally stunned; she hadn't expected that her macho space cowboy would ever commit to their relationship.

After a pause, Tom prompted her. "Lizzie, I can fly back to Dallas in the time you're taking to answer."

Elizabeth stepped forward and took the ring from the box. Tom stood up, and she moved into his arms.

"Don't fly away, cowboy. The answer is yes."

They embraced and kissed—a long-awaited but, until then, unspoken commitment. Applause came from those within earshot who had been watching.

"Well done, son," Tiberius chimed in.

"Don't you mean grandson?" Zee added.

"So, Tiberius," Tom said, still holding Elizabeth in his arms, "*The Marriage of Figaro* you said ends with a double wedding."

All attention turned to Zee, who was now bright red with embarrassment.

"I'll deal with you later... grandson," Tiberius said with a genuine sternness. Then turning to Zee, "I should be so lucky" with a noncommittal and flippant tone.

Zee laughed; no one else did. Then disingenuously, "Who, me?"

It was a joyful evening for the President and his granddaughter at the gala, and this time, Tiberius welcomed the gathered media to capture the special occasion. By the next morning, all the news blogs carried the story prominently, with the lead headline reading:

PRESIDENT'S GRANDDAUGHTER BETROTHED

It was a happy night indeed, as the President celebrated his granddaughter's engagement to General Tom Burke. Photos from the event show the President—now ninety years old but still remarkably fit—his granddaughter, General Burke, and an unidentified guest. For anyone who's been living under a rock, yes, you read that correctly: the President is ninety. What I'd give to have his physique and good looks! Perhaps, Mr President, I could have a go in your anti-ageing equipment.

Over breakfast the next morning:

Tiberius threw his tablet back onto the kitchen table nearly spilling his coffee. "*Ninety years old.* Sounds like a death sentence. You see this is why I don't like having my picture taken."

Zee's tablet joined his tablet on the breakfast table a moment later, visibly annoyed. "*Unknown guest.* I don't even get a credit. I'm a nobody."

CHAPTER SEVEN

Accursed Politics

In the years that followed, the Federation flourished. Their new capital on Proxima Centauri B, now known as Elysium, had grown to over five million inhabitants, thanks largely to the introduction of regular warp-capable shuttle transports providing direct service between Earth, Mars and Elysium, as well as the opportunities for personal wealth offered to new migrants. Elysium had become the centre of a massive trading empire, fostering substantial and sustained economic growth throughout the New World. The Federation now had colonies on twenty-seven star systems, moons, and orbiting stations.

Tiberius had abandoned all manufacturing on Earth but maintained vibrant trade with that planet through its consulate in Dallas, Texas. Earth currency meant little in the New World, but it could still purchase exotic produce from Earth not yet farmed or mined within the Federation—things like truffles, caviar, certain French wines, spices, shellfish, art, and antiquities. Tiberius was determined to preserve the great accomplishments of human culture for fear of their extinction, particularly works of high art. The newly built Museum of Art and Antiquities on Elysium was already attracting great interest from residents and visitors alike.

As part of its program to socially distance itself from Earth, the Federation sold its mining and tourism interests on Earth's moon without compromising the secrecy of the technology used there. All

Federation equipment was withdrawn from the moon prior to the sale. Earth's nations had eventually developed rudimentary gravity-management technology, and Tiberius's patents were being widely abused. Privately, Tiberius was not overly distressed that his gravity-management technology had become public; it at least meant Earth's nations were no longer polluting their atmosphere with rockets and petrol-driven cars. Many attempts were underway on Earth to mimic the Federation's faster-than-light travel technology, though none had succeeded. Various crude, non-Federation shielding systems were now in common use.

Most Earth *democracies* had fallen foul of the invasive corruption perfected, as history books noted, by the Biden administration of the early 2020s, and a one-party system was now common in all such "free" societies. Given the success of what had become known as *The Biden Doctrine*—elections manipulated via financially incentivised media and partisan local district attorneys and judges to suppress opposition—most democratic countries inevitably followed suit. There was now little difference between states ruled by dictators or demagogues and those calling themselves free. In America—whose democracy was supposedly envied worldwide, at least according to its captive media—vote harvesting, ballot-box stuffing, the use of public monies for political purposes and the legal harassment of potential opponents had led many citizens to conclude that voting was pointless. Despite the waning public interest in voting, successive elections still reported massive surges in voter numbers, including those of many deceased Americans. The old Superman motto of "Truth, Justice, and the American Way" had become merely about that last sentiment; America had long since abandoned the first two.

Central to this decline was the fact that a democracy couldn't function properly without the scrutiny of a free and independent media. After Tiberius sold off his media interests, all press organisations were now owned by companies pursuing their own objectives and were not motivated to produce fair or informative news. These companies had their own private commercial agendas, and the pursuit of those agendas was best served by maintaining a single corrupt political party in power. Earth's economic growth was stifled by that demagoguery, which prioritised paying off those in authority rather than pursuing innovation and progress. Ultimately, the loss of an independent press seemed inevitable, and the concept of journalistic integrity became an anachronism. Why wouldn't large multinational corporations buy up media outlets—most of which were operating at a loss—if that investment helped them pressure governments to serve their broader financial interests? Unholy alliances and symbiotic relationships thrived, while public interest sank to a punchline at post-dinner gatherings in the homes of the rich and powerful.

Even so, these same media companies continued to receive Pulitzer Prizes for political hit pieces that were later proven entirely fallacious—prizes that were never rescinded, even when the fraudulent nature of those works was eventually uncovered, generally too late to alter public policy. Meanwhile, those media companies produced movies in which journalists were portrayed as heroically, relentlessly pursuing "the truth," even as the actual notion of news integrity had long since been extinguished in real life. Such films and documentaries transparently aimed to reassure the public they were being given real facts—courtesy of the same corrupt media.

Tiberius's disdain for politics was not born of any particular leaning left- or right-wing ideology but rather from a hatred of misdirection, lying, and hidden alliances aimed at subverting public opinion. He believed that publicly visible oversight by well-qualified administrators was preferable to the seedy world of politics running deep and unchecked, especially when the media—who were part of the game—were tasked with acting as watchdogs. A system with auditors and reviewers, constantly being replaced or rotated to avoid entrenched relationships, along with stiff penalties for any auditor found to be favouring one person or party, would, in Tiberius's view, yield a far better outcome.

It was Winston Churchill who supposedly once asserted that "democracy is the worst form of government, except for all the others." For Tiberius, the first part was possibly true, but not the second. Democracy was almost always infected by corruption and misrepresentation, just as much as all the other forms of government, and in his view, more deceptive and less self-aware. Tiberius had designed a form of social management akin to that used by a public company, with directors and management appointed on merit and subject to multiple layers of transparency and review. This system was supplemented by electronically obtained consensus on specific issues from the registered general public—anyone over the age of fourteen could register to participate in such policy polling. While the results of these surveys did not legally dictate policy, failing to act upon a clear majority view on any particular issue did invite public scrutiny. These polls were tightly controlled regarding who could participate, and they carried weight only if a definitive majority was established. Administration, combined with appointments based on proven ability rather than image, and accompanied by transparent and publicly available performance analysis, proved highly effective—even at the local level. No parties or factions could form to secure promotions for their own members in order to impose a group or party agenda. Anyone could apply for public positions, but only the most qualified were chosen, with all relevant credentials required and performance made public.

Tellurium had been re-deployed to Mars; still in orbit, it serviced Copernicus and facilitated trade with the rest of the Federation. Copernicus had expanded and continued to process substantial resources from the asteroid belt that encircled Earth's solar system. Tiberius had turned his attention towards looking for an Earth-like planet where the globes would not be required. The Kepler planets, long determined to be the most likely Earth equivalents, were still considered to be too distant—Kepler-452b, the most intriguing of them, was over 1,400 light years from Elysium and almost certainly, Tiberius thought, in alien territory. There was, however, one system just thirty light years from Elysium—the TRAPPIST-1 system—which had rightfully attracted a great deal of Federation interest. Not only were all seven planets in that system Earth-sized, but three of them were in the star's habitable zone. Some computer modelling suggested these planets might have developed like Venus, making them too hot for water, but it was believed TRAPPIST-1e could still be hospitable to life. In the absence of more data, this was impossible to confirm, but the Federation planned to investigate within the next two months. Gliese

12b, also around thirty light years from Elysium, orbiting a red dwarf and almost identical in size to Earth, was similarly indicated to have the right temperature to support life.

The Federation had developed its own currency, which was exclusively electronic. Capitalism inevitably took over as the driving force of the economy—just as the Chinese discovered after their dalliance with communism, true prosperity could not be achieved without some form of self-interest. There was no income tax, but certain sales taxes existed more as a deterrent than as a revenue-collection necessity. The Federation was hugely profitable and produced nearly all its own goods and materials, so there was little need for taxation. Businesses paid employees from sales revenue. Government-run businesses were few, but where they existed, they too collected fees for services rendered. Basic rental accommodation was free for everyone, as was a food stipend for essential items. Thus, basic rent, utilities, primary education, and healthcare were covered at no cost. Everything else had a price.

The price of booze and smokes were deliberately inflated by sales tax, with that revenue going directly to the Federation Infrastructures Fund. Smoking was not banned in most areas except hospitals, childcare centres, schools, public transport, and restaurants (including bars contiguous with restaurants). Several standalone bars and taverns had success in banning smoking, although it was not a legal requirement in bars that did not serve food. Numerous cafés, however, offered cigarettes, cigars, and marijuana alongside coffee, alcohol, and absinthe; these venues were popular with artists, writers, and social thinkers. Such creative solons were strongly encouraged by the Federation.

The absence of a total ban on such substances had little negative effect. A compulsory, free, quarterly visit to a public health clinic—spending five minutes in a detox tank—eliminated toxins, cancer cells, and unwanted bacteria and viruses, greatly reducing both personal health risks and systemic healthcare burdens. During that same procedure, the individual's body mass index was regulated to around twenty-four per cent, so obesity and its associated impacts on productivity and well-being were not a concern in the Federation. The fat-reduction process involved increased urination and faecal excretion for about seventy-two hours post-treatment. As a result, this treatment was unpopular—even requiring the use of a nappy at times—but no one seriously objected, given the health benefits and improved quality of life. Once a person reached the required weight, quarterly treatments were far less disruptive, so there was a strong incentive not to overeat between sessions—thus avoiding the unpleasant consequences of a forced weight-reduction procedure. In cases of severe obesity, multiple treatments were administered, usually in a residential clinic setting.

Whilst smoking and drinking were all permitted (including marijuana), public intoxication that resulted in mischief or property damage would lead to incarceration. In the Federation, incarceration was always short-term—usually less than a week—serving more as an inconvenience and embarrassment than a serious method of behaviour modification. Any form of public aggression, for any reason, resulted in incarceration. Opiates were not available for sale to the public. Turning up for work under the influence of alcohol or marijuana could lead to incarceration, depending on the circumstances, and three such offences triggered compulsory rehabilitation, which involved a two-week stint in a live-in facility with no access to any drugs or stimulants. Further or repeated offences, or the perpetration of more serious offences, would result in deportation. Given that the vast majority of Federation citizens were migrants, deportation was an available, albeit extreme, option that was used regularly. Some officials joked that Earth would end up being full of nothing but Federation deportees.

How to correct antisocial behaviour was the hot sociological topic of the day, with most citizens not in favour of deportation as the solution. Alternatives were being sought, the most controversial of which was manipulating a citizen's genetic makeup if it were proven that faulty genetics was the root cause of any aberrant behaviour. The Federation had the technology. Tiberius feared this could send society down a dark path—open to abuse and it represented a forced removal of free will. The genetics behind most antisocial tendencies had indeed been identified at the molecular level and could be addressed clinically, but that procedure was not yet approved.

Zygote screening—that is, the screening of newly fertilised human embryos prior to their development beyond two dozen cells, and before implantation in the uterus—had become compulsory for all citizens seeking to procreate. The goal was to address any antisocial predisposition before birth rather than wait for it to manifest in adulthood, potentially causing harm to innocents. The zygotes themselves were not modified; however, couples were required to fertilise several eggs (as many as possible), then the zygotes were screened. Any malformed embryos, or those carrying genetic markers for socially harmful behaviour or genetic diseases, were simply discarded prior to implantation. From the remaining viable zygotes, parents could choose gender but no other attributes. In the growing Federation, there was no limit to the number of children any set of parents could produce.

The question remained whether it was ethical to enforce genetic modifications on an adult human—except for legitimate medical purposes—without the individual's permission. The age-old debate of nature versus nurture receded into the background because the Federation possessed a clinical fix regardless of how the behaviour originated. Whilst the issue of corrective measures for aberrant behaviour was pressing at that moment, it was thought that over time—as the populace became increasingly home-grown—deportation would become less feasible, and the effects of the zygote screening programme would likely eliminate much of the problem altogether. The Federation recognised that the ability to deport was transient: more and more citizens were born in the Federation or had lived there long enough to make deportation inapplicable. Moreover, sending a felon back to Earth opened the possibility of them reoffending and harming innocents elsewhere. Although the deportee's full file was handed over to local authorities, Earth police forces were often incentivised—due to budget or political constraints—to minimise workload; many deportees ended up released into society without any real oversight.

Citizens were prohibited from owning any kind of guns, and the police force was unarmed apart from batons, stun guns, and standard restraints. Civil defence (including the police) and the military were all part of the same department in the Federation, a structure that was designed for efficiency, clear communication, and effective coordination. The ultimate head of that department, The Department of Civil and External Defence, was yet to be appointed, but below that role, the structure was well settled. There were two divisions: The Division of

Military Defence, led by Tom Burke, and The Department of Civil Defence, which included the police, was led by Jenene Svensson, a recruit from Myndigheten för samhällsskydd och beredskap (MSB), the Swedish Civil Contingencies Agency. Often, both divisions were housed in the same building at the local level and could even be headed by the same individual, depending on the size of the station in each community.

Given the generosity of free social benefits, the Federation could be picky about who they allowed to immigrate. Combined with the fact that sneaking across a land border illegally was impossible—there wasn't one—this meant that new arrivals were well-vetted, generally productive, well-intentioned individuals. The opposite problem, however, had arisen which was citizen bludgers—people who simply took advantage of free rent and basic food without working. Several social measures were put in place to discourage such behaviour. Firstly, counselling was compulsory for anyone who did not work unless they were ill or geriatric or caring for a child or a person with a disability. Secondly, non-workers could not legally purchase certain goods or services—including alcohol, marijuana, or cigarettes—and it was against the law for anyone to provide these goods to a non-worker. Thirdly, non-workers were sometimes required to serve in the military. Everyone had to serve between the ages of sixteen and seventeen (as part of their tertiary education), but a non-worker might be required to return for an additional twelve-month term, or a first term if they were not in the Federation at sixteen. Ultimately, social pressure was the overarching solution; this was a brave New World, and everyone was expected to help build it.

Education was free at all levels in the Federation, right up to and including university. There were now three well-regarded universities in the Federation in Copernicus and Elysium with two more under construction, one of which was in Principium. The curriculum focused mainly on hard sciences (including medicine), public administration (including Federation law), accounting, languages and engineering. Humanities were not offered, apart from history, art, and design. It was felt that someone could always read a book on studies of humanities, of which all that were ever written in all languages were available online without censorship or cost except for pornography and graphic violence. A Fedorite could still go to an Earth-based university, if they had the money, but degrees in subjects not offered in Federation universities were not recognised when seeking a job in Federation space. Earth-based universities were largely regarded as not offering useful practical training in any field of endeavour and were considered as simply providing a "brainwashing production line" that forced students into being Marxists, dropouts, or agitators, and they charged a large fee for the privilege. In any case, the technical courses offered in Earth universities, including medicine, were considered outdated. A graduate from a Federation university or tertiary institute was expected to be able to walk out of school into a job in their chosen profession and be immediately able to perform.

Overall, peace reigned supreme in the Federation. Citizen morale and satisfaction remained high; the environment was clean, and the weather was always excellent. There was even a complete absence of bothersome insects—fleas, flies, mosquitoes, and bed bugs, all of which did not exist inside the globes. Only pollinating bees were present, confined to agricultural domes. Everyone could find work, and social amenities were abundant. Tiberius's dream had largely become reality, and he was now eager to extend that dream deeper into the near galaxy.

CHAPTER EIGHT

The Bessel Discovery

Word had come back from the *Denderah*, in orbit in the Sirius System, that the examination of Bessel had yielded important information. They had requested a confidential meeting with Tiberius, Georgina Devante (the Director of Mining), and Jack Lee (the Federation's Head Chemist). That meeting had just gotten underway on the *Denderah*. Devante and Lee had arrived on-site two days earlier to examine the material extracted from Bessel's surface and assess the viability of mining there.

Tiberius: "Well, this has got my attention—what's with all the cloak and dagger?"

Devante: "Deservedly so. What we have uncovered on the planet below is a game changer."

Lee: "It's a new element, Tiberius—completely new, never seen before. And it's a beauty. Everyone here has been calling it Besselite, and we may as well stick with that. It's as good a name as any."

Tiberius: "A new element is exciting, but we always expected to find material out here we hadn't seen before. Why is it a *beauty?*"

Lee put an image up on the meeting room's large screen—a microscopic examination of the element down to the molecular level.

Lee: "You can even see in this still what I'm talking about, but look at this."

Lee changed the still image to a video.

Lee: "It's almost as though it's alive, but it isn't. It is completely inert—there's just so much energy captured within the molecular structure that it can't sit still."

Devante: "We've done some small-scale tests, and it appears that if the material is added to our shield array generator fluid, the strength of the shielding is improved by at least one hundred times. Following that result we ran further tests mixing the material with the Helium 3 that goes into our fusion reactors and again, even at extremely small amounts, we got a similar improvement in the energy output from the reactors. Both models are still running, so we don't know how long the improvement lasts but the Besselite hasn't degraded after twenty-four hours."

Tiberius: "What made you think of doing those tests?"

Lee: "Just by looking at it, Tiberius. It's bursting with energy, screaming to get out."

Tiberius: "How much of it is down there?"

Devante: "Pretty much the whole planet. That information is based on drilling samples, you can't scan through this material. The planet seems to have a small iron core, but the rest of it is made up of... Besselite."

Tiberius: "Extraction and storage?"

Devante: "We need to do more work, but the material seems to flake off easily when we put our scrapers over it and containment hasn't been an issue thus far. We have several different types of containers full of the stuff sitting out in the open on the planet to gauge what happens to the containers when the material sits in them for a while. The answer seems to be that it doesn't react with any of the containers in any way. So, at the moment, it looks like mining and transportation costs are going to be minimal."

Lee: "Clearly, it doesn't react with itself either. It's just sitting down there in a huge black ball. To the naked eye, there's nothing visibly remarkable about it. Our scanners picked up nothing because it doesn't return a signal. The Denderah saw it visually, and only Captain Travice's thoroughness led us to investigate more closely."

Tiberius: "How hard is it to integrate it into our shielding systems? I'm always interested in improved protection and defence."

Lee: "We did it here in a matter of hours and it worked first time, albeit on a small model—but it looks scalable. We could probably roll it out to the fleet and to the globes in a matter of weeks, once it's fully tested and we get the go-ahead from you. I'm no commercial genius, but this element strikes me as super rare and super useful. Perhaps this is the only place it's available in the universe. I know that sounds like a big call but hear me out. We have never seen it on Earth or in Earth's solar system, or in the asteroid belt around Earth's system—and we've been mining there for years. Some of those asteroids come from different parts of the galaxy. So, it isn't present anywhere else out to eleven light years from Earth. I'd say it is not only rare but potentially unique, available only at this location. This planet has had an extraordinary "upbringing," which is why this stuff formed. You have always said that we will meet other developed species; it would be nice to have something to sell them."

Tiberius: "Dr Lee, you know when Jack Kennedy selected his inner cabinet he often said 'you can't beat brains'. It didn't do him much good, perhaps they didn't have enough brains, but you just put forward an excellent suggestion. It is entirely plausible that this discovery is unique, perhaps not universally unique, but that statement seems to be correct—at least in the near galaxy. It would most certainly be of interest to other species."

Tiberius thought about the next steps.

Tiberius: "Get a load of it down to the Apollo product development people and have them go over it and check for any safety issues. Hush, hush of course. Tell them I am keen to know how quickly it degrades in the shielding systems. I'm going to go and congratulate Captain Jarvice on her *thoroughness* and get her to take Bessel off all the star charts. The interesting thing is that we couldn't see it from a distance because our scanners are blind to it. We had to be right on top of it to know that it was there. So, nobody else is going to find it anytime soon. Sirius is generally considered by Federation cosmologists to be of no commercial use. Chances are we can have this all to ourselves if we are careful."

Now with Captain Jarvice…

"What caused you to take a closer look at the moon below us?"

"You sent us out here to explore. I was just doing my job."

"It looks barren and otherwise unremarkable from orbit. Good instincts, Captain."

"Call me Deborah."

"I am putting together a four-starship expedition to the Trappist System, Deborah—roughly forty light years from Principium. We'll need to do a lot of mapping from there to move forward. I want you to head it up. I will have the FDF forward your promotion to Colonel when I return to Principium. I will have to clear it with Tom Burke, but until then, I want you on station here right up to when the mining operation is set up and secured."

"I don't know what to say."

"You've earned it. What you have found here means we can move forward deeper into space, confident of our security, presuming our initial analysis of what Besselite can do holds up."

"How far out do you plan on going?"

"I guess the answer is all the way, but I think from here, near term, onto Kepler 452, so deep space, 1800 light years. I think Kepler 452b is our best bet at finding an Earth-like planet, so possibly our best bet of finding it already occupied. That is where the line is in my head after which it might become a question of where we will be allowed to go rather than where do we want to go."

On his return to Principium that Sunday afternoon, Tiberius found Elizabeth at his house, deep in conversation with a couple of wedding planners. She barely acknowledged his arrival except for a distracted wave. Tom was in the kitchen, reading reports and nursing a coffee, looking thoroughly bored.

"I'm glad you're here, I wanted to talk to you," Tiberius said, going straight for the coffee maker.

"Shoot." Tom put down his reading pad. "And… hello."

"I want to put a four-starship fleet together for an expedition to the Trappist System."

"Forty light years, that's the farthest out we've been." Tom's interest was piqued. "Certainly reachable now, less than a day, but we'll need to do a lot of mapping as we go."

"I want Deborah Jarvice to head it up, the skipper of the *Denderah* currently on station in the Sirius System. That would mean a promotion to Colonel. You cool with that?"

"You're the boss. She has a flawless record, so… sure. Love to do it myself."

"You're needed elsewhere. One other thing and it's important and confidential." Tiberius came over to the kitchen table and sat, having collected his cup of coffee.

"Everything you tell me, Tiberius, is confidential, unless you say otherwise."

"There has been a development in the Sirius System. We've uncovered a small planet in orbit around the two stars. We've named it Bessel after the German astronomer who first optically charted that system."

"I thought they'd found nothing. There's nothing on the charts other than the binary stars." Tom gestured towards the reports that he had just pushed aside.

"Glad you're staying abreast of matters. I had them take Bessel off the charts because of its mineral make-up; I don't want anyone else to find it."

"Who else would…"

"They've found that it's made up of a new element, one that could seriously enhance our shielding and power generation."

"That's great news, Boss."

"The material has been sent down to our product development people on Apollo to see if our initial expectations prove out."

At that moment, Elizabeth strode in, seeking Tom's approval for a decision she'd just made about their wedding invitations.

"How come you get to do all the planning for the wedding while I sit in the kitchen? Seems a bit sexist to me."

"You want to do it?" Elizabeth asked as she walked over and gave her grandfather a kiss, then stood in front of Tom with her hands on her hips.

"No."

"Then shut up. I'll bring you the key decisions we've made, and you can veto what you want."

"It's all you, baby. I was just joking."

"Wise decision," Tiberius suggests to Tom.

"Grandad, are you sure you're OK with Mum and Dad coming?"

"Of course. It'll be good to catch up with those two arseholes."

Tom laughed out loud; Elizabeth didn't.

"Just kidding, but your father never calls me, and I assume she doesn't tell him to."

A stern look from Elizabeth that included a look of *as if you call them.*

"What about your ex-wife?"

"God, no. Sorry, but I guess you have to ask her though—grandmother of the bride."

"What about your daughter, Ms Judgemental?"

"That's a hard no. But don't forget to invite James and Mrs Mac." Tiberius got up. "Tom, you'll get that promotion notification over to HQ tomorrow and start the logistics for Trappist?"

"Yes, to both."

Tiberius took a swig of his coffee, got up and put the cup in the sink and went to get a shower, patting Elizabeth on the shoulder, still frowning, as he passed.

"Grandad, maybe Mum and Dad could have a go in your tank whilst their here? Especially Dad—he hasn't been well," she said, grimacing.

Tiberius stopped walking, not yet out the kitchen, but didn't turn around. "He should see a doctor."

"Grandad?"

After a pause—still not turning, feeling ambushed—he dropped his head. "Sure. Tell them to bring their medical records." He kept walking, then, after just one more step, he stopped again. "That reminds me—it's time to put the cats through again."

Elizabeth, thinking there was gossip afoot regarding the promotion Tiberius had just referred to, turned back to Tom after Tiberius had left the room to follow up on what she had overheard.

"What promotion? Not Zee?"

"No, the skipper of the *Denderah*, Deborah Travice. Although, she's a hotty too, if that's what you're after—a bit older, taller, and way scarier. If he's promised her a promotion, I am not going to be the one to tell her no."

"I'm so glad you notice such things—especially her being hot," Elizabeth said as she came over and sat on Tom's lap looking for a kiss, then becoming pensive. "I'm not sure I want my parents to be my age."

"Your grandfather is. Why not make it a set—the four of you? It'll be cute. You could wear matching sweaters."

"We wouldn't be quadruplets, arsehole." She kissed him, then stood up. "Why did he hesitate about letting Dad into his tank?"

"Eternity is a long time, sweetheart. They might not be ready to face it."

"I guess."

"And in my view, his hesitation is warranted. You have to remember, he got a raw deal from his own kids. He put everything into their upbringing—everything—and they had the audacity to give him the cold shoulder over some rubbish about who hurt who in the divorce, after they'd fully investigated one side of the story."

"You're such a sweetie." She kissed him on the head.

Tiberius had sold his property in LA. The Australian construction site had been decommissioned and sold off and all that was left in Dallas was the consulate and a well-shielded defence force base called Defence Station Burke, named after Tom's dad who had, the year before, died in a training accident involving the new third-generation defence force fighter spacecraft. The death of Fitzgerald Burke was a sobering reminder of the dangers inherent in what the Federation was trying to achieve in deep space. Tiberius had cut all asset-related ties with Earth but was still having trouble cutting the remaining, and ever-present, emotional ties with his home planet. Commercial trade with Earth was still in place and thriving, all business being conducted through Tellurium One and the Dallas consulate. However, Tiberius's concerns about leaving Earth behind were dissipating because the new push out to the Trappist System meant that there were more interesting matters to consider.

Tiberius and Lee had reconvened at the product development lab on Apollo Base, Mars, to discuss the test results of the Besselite material.

"It does degrade, Tiberius, but very slowly. We estimate that the standard shielding for a five-kilometre diameter dome would have to be refreshed with Besselite every twelve months. But the amounts of Besselite needed are miniscule, smaller than I initially thought would be required."

"Well, that's not a burden. Any safety concerns?"

"None. The material is easy to handle with our existing equipment and our tests have shown that human contact with it, even directly, has no consequences."

"We'll continue to have workers using the stuff fully suited until we've been dealing with it for a while, probably even after that time."

"Agreed."

"And the rollout?"

"We have drafted a schedule for your approval. It's been sent to your inbox."

"Give me the overview."

"We aim to complete the upgrade to the globe shielding within fifteen weeks, then the starships another twelve weeks after that."

"Reverse that order. Start with the four starships allocated to the TRAPPIST system expedition. And can't we ramp up resources to get it all done faster?"

"We have to train everyone, Tiberius. This is all new."

"I want it all completed in ten weeks—done properly. Bring in the military if you have to."

Lee hesitated, but Tiberius's expression made it clear there was only one acceptable answer. "Understood. But you'll need to increase collection and processing."

"I'm heading to the *Denderah* now to review the mining setup and security with Devante. I'll make sure you get the material you need."

Three months later, Tiberius and Tom Burke were standing on the stage in the large meeting hall on the *Denderah*, preparing to address the crews of the four starships assigned to the Trappist expedition. The shielding and powerplant upgrades were complete—although three weeks over Tiberius's tight schedule. The starships *Denderah*, *Centauri*

One, Rigel One and *Endeavour* were all in orbit around Novum Principium in the Ross System.

Tiberius stepped up to the microphone.

"It was quite breathtaking when my boat approached these four beautiful craft orbiting so close together. It reminded me just how far we've come—and, in contrast, how far you're about to go. TRAPPIST is forty light years from here, the furthest any human has ever travelled. You truly are the intrepid explorers of our generation. You've been hand-picked from an impressive pool of flyers. I'm envious, and I know the General here is also jealous of the opportunity you've been given.

"You each have your specific assignments, and we expect you to carry them out excellently. As you know, you'll be stopping every parsec to update our star maps—so, hops of 3.26 light years." (A translation of that distance—3.086 × 10^13 kilometres—flashed on the hall's overhead screen.) "Once you make each stop, you'll remain there for twenty-four hours to map, then move on to the next. Colonel Travice will send those maps back to us at the end of each stop.

"You can all use the map-update shuttle for personal communications back to Principium, and from there to the rest of the Federation, so you won't need to feel isolated at all. Once you reach the TRAPPIST system, and the route has been fully mapped, you'll quickly be joined by the resources needed to establish a colony as soon as you identify a suitable site. We're all thinking of you and know you'll do us proud. So, I'll simply say: *bon voyage.*"

Tiberius looked at Tom to see if he wanted to say anything. He shook his head.

"Colonel."

Now Colonel Travice.

"To your stations. Let's get out of here, we've got places to go and worlds to explore. Dismissed."

After pleasantries and a lot of hand shaking, Tom and Tiberius went back down to the planet and dropped in on Elizabeth in her office at the Principium Town Hall.

"Hey, babe." A kiss for them both from Elizabeth. "The guys get away OK?"

"As we speak."

"To what do I owe this pleasure?"

Tiberius: "I've been speaking to the curator at the National Opera House and they are prepared to make available a Saturday night late next month for you to have your wedding in their foyer. They have to shut down the main theatre for an acoustic upgrade over that weekend, so they've offered us the foyer. Thoughts?"

"That place is huge," Elizabeth responded. "Just how many guests do you want to invite?"

"I was thinking, given we now have the space, we can invite a number of senior Federation officials, make it a state affair."

"Grandad, I'm not sure I want my marriage to be a *State Affair.*"

"Sweetheart, you know they consider us a *royal family.* I cringe at the concept, but I think it would be a unifying moment of national significance."

Tom: "That's only eight weeks away, Boss. Can we organise that in time?"

"If we send the invites out this week, sure. I've gotta go, I'm meeting Zee for dinner back in Copernicus. Think about it. I'll need an answer by tomorrow."

Now with Zee at dinner, Tiberius was explaining the National Opera House offer to host the wedding.

"I think it would be great," Tiberius gushed. "They are set up to cater large events. There would be an out-of-work orchestra available that weekend because of the renovation of the main theatre. They could play Sull'aria as a reminder of Tom's proposal at *The Marriage of Figaro.* It's perfect."

"That place is huge. You could comfortably seat fifteen hundred people for dinner in that foyer—more."

"You'd have enough for two weddings, at the same time, right?"

Zee stopped chewing, mumbling through a mouth full of Sole Meunière. "What does that mean?"

"Just saying." Tiberius kept eating. "With the expanded list of invitees, all the right people would be there, you know, if, say, the President wanted to get married at the same time... or something."

"Tiberius, don't you fuck around with me." Now clear-voiced, having swallowed her fish.

"Relax. If I was going to ask you to marry me, you would know it. For starters, I'd have a ring." Tiberius ruffled through his breast pocket and put a ring box in the middle of the table.

Zee dropped her fork with a clang, dumbstruck.

"It would be a beauty, too. Mined from the asteroid belt near Ganymede. It would be massive, at least seventy carats, minimum, bigger than Elizabeth Taylor's ring. I know you like the old movie stars."

Zee opened the box. It was empty.

"You prick. That is not funny."

Without missing a beat, Tiberius pushed the actual ring across the tablecloth: a massive blue diamond, the look of it made clearer by the white linen. He just kept eating. Zee went backed to being in shock.

"Prick, eh. Not sure I want to go through with it now."

He set his knife and fork down, seeing she'd had enough of his humour, wiped his mouth, and stood. Zee, her mouth still open, watched as he picked up the ring between his thumb and forefinger. She instinctively reached out for it, not wanting it to get away, and then clasped her hands over her heart, anticipating what was coming. Holding on to the table for balance, Tiberius got down on one knee.

"Zee, would you be prepared to marry a nonagenarian?"

Zee stood, then dropped to both knees, shuffling closer to Tiberius, and hugged him excitedly.

Then looking up into his face she replied, "in a heartbeat."

They kissed, hopes fulfilled and desires consummated. Other diners, realising what was happening, began to applaud. Tiberius stood, helping Zee to her feet, and beckoned to the waiter.

"Champagne for everyone, my good man."

Eight weeks later, the wedding became a major social occasion, drawing media attention from across the Federation—and from Earth, too. The local media coverage read:

THE PRESIDENT IN DOUBLE WEDDING

Lieutenant Zoe Jefferson, Zee to her friends, married Federation President Tiberius Xander in a lavish ceremony at the National Opera House on Saturday night. The couple were joined in a double wedding by the President's granddaughter Elizabeth Xander, currently Mayor of Principium, who married Brigadier General Tom Burke, the Head of the Federation's Defence Forces, he resplendent in full uniform. Both brides were dressed by up-and-coming Martian designer Angelica Rossi, and the President's tux, wonderfully structured to show off his magnificent physique, was created by Bowden Taylors on 14th Street in Schöneberg-Globe in Copernicus. No expense was spared, and no key Federation official was left out. Beautiful weather, of course, by arrangement, and the two couples struck a majestic scene, the envy of any royal affair on Earth. All-in-all, it was a grand day for the President and his family and indeed for the Federation itself.

Also, media from Earth covered the event.

FEDERATION PRESIDENT MARRIES

Great pomp and ceremony were on display at the National Opera House in Copernicus on Mars as the so-called Federation "coronated" its king and queen in a double wedding aimed, no doubt, at consolidating the Emperor's—sorry, the President's—rule over this fledgling non-democratic state. The bride is considerably younger than the President and a subordinate in his Defence Forces, so one must wonder if any coercion was involved in securing her agreement to marry; she is, after all, a beautiful woman and he is over ninety years old. The only thing missing was the horse-drawn golden carriage. Here's a clip form a recent interview with Emperor Tiberius:

[The clip shows Tiberius talking to an interviewer: "Earth politics is corrupt. There is no difference between dictatorships there and so-called democratic or free societies."]

It all sounds to this reporter as though this technologically advanced dictatorship plans to remodel, potentially by force, our way of life here in America.

OFFICAL STATEMENT IN RESPONSE TO THE EARTH MEDIA REPORT OF THE PRESIDENT'S WEDDING.

It is the view of the Federation that all of Earth's governments, democratic or otherwise, to varying degrees are corrupt and deceptive in their behaviour, just like the reporter lodging this fallacious report. This kind of sleazy reporting is a major part of why the general populace on Earth is so poorly informed and, as such, the shoddy media on that planet is damning it to repeating its multitudinous past mistakes and is enabling the continued political delinquency that has plagued it so debilitatingly in the past. It is a source of amazement to us that the citizenry of Earth's nations remains accepting of that corruption and allows that situation to continue despite the blindingly obvious available evidence and the presence of more productive alternatives. If Earth's commentators and influencers were reaching for a higher plane rather than dragging their societies into the gutter, then perhaps those societies would now be more advanced like that of the Federation.

The Federation has no intention of interfering in Earth politics but has every intention of simply leaving them to it. The Federation abhors violence of any kind and, unlike the USA, has no offensive weapons nor any intention to engage in conflict of any kind with any country. As previously demonstrated with Russia's attempt to capture the Federation's orbiting space station, Tellurium One, we will vigorously defend ourselves if required.

CHAPTER NINE

The Martian Confrontation

By this time, the USA and China had each developed their own rudimentary gravity-management systems and had used them to build space-capable craft that enabled further exploration of Earth's solar system. Neither nation had yet mastered faster-than-light travel, but both were close, devoting significant resources to that pursuit. Tensions had arisen over the Federation's claims to all the planets it had colonised and declared part of the Federation. Both the USA and China refused to recognise those claims, establishing bases on Mars—not far from Copernicus City to further their own interests and undermine the Federation's claim to the planet. Talks were underway about dividing Mars into separately owned states, but these discussions were stalling badly—particularly as China insisted it owned the entire planet, including the regions occupied by both the Federation and the Americans. The Federation, for its part, believed it had already colonised Mars but was open to sharing territory, recognising that one day it might need to share other planets with newly encountered species. Increasingly Tiberius was beginning to think of Earthlings as "other species."

The main underlying concern had become that both the USA and China had brought offensive weapons to their bases on Mars. It wasn't difficult to interpret that as an act of aggression, but Tiberius was at this point prepared to wait and see.

All of this occurred against the backdrop of a growing exodus from Earth to the Federation. Owing to its advanced construction technologies, the Federation could build and fit out globes in a matter of weeks, and it was taking on over ten million Earth migrants each year—selected from among twenty million applicants in the past year alone. A significant proportion of those accepted were from poorer Earth nations, though the Federation always paid close attention to each applicant's skillset, likely productivity, and basic personal attributes. Tiberius believed that citizens of "free democracies" could, in theory, use their vote to remedy their local predicaments instead of leaving the planet, but he held out little hope that they would do so. He doubted the electorate would ever reject the pervasive corruption, particularly when so many corporations benefited from it and exerted massive influence over the media in partnership with any political party granting them favours—never mind the welfare of the general population. Tiberius was always mindful of the fact that he, too, had fled Earth, having fully given up on improving humanity's condition there through democracy or negotiation.

China and America had developed rudimentary shielding technology —rudimentary even compared to the Federation's pre-Besselite systems. They had achieved those advances largely by abusing Tiberius's patents. Tiberius had effectively written those patents off, concluding that pursuing the offenders would ultimately be fruitless. Nonetheless, he ceased selling advanced gravity-management products to Earth-based clients and had never sold them any Federation shielding technology. Having brought Earth back from the brink of extermination with his gravity-management transport systems and fusion reactors, Tiberius would now no longer benefit significantly from those same technological advancements on his home world. Even so, both the USA and China continued to rely solely on stolen gravity-management systems and shielding technology for their spacecraft—something Tiberius rationalised was still good news for the environment. He considered imposing a total ban on product sales to those countries but decided against it, given the importance of gravity-management vehicles and fusion reactors for environmental protection, as well as the health benefits provided by his scanning chambers.

Then one day at a defence outpost outside Copernicus City, Mars.

Scanner Operator: "They appear to be sending in tank-like crawlers from both the American and Chinese bases."

Sergeant: "The scans say they're carrying tactical nuclear weapons— you know, the 'little ones.'"

Base Commander: "There's no such thing as a little nuclear weapon, Sergeant. Contact Defence HQ and make sure General Burke is informed."

Within thirty minutes, Tom was standing beside the outpost commander, binoculars in hand, watching the crawlers digging in approximately fifteen kilometres from the edge of the post—around twenty kilometres from Copernicus. All Defence outposts were equipped with fighter-craft docking replicators, so Tom had flown directly to the station.

"What the fuck are these arseholes up to?" Burke commented, largely to himself. "Get the Director and Tiberius on teleconference, please."

As Tom was briefing Tiberius, all American and Chinese units started firing in a coordinated attack.

"They are aiming at the two new construction sites. Are they shielded?" the Post Commander asked.

"We shield before we start construction, so, they will find that this is pointless," Tom said, with Tiberius and a handful of the Federation Directors watching online.

"Not to them, I'm guessing," Tiberius said calmly. "To them, the gun is always the answer. Let them play out their stupid war game. They'll get tired of it."

The soldier manning the scanner piped up. "Their shielding is not handling the blowback from the nuclear shells exploding against our shields. If they keep this up from their current positions, they're going to kill themselves."

"Fuck 'em" was, as usual, Tom's attitude.

"Look," Tiberius ordered, "send them a message that they are wasting their time and that we think their shield won't hold up."

"And tell them to fuck off," Tom added.

But before either message could be sent, "We're receiving a communication from them. I'll put it on speaker."

American Voice (through speakers): "Do you wish to surrender?"

Everyone in the outpost burst into spontaneous laughter.

Then Tiberius said, "Wait, wait. Send them this and only this in reply: *Nuts.* The Americans will understand the reference if they remember their history from World War Two."

Tom puts his hand up as if to answer a question from the teacher. "Battle of the Bulge, late in the Second World War, the Germans had McAuliffe, who was the acting division commander of the 101st Airborne, surrounded in a small French town with his men. The Germans asked them to surrender, that was McAuliffe's response: '*Nuts*.'"

"You know your history, Tom, congrats. Can we get a reading on the effect the shelling is having on the new shields?"

Scanner operator: "Nothing."

"You can't get a reading?"

"No, I mean yes, I can get a reading, but it is having no effect whatsoever. I mean none, zero. It's making a mess of the terrain outside the shielding, but that won't bother the globes either, or their stability. They are self-supporting, they could levitate if they had to, and the residents know that."

Tiberius expands on the answer from the scanner operator. "We'll have to fill it back in to let the globes sit down without needing energy to hold them up, but we can attend to that after these bozos back off. They could blow the planet out from under Copernicus, and we'd just relocate the whole city."

"Hopefully that won't be necessary," Tom adds, "but these pricks are going to blow themselves up if they keep shelling."

"I was wondering how we were going to test those new shields. I'll have to send them a thank you note. Look, keep us up to date and let us know when they wriggle off back to their bases, please. This is immensely disappointing but not surprising, although I am happy with how the shields are performing."

"You don't want to squash them or something?"

"No need for loss of life, Tom. Keep us informed." Click.

After a while, a crowd started to gather inside one of the new globes to watch the fireworks.

"Should we move them back, General?"

"No need. Let them watch these idiots, what the old-world leadership has to offer its citizens."

"Look, look!" The scanner operator was on his feet, standing at the window, pointing at someone in the growing crowd. "There's someone selling popcorn."

Tom shifted his binoculars to look at the audience. "OK. That's a beer truck that just arrived; this might get out of hand. Wait, there is a couple of taco trucks right behind him. It's just going to be a party. Ain't capitalism grand."

"And here comes another guy with a truckload of folding chairs," the post commander added.

"One guy has made a *fuck you* sign. General, can they see that?"

"The globes are completely transparent so, yes. This is fucking hilarious. If Oppenheimer could see this," Tom mused, "he wouldn't have felt so guilty about developing nuclear weapons. It reminds me a bit of accounts from the Battle of Manassas, the first battle of the American Civil War, when well-to-do Washington citizens rode out in their carriages to watch what they thought was going to be the only battle of the war and to have a picnic. They soon learned that the war wasn't going to be any picnic."

"One guy's got his bare arse up against the glass. Won't he get burned?"

"There is no radiation getting through the shields, so, no."

"Look, two of the American tanks are heading back."

The crowd goes wild.

"Can we get audio from inside that globe?"

The scanner operator flicked a switch and uproarious cheers and laughter burst through the sound system.

"That's a real crowd pleaser. Do you think the Yanks will come back for an encore?"

"Don't think so. I wish I could join the crowd," Tom said out loud. "I'd send the police over there to calm them down, but I agree with their sentiment. It's a triumph without us firing a shot. Like a war never fought but won anyway. Tiberius was right all along about offensive weapons."

Diplomatic objections were vociferously lodged. Sanctions were imposed to no discernible effect. Tiberius knew that this was not the end of it.

The Federation was never admitted to the United Nations but Tiberius didn't care to belong to a chamber full of hot air, populated by members doing nothing about the real problems of the planet who were almost entirely subsumed with their own self-interest. As usual, there was no action taken by the UN against China and the USA for the Martian attack primarily because both China and the USA had veto power to squash any resolution, reinforcing Tiberius's view of the uselessness of that organisation. In any case, the Martian conflict shrivelled down to nothing as did discussions about ownership of the planet, and indeed, the Chinese and American bases later that year reduced in size. The Federation formed the view that discussions about ownership of the land was irrelevant to its own plans. There was nothing that the Americans or Chinese could do on Mars, and after the failure of that attack they certainly had nothing further to prove by being there. The Federation city, Copernicus, was economically driven by mineral processing of material delivered by mining output from the asteroid belt. It also had globe construction and a myriad of small businesses serving the Colonies with goods and produce; the Chinese and Americans had none of those things to sustain, economically or otherwise, a presence on Mars either because of the lack of the technology or the fact that, for them, those businesses were all based on Earth. There was nothing left to explore on Mars that the Federation hadn't already explored, mapped and mined. The planet itself offered little further commercial prospects outside of the Federation city and base, so there was nothing for the Americans and Chinese to do there except pose. But that attack did indicate a seismic shift in American and Chinese attitudes towards the Federation, one that would rear its ugly head again in the future.

Subsequently, the defence base in Dallas was closed with all willing personnel being transferred to Elysium. Those actions further distanced the Federation from its mother planet.

CHAPTER TEN

Hello There

In the four years that followed the Martian conflict, the Federation had left behind all concerns about the petty squabbles it had with Earth and focused on colonising the near galaxy. They had sent probes to Gliese 414A in Ursa Major, Gliese 806 in Cygnus, Upsilon Andromedae, and as far out as Mu Arae, fifty-one light years from Earth where they had found orbiting the planet Quijote, itself a gas giant, a large moon that was immediately habitable using the globes, but it was thought potentially, longer term, that it might be habitable in the open. That moon, rich in usable minerals, soon hosted a Colony that proved popular with the Federation's now-substantial community of prospectors. It was the miners on Quijote-1 who coined a new nickname for Federation citizens—"Newcons" instead of "Fedorites"— and this term quickly spread throughout the Colonies (including Mars) inhabited by Newcons in Federation space. By now, the Federation's population exceeded one hundred million people.

Included in that list of planetary acquisitions was four colonies in the near space around Trappist-1, including on the fourth planet of that system, which they had renamed Borealis, because of the odd light given off from the Trappist-1 sun. They had established what had become a large colony in a very short period. They called the city New Dallas, over fifty light years from Earth, in honour of the role Dallas, and indeed Texas, had played in the Federation's early development. It was in Tiberius's house in New Dallas that the family had gathered for their now-regular Sunday lunch. Tom and Elizabeth had a two-year-old son with them, whom they had named Sunrise, inevitably to be shortened to Sunny by his future classmates, and Elizabeth was pregnant again with their second child. Zee and Tiberius were still undecided as to whether they would have children.

After their lunch, as they waited for their dessert to be served, Tom put forward a question that he had been puzzling over for some time.

"How did you crack the faster-than-light travel thing, Boss?"

"That would require a long answer, too long for here. But if you want to start down that path, begin with the fact that time doesn't appear in any cosmological mathematical equations. It is presumed to exist but nowhere is it moving, so it doesn't factor into those equations. Notable it's never seen to be moving forward. Start there and see where that takes you."

Tom looked puzzled. He decided to do more reading before speaking again, given that it didn't sound quite right to him. Then Zee, thankfully, changed the subject to music.

"Tee, give us a tune on that grand piano over there. You must have brought it all the way from Earth for a reason."

"Yeah, Grandad," Elizabeth agreed. "That's a great idea."

Tiberius —who was gifted with a naturally fine singing voice from his days in the boys' choir at the Church of the Little Flower in Dallas—had never been formally trained in piano. Instead, he'd used his rejuvenation tank to install the necessary muscle memory. He felt a twinge of guilt as he sat at the keyboard, thinking he hadn't earned the right to play, but he dismissed the thought as quickly as it arose. It was, after all, his technology.

He began to play.

"This is for the most beautiful woman I have ever met…" everyone turned to see a big smile rising on Zee's reddening face "…who unfortunately can't be here today."

"Hey!" Zee exclaimed reflexively, never quite accustomed to Tiberius's brand of humour. He relished provoking a reaction in those around him was part of his DNA. His daughter always found it irritating.

"Oh, Zee, unclench. This is for you."

He began to sing 'At Last' (by Gordon and Warren):

At last
My love has come along

...

Zee came over to the piano as he sang and sat next to Tiberius. She put her arm around him and her head on his shoulder as he played. Tiberius continued, now looking at Zee.

*And here we are in **Heaven***
For you are mine at last.

Vigorous applause, but Tiberiu

Vigorous applause, but Tiberius immediately got up to return to the table after giving Zee a kiss, waving off requests for an encore.

"Ah! Dessert," Tiberius declared, walking back to his seat. "Thank you, James—you saved me from further embarrassment. Join us, please—you deserve it. That was an excellent lunch."

Sunny, Tom and Elizabeth's son, was due to start school early the following year, when he would turn three. In the Federation's school system, students graduated from what Earth called high school at around fourteen years of age, and they did so with a level of knowledge more advanced than any Earth high school offered. They then moved on to skills-based tertiary studies in their chosen field—some becoming doctors and engineers in Federation universities. That study was paused at sixteen whilst students attended compulsory military enlistment for one year and resumed thereafter for those that required further tertiary studies to enter the career of their choice. The military enlistment was considered more of a benefit to self-discipline and personal fitness than preparedness for any war.

Lately, almost no one chose to attend Earth-based universities, as they were seen to offer little of practical value—unless one specifically wished to learn why Earth was so dysfunctional, particularly the so-called Ivy League American institutions, which were perceived as peddling "woke" or Marxist agendas, those universities having long since given up on their once famous reputation for broadening the mind of their students. Even their technology courses were widely judged outmoded, offering hardly more than a Federation high school education. In the Federation, it was believed children could learn far more quickly than the slow pace enforced by Earth's school systems. Consequently, they graduated high school at fourteen, completed transitional or trade courses by sixteen, then their military enlistment, and sometimes proceeded to university. A university degree was less prized than it was on Earth; being productive was what mattered most. Nonetheless, some pursued a doctorate, including a medical degree, usually finishing by about the age of twenty-two.

For a Federation medical doctor, cutting skin and the use of needles was considered barbaric techniques. A medical graduate left a Federation university well-versed in both new and traditional technologies— the latter studied largely to appreciate historical practices rather than for their use. They finished with no personal debt; the services they provided were heavily subsidised by the government through universal health insurance, with add-on cover offered by privately owned, licenced insurance companies.

Meanwhile, Tiberius—eternally preoccupied with next steps—now felt sufficiently confident in the new shielding technology to deploy colonists straight onto newly discovered suitable planets, moving even deeper into previously unexplored space.

Early the next morning after their Sunday lunch, Tiberius and Tom had decided to sneak in a quick nine holes of golf before work. A golf globe was typically one of the first structures erected in any new colony; this one remained a bit rough due to the youth of its vegetation, but it was still playable.

"There's going to be a PGA-sanctioned tournament on Elysium next month—the Federation Cup," Tom remarked.

"Thank goodness Earth sports aren't so political these days," Tiberius replied.

"That course is wicked."

"Especially if we arrange for rain on the Thursday night before the tournament and some hefty winds on the Saturday. I've got it on good authority… that's precisely what they'll be facing."

"Yeah, your authority."

"Time to show them how things work in the New World. That'll sort those fuckers out. Good PR for once."

Tom's communications device rang, cutting their golf round short. Within minutes, both men were enroute to the Defence Control Room on the outskirts of New Dallas, picked up directly from the course by a Defence Force shuttle. There, Amanda Hoffing, the station's duty officer, began her briefing.

"It's not a configuration that I recognise, Mr President," she said, referring to a medium-sized ship that had just dropped out of warp and taken orbit above Borealis. Footage of the craft, relayed by one of the planet's communication satellites, filled the big screen.

"Is it just one ship?" asked Tiberius.

"Nothing else is showing on our scanners."

"Could it be Earth-based?"

"They have nothing as advanced as that craft, Tiberius."

"Then this could be that *oh shit* moment that we've talked about. Try hailing them."

"Hailing unknown orbiting vessel. Please identify yourself."

No response.

"Do it again, a little more firmly," Tiberius suggested.

Tom took the communicator. "Orbiting unknown craft, this is restricted space. Please identify yourself and state your intentions."

Silence lingered—then suddenly:

Voice (crackling over speakers): "Apologies… sorry, we had the wrong translator loaded. This is the starship Amna#hsg*fterr. We are The Tearn."

In the background, another voice could be heard berating the comms officer: "You know they're English speakers!", prompting the captain to turn and politely ask them to be quiet.

"We would like to meet with your President, Tiberius Xander."

"How the fuck do they know me?" Tiberius said quietly to the post commander, unheard by the crew of the orbiting ship. "Are they armed?"

"Our scanners say no, Mr President."

Tiberius clicked the communicator on. "This is Tiberius…"

Tom put his hand over the communicator. "What the hell are you doing? Don't let them know you're here."

Tiberius took the communicator back, gently removing Tom's hand. "Settle down, Tom. This was inevitable. I'm not going to start a relationship with them with a lie." He clicked it back on. "With whom am I speaking?"

"I am Standart, which is the best translation I can offer you. I am the Captain of this vessel. Sorry for the intrusion."

"How do you know my name?"

"The whole galaxy knows your name, Mr President."

"The whole galaxy, Captain?"

"Yes, there are seven nascent species known to exist in this half of the galaxy, including you and Earth, since you now count yourselves as two different species—although you are genetically one. Three of those seven planets are not yet capable of space travel, but each are under the guidance of one of the developed civilisations, mostly willingly."

"What does that mean?"

"Well, two of them have been forcefully taken over by the Tracalonians; they are a warrior species."

"But you are a peaceful civilisation."

"Of course. Like you, we are not armed. The same can't be said for your home planet, though."

"The Federation has no association with Earth any longer."

"We're well aware of that. It's precisely why we'd prefer to talk to you, not them. Would you like to come aboard to discuss matters, or would you rather we come down to the planet? Your choice."

"Give me some time to confer with my colleagues. The answer is yes, we do want to meet—but we've only just made contact, and we need to consider our security." Tiberius clicked off. "Tom, call a Directors' meeting and advise them immediately that we have alien visitors. Ask for complete confidentiality until we decide how to handle this."

Twenty minutes later, an online meeting with the Federation Directors revealed mixed reactions to this sudden development.

Tiberius: "We can't ignore it; they're here, knocking on our door. Thank God it wasn't the 'Troglodytes'—or whatever he called that warrior species."

Tom: "Tracalonians."

Jenene Svensson, the Director of Civil Defence: "Yes, we must meet but we must keep you safe, Mr President."

Tom: "Then not on their ship."

Devonte Jones, Director of Sales and Marketing: "Could be some excellent trading opportunities here, both ways."

Tiberius: "That's the spirit, Devonte."

Jenene: "A separate globe, perhaps. We have one nearing completion on the western outskirts of the city. We could get the construction crews out of there; I think the docking portal has been installed."

Fred James, Director of Product Development and Construction: "The docking replicator has been installed, the globe is fully pressurised. We are just starting to build, but there is a hall nearing completion. We could set that up for the meeting."

Jenene: "The globe is, of course, separately shielded. If we let them in there, and by them I mean them personally, not their ship, we can limit the risk. If they try and blow it up like the Russians did to Tellurium, the damage, other than potentially to the attendees, would be minimal to the city."

Tom: "Tiberius is an attendee."

Tiberius: "But as you know I am fully shielded, which has been upgraded with Besselite. I might get knocked around a bit so, given that possibility, I think I have to be the only one there from our side."

No further objections were raised.

Tiberius: "It's agreed, then. I alone will attend; the rest of you will be online with both audio and video. Tom, let them know we're setting up a venue and will provide coordinates and docking protocols. Fred, please get that hall ready ASAP, including all the electronics."

At the meeting with the Tearn.

Tiberius: "It seemed prudent for me to attend alone, for security reasons, but the rest of our Board is on the large screen behind me. I hope that's acceptable to you."

Captain Standart: "Certainly. That's fine; we understand your caution, though I assure you it's misplaced. This is my Second-in-Command—a Lieutenant in our squadron—and my Chief Engineer. Their names wouldn't roll easily off your tongue, and in our society, mispronouncing someone's name is an insult. 'Lieutenant' and 'Chief' will suffice."

Tiberius: "Pardon my ignorance, but the Lieutenant is female, correct? She appears very female to me. Do you have different genders?"

Standart: "Yes, two biological genders, much like you, and yes, she is most definitely female as you correctly observe."

Tiberius: "If it's not offensive to say so, you look more like us than I ever expected an alien species to look."

The Tearn were olive-skinned, with body shapes and features similar to humans, though they had larger eyes—not the exaggerated "little green men" look of Earthly science fiction. Standart and the Chief were completely bald, while the Lieutenant had long, braided white hair extending all the way to her waist.

Standart: "That's no offence. We find your species handsome as well. In this region of the galaxy, all developed species are humanoid—except for the Tracalonians, who evolved from reptiles."

Tiberius: "Your translator is remarkably fluent, including some human jargon."

Standart: "We have developed it over many of your years."

Tiberius: "We also have electronic translators, but only for our own human languages—all of them, in fact."

Standart: "We'll swap them, then. It will be our first trade transaction."

Tiberius: "Thank you—sounds good. So, why are you here, and why now? You've obviously been observing for some time."

Standart: "Yes, we've been watching for quite a while. We once had face-to-face contact with an Earthling—a rather remarkable human. It went well, but we decided to let the planet mature before pursuing formal discussions with any of its governments. Earth was fortunate we found it first; if the Tracalonians had stumbled upon it, you'd likely be quite accustomed to lizard stew by now."

Laughter rang out among the Tearn crew, though Tiberius only smiled politely.

Standart: "To our surprise, Earth's development produced the Federation rather than a maturing of Earth's species as a whole."

Tiberius: "Yes, the politics on Earth proved impenetrable, it was better to start again, at least that way well-meaning Earthlings have options. It's good to see that you guys have a sense of humour, the lizard stew joke." Smiles all around. "But, again, why make contact now?"

Standart: We have a proposition: a joint project. We've identified an uncolonised planet about one thousand light years from here—much like Earth was a few thousand years ago. Its flora is reminiscent of Earth's from that era; however, it has no sentient life and no fauna. We can share our star maps with you in order for you to see where it is. We want to colonise it in the open, so your globes won't be necessary. We'd like you to join us."

Tiberius: "Join you?"

Standart: "Yes, a combined colony, and by 'combined' we mean mixed, not segregated."

Tiberius: "Sounds fascinating. Why us?"

Standart: "It is a logical next step for you, and us, and in the view of our Council you are ready, and by *you* I mean the Federation, not Earth. You are the most suitable candidate of the developed beings. Besides…"

Tiberius: "Besides?"

Standart: "Your shielding is magnificent—far better than anything else in the galaxy. We can give you technology to shield an entire planet, which would be critical if we're living out in the open. Individual globes won't be required on this planet, so without full planetary shielding, we'd be vulnerable. Its atmosphere suits both our species; gravity's Earth-like, which suits us—one reason we're roughly your height—but we still need planetary defence."

Tiberius: "You think the planet will need defences?"

Standart: "Of course, you can never be too careful. And it would be helpful in climate management."

Tiberius: "Pardon if this inference is off-base, but… you're implying our species could be genetically compatible?"

Standart: "Our people aren't sure. We've considered that question and we think the answer is no, but with a little medical assistance then maybe. They have speculated that the genetic combination, us and you, would most likely yield an excellent outcome though, even exciting.

Our genetic pools have been separated since the beginning of time which makes for great opportunity if they were combined."

Tiberius: "They're not going to be able to fly, are they?"

Standart: "I agree a sense of humour makes for better company. No, our projections say that they would be smarter, stronger, with enhanced longevity, but not superheroes, no. We have monitored some of Earth's television broadcasts over the years, mainly to test the translators, especially the science fiction movies and television shows. There was a character on one of those telecasts named…"

Lieutenant: "Spock, from the planet Vulcan. I loved that show, what I saw of it, but I am sure they didn't deliberately write it as a comedy."

Chief: "Yes, teleportation for one thing, as if that's possible. Hilarious."

Laughter from the Tearn and, this time, Tiberius joined in.

Standart: "Yes, Spock, superior strength, intellect, peace loving; they are thinking something like him as the progenies, without the ears."

Tiberius: "If it works at all."

Standart: "Yes."

Tiberius: "A new species? That thought has never entered my head. Are you suggesting forced fertilisation?"

Standart: "No, no—nothing so barbaric. We also value the family unit and personal freedoms. That's why I said 'mixed colony,' not segregated. Just let them live in proximity and see what happens. If couples do form and want children, we can help medically. We'd limit genetic choices to health factors, then let nature lead us."

Tiberius: "If it doesn't work—culturally or biologically—then what?"

Standart: "Then we have an excellent cultural exchange, at least."

Tiberius: "I didn't see that one coming. Trade deals, sure— but marriage? Sounds like a good way to mess up our brand-new relationship."

More laughter—apparently marriage was as tricky a proposition for the Tearn as it was for humans.

Standart: "So, let's start with just a new friendship then?"

Standart stood and put out his hand to Tiberius, which he welcomed and shook with both hands to the applause from the Board and the Tearn crew.

The image of the handshake was captured for posterity.

It was a brand-new day in a brand-new world eighteen months after first contact. Tiberius had come down to inspect progress on Hope, the combined Federation and Tearn world, and was standing out in the open near the almost completed Town Hall, breathing in the new clean air, overwhelmed by a sense of accomplishment. *Hope* was a word that both species could pronounce and the Tearn had acquiesced to using an English word for the name of the planet because of the underlying sentiment it conveyed. It was Tiberius's first visit since construction had begun.

He was amazed at how the concept of this new community captured the imagination of Federation citizens. Applications to participate had poured in. Tiberius wondered if perhaps people were finding the globes claustrophobic—though he'd never seen evidence of that, and the domes were certainly vast enough to avoid feeling cramped. More likely, it was the pioneering spirit: building a life under open skies on a virgin planet, far from Earth's failures, with freedom to roam was irresistibly compelling.

The new planetary shielding satellites had been installed, and as a result Tiberius had shared his shielding technology with the Tearn—but not the location of Bessel. He sold them Besselite at a reasonable price (including a profit, as the Tearn were also capitalists), and in return he acquired Tearn scanning systems, subspace communications technology, and the means to shield an entire planet. Subspace communication was something Tiberius had previously dismissed as impossible.

Now he was installing planetary shielding on all worlds with Federation colonies—including, importantly, the secure protection of Bessel.

The new inhabitants of Hope had begun arriving in droves as soon as the housing became available. As discussed at the first meeting, the houses were arranged so as to have one Tearn household next to a Federation household.

Tiberius felt a tap on his shoulder and turned to find it was Standart.

"Quite something, Mr President?"

"It certainly will be, Standart —assuming all goes well. And call me Tiberius." He gestured to the crystalline sky. "Look at that—the colour's like crystal. Feel that sun on your face... not like an artificial sun. You can almost feel it doing you good."

"Blueish sky, just like Earth and Tearn, because the gases are basically the same and yield that blueish colour under a yellow sun... and crucially it has no pollution."

"Let's keep it that way. But your sky is just as clear?"

"We developed the technology to clean up the atmosphere. Your ex-friends on your home world never bothered to develop that technology, they were too busy whinging about the problem. I forgot you've just flown in from Tearn, your second visit there, the first was to make the agreement for this colony?"

"Yes, Tearn is a beautiful world, Standart, and your people are so accommodating. The personal translating devices you designed respond almost immediately to the spoken word."

"You can always turn it off if you don't want to hear what they have to say."

"I know you're joking, but I have done just that, to listen to your native tongue. It is pleasant-sounding, though many words are unpronounceable for me."

"That won't be an issue here; we'll ensure everyone has a communicator."

"We must open a marketplace, a large one, with both cultures selling their wares and foodstuffs. It would be quite the tourist attraction, and it would also promote integration."

"Indeed. Do you think we'll need a common currency, Tiberius?"

"No, just an exchange rate. Everything is electronic. We'll float the exchange rate in due course once the volume of money being exchanged between us warrants it. Have the rate reflect the value and volume of the goods being sold between the two cultures, including at the trade level." Standart agreed. "You seem to be able to get your mouth around English without issue. You don't use a communicator."

"English is a simple language with no syllables drawn back into the throat like with Tearn. Some of the Newcons will give it a go, I am sure."

"And make idiots of themselves much as I did when I first spoke Japanese."

"Tearn is not as simple as Japanese either."

"I know, but the two languages have this inextricable link to the social system, what word you choose to use in any sentence depends on the social standing of the person with whom you are conversing: male, female, younger, older, boss, or underling. In Japanese, you must tread very carefully to ensure you don't insult people by using the wrong noun or verb that might be inconsistent with their social relationship with you. From what I can gather, Tearn is the same."

"Indeed, very observant." Then changing the subject. "Speaking of conversing, what are you doing tonight for dinner? I would like you to meet my wife, Zara. Did you bring Zee?"

"Yes, she came with me. Zara's a Newcon variation of your wife's name?"

"No, it's just Zara."

At dinner that night, in the private dining room on Standart's ship.

"We'll have four small courses," Standart announced, "two 'Newcon' dishes—my cook's best interpretation—and two Tearn dishes, accompanied by a Tearn alcoholic drink called Tibit, derived from the esr#@ta tree on my home world."

"Zee, what's that tree called again?" Tiberius teased.

To everyone's amusement, she attempted to pronounce it.

"Not even close," Tiberius said, as always ribbing her.

"Zee, you'll make an excellent Tearn speaker… in due course," Zara reassured her. Communicators weren't needed tonight, as both Standart and Zara spoke fluent English.

"How many Earth TV shows did you watch?" Tiberius asked, noting their effortless use of idioms. "You've really nailed the colloquialisms."

"We studied them," Standart said. "We knew you'd be our next contact."

"But you mentioned you'd already met a human."

"Three, in fact, over a period of years—not me personally, but our species. We've kept an eye on Earth for quite some time."

Tiberius tucked that information away, making a mental note to explore it further later. Tonight was for socialising, not interrogation.

"So, Zara," Zee asked, "tell us your story. How did you meet this character?"

"I'm a biochemist, and I was working at a hospital when they brought in this scoundrel—injured in a clash with the Tracalonians. I had to do some tests; we met, he begged, I caved."

"So you and the Tracalonians have actually been at war?" Tiberius interjected, interested.

"There was a treaty signed about thirty years ago, but yes, it got very messy there for a while."

"You've been in battle. My respect. I've never had the privilege. I respect your sense of service to your community."

"I'm not sure I'd call it a *privilege*. It's hours of mind-numbing boredom followed by pants-wetting fright."

"Language, Standart," Zara chastised.

"Apologies to the ladies."

"If I may say you don't look old enough to have been fighting wars thirty plus years ago," Zee observed.

"Your husband is not the only one with a cell regeneration chamber, Zee."

"Good to know." She glanced at Tiberius, contemplating whether it might be time she tried his tank. "So you two have been married over thirty years?"

"It's easier to keep a relationship going for a couple if they are constantly renewing their vows and, importantly, renewing their age and youthful energy to sustain those vows."

That being confirmed, Zee said to Tiberius, "You'd better give me a go in that tank of yours then."

The wine was served, and all parties paused to assess the beverage.

"Oh, that's smooth, with an extremely interesting aftertaste," Tiberius offered. "This ka-ka-whats-it tree has a sweet fruit."

"That's a much closer pronunciation of the name."

"Bullshit," Zee interjected, "that's worse than my attempt. Apologies to the ladies."

"It's not a fruit; it's a bean. You know, if the experiment on the planet below works out, we should grow some of these esr#@ta beans. And we should open our borders—your people can move to our colonies, and Newcons can migrate to Tearn."

Tiberius thought carefully before answering.

"So your plan is to take us over by stealth?"

Laughter ensued but cut short, the group mindful of how new and delicate their relationship still was.

"You're joking, right?" Standart asked.

"Sure. We should both vet any applicants moving either way."

"Of course."

A slight tension hung in the air, so the conversation drifted back to safer social topics—fitting for a first dinner between two newly acquainted species.

"Do you keep pets?" Zee asked.

"Yes," Zara replied. "Not like your cats or dogs—those species don't exist on Tearn—but small mammals that might remind you of otters. They aren't aquatic, but they love our pool."

"We'll have to get you a pair of cats," Tiberius chimed in. "Cats are the preferred pet of intelligent humans."

"I take it you keep cats."

"Yes, they're both nearly forty years old now."

"They live that long?"

"No. About fifteen years usually. I put them through my chamber."

"You modified the cell regeneration chamber for cats?"

"Yes."

"You'll have to share that reprogramming with us. The *otters* only live for about eight years, and for our pair their time is just about up."

Zara sighed. "Don't say that, Standart. We love them, but they're too clever for their own good. You need two separate locks on your pantry door or they'll break in. One of them dragged a box over the other day so he could stand on it and fiddle with the locks using both hands."

"What's his name?" Zee asked.

Zara gave Zee a look implying *you wouldn't be able to pronounce it.* She let the question pass. "We have a pair, but they're desexed—there are plenty on our planet."

"That's a lovely dress, Zara," Zee observed, looking for a subject more to her liking. "You could certainly sell your fashions in the marketplace once it opens."

"Tearn fashions will be available before then. At least two of our clothing retailers plan to set up on Hope soon."

From there, the group chatted about fashion, cooking, spices, and entertainment, and by the end of the evening, everyone felt warmly connected—satisfied by both the meal and their new friendships.

CHAPTER ELEVEN

The Shared Soul

Within four years, Hope had become a shining example in the near galaxy of what can be achieved with acceptance and reconciliation between species. The houses were being occupied as fast as they could be built. There were almost five million occupants of the planet already, split into four cities, with Hopeton as the capital. There were approximately equal numbers of Tearn and Newcons, even Tiberius and Zee had bought a small ranch just outside Hopeton on which, with some help from employed Tearn workers, they grew both Newcon vegetables and Tearn edible plants. They had hopes of selling any excess produce in the now vibrant Hopeton open market that operated seven days a week because of demand from an enthusiastic domestic market and from tourists, some of whom had come specifically to visit the market.

The tourist trade was flourishing on Hope not just because of the popularity of the produce market but because of the hotel and spa resorts that had sprung up in and around the Hopeton environs. One such resort, which had become famous for its health and relaxation resources, was located about fifty kilometres out of town on a hot spring in the foothills of the mountain range that surrounded the town. Many people visited the planet because they wanted to see firsthand what a mixed species community looked like and how it functioned. There was a deep-seated fascination amongst both Tearn and Newcons for the mixed community concept and a hopefulness, pun intended, that it would be successful.

The restaurants in Hopeton and the other towns on the planet had become legendary amongst culinary experts with chefs moving to Hope to explore the opportunities of a fusion between Newcon and Tearn cuisine, inventing new dishes that included the produce from two diverse and fully developed societies. As a result, farming had become a major economic driver for the planet, included in which were several ex-Texan ranchers who had begun to experiment, fully endorsed and assisted by the government, with crossbreeding Tearn and Newcon livestock.

Hope had adopted the Newcon measure of time and metric size and distance because of its similarity with Tearn metrics for those constants. In other instances, such as temperature and pressure, the Tearn methodology had become accepted and universally used. Standardisation of those measurement tools was necessary for many reasons, but critical amongst them was their use in the new architecture that had started to grow up on the planet. There were architectural firms based in Hopeton that had both Tearn and Newcon partners whose work had become highly sought after not just on Hope but in several cities in the Federation and on Tearn. Their designs and engineering were considered not only unique but also vibrant in both aesthetics and function. Additionally, both the Federation and the Tearn had opened manufacturing facilities, mostly electronics, on Hope to assist the economy and employment. However, the unemployment rate was virtually zero, not only because of those new manufacturing jobs but because of demand from the tourism industry, mining, farming, and construction.

In the four years just past, Tiberius and Standart had become close friends, and their families often got together to share company and discuss the issues of the day. The two of them had worked together on numerous projects on Hope and had come to rely on each other's judgement and opinions. Tiberius had decided to make his personal headquarters on Hope. The offices were only partially built, but on this particular evening, after a long day, Tiberius had invited Standart to see his as yet undecorated office to get his opinion on the proposed decor and for a discussion on progress more generally on the planet. Tiberius had moved in some essential furniture like a desk and a liquor cabinet, and two leather high back winged lounge chairs which were, for the moment, sitting facing an open gas fireplace with ceramic artificial logs, which was in full operation.

"So, we are friends, right?" Tiberius asked as Standart sat on one of the lounge chairs and Tiberius went over to his bar to fetch them both a drink. "Any residual suspicions?"

"None. Yes, friends. Our relationship makes me wonder about the universality of nascent beings. I still have the occasional double take when I see who I'm talking to—your appearance, I mean."

"Sure. I've actually got used to your bug-eyed face."

"Charming."

"This is the first batch of whiskey from the distillery on Elysium. Five years, oak barrels, Elysium home grown oaks and barley by the way. Try it."

Standart complied and took a sip and scrunched up his nose.

"My first impression is that it's too aggressive on the palate."

"It's early days for this batch. I just had to try it, though. It's not as smooth as that bean shit that you live on, but it's far more complex. Give it another ten years, I'll convert you."

"Bean shit."

"Over on Principium, there's a new winery gaining popularity—a big plantation of Weber Blue Agave, aiming to make tequila."

"You Newcons keep surprising me with your thousands of alcohol variants. It's the alcohol you're after, right?"

"Not just the booze—there's passion in how it's made, and the taste can be beautifully nuanced. I have a second batch of that same whisky if you'd prefer."

"Is it any less harsh?"

"No."

Tiberius got up and took Standart's glass to get him a new drink.

"So, try this," Tiberius said as he went back over to his antique drinks trolley. "I bought the last three cases available on Earth of this Glenfiddich Grande Couronne Forty-Year-Old Single Malt Scotch. Cost me a fortune. Talk about passion."

Tiberius handed him a new glass with two shots of whiskey, straight.

"It's better than that bean shit, right?" Tiberius suggested pre-emptively.

"I love my Tibit," Standart took a sip of the Glenfiddich, "but I could get used to this one."

"I'll give you a case. By the time you're done, you'll be a convert." Tiberius settled back into the chair beside Standart, both facing the fire. Tiberius also had a glass of the Glenfiddich, the bottle placed nearby in anticipation of a long talk. "I bought a hundred acres up in the hills from another Texan. He was running cattle and needed a bigger farm."

"I heard. And I know about his meat production too—the steaks are excellent. No wonder he's keen to expand. Prosperity all round on Hope, it seems. Cheers."

"We should start a winery ourselves. Maybe buy out a vineyard in Bordeaux and get one of their vintners to move here, bring their famous vines."

"Next, you'll be breeding sturgeon for caviar."

"Pass. But we do have two goat farms producing great cheese on Elysium. There are quite a few of Earth culinary artisans making their way to the New World."

"Sure, but I wouldn't even know what a wine plant looked like, let alone grow them."

"Grape vine. Just saying we should do it." Then more seriously. "It's interesting that no debilitating viruses or bacteria have developed on this planet so far. Their development must be related to a humanoid or mammal presence, do you think?"

"There are some plant-based bacteria here, in the soil mainly, but much of the bad stuff must come from poor hygiene of the indigenous fauna on each of our planets. And yes, that is an interesting observation."

"We'll have to get our scientists to look at their evolution now that we have a clean slate to start."

"There's no one sitting out in the open eating monkey brains, to put it in Earth parlance, just begging for cross-species contamination. So that won't be the source of any pathogen."

"Our ancestors, both ours and yours, caused the development of harmful viruses and bacteria on our planets, do you think?"

"Not enough data. Tearn has as many harmful bacteria and viruses as Earth, not that it matters now with the medical chambers."

"This planet hasn't yet produced any fauna at all. That's remarkable to the extent that it relates to what is generally believed to be a planet's development."

"A planet can develop along certain phylogenetic lines that don't restrict what happens later in its future existence."

"You sound like your wife. We've been assuming that evolution brings with it a full suite of flora and fauna but it seems that doesn't necessarily apply."

"Very interesting hypothesis. It was, however, flora first on Earth. What if mammals, fish, birds never develop here, except for the ones we introduce."

"The flora on this planet has never had any exposure to animals."

"It does point to the impact of what we call advanced life, not just modern Tearn or Humans, it goes back to the beginning of developed life's impact on a planet's survival."

"So, it was the mammals that fucked everything up, or are you referring to us humans, or Tearns? It's relevant to our exploration of the galaxy."

"I'm saying all mammals had an impact. We are here in the open on Hope. Probably it's a good time to have a good look at that process."

"I think that there is an even more interesting, perhaps related, question."

"Being?"

"If we are talking about the presence of advanced life, nascent beings, and if you believe, I mean the all-inclusive *you* meaning both our societies in general, that each nascent entity has a soul—is it possible that one soul inhabits multiple beings?"

"How did you get there?"

"We're talking about starting with nothing on this planet. Where do the souls come from? Do they just evolve? That issue has recently got my juices flowing. Earth's Buddhists talk about a soul returning after the death of its host in an attempt to become a better, more fulfilled being, and to progress eventually towards perfection. If you believe that, why not have one permanent soul inhabiting multiple people and using each of them to gain enlightenment. What if there is one soul that inhabits us both, you and me, two people from entirely different planets. You don't wonder about that stuff? You don't ever wonder how is it that you and I get along so well, even from the very start? What if souls don't die? What if they just spread out? Or what if there are only a limited number of souls that have existed since the beginning of ancient life?"

"So, you're a philosopher now, not a scientist?"

"Both, and I choose this direction for this evening's discussion."

"OK, I'm game. So, you're saying we're soul mates."

"Maybe. One of Earth's ancient philosophers, Plato, asserted that humans originally had four arms, four legs and two faces. Zeus, their god, became afraid of human power so he split them all in two, destining humans to a life of trying to complete themselves, find their other half."

"So that's why we get along, we're two halves of the same person. We're not even the same species."

"Just giving you some background. We humans did have some deep thinkers, even twenty-five hundred years ago. I think there are some people who don't have a soul, maybe to get one you need to be part of a community or do something productive or have passed some kind of test. If true, that leads you to the question of how many souls are available. On my planet, ex-planet, there are people who believe that they have had a previous life. What if they just got a used soul?"

"Tearn spiritual teachings allude to each person having a soul, although we call it something different. That *soul* goes off to be rewarded or punished depending on the life that was led by the person that possessed it."

"It's interesting that the same proposition developed separately on two planets. You believe that?"

"No."

"Is religion a big deal on Tearn?"

"It exists, but most Tearn are what you'd call agnostic."

"Lately, I've been toying with the notion that there's only one soul inhabiting all nascent beings. Is that religious—or even feasible?"

"It's hypothetical, and maybe ridiculous. What about the Tracalonians?"

"Yeah—see, arseholes don't get souls."

"Of course not." They both laughed. "So where does that lead you?"

"I think it leads me to the belief that there are no souls, just a spirit within each of us produced by our own intellect."

"Deep."

"Not sure yet, I haven't thought it all the way through, but I will."

"Moving on then. You're thinking about raising a family on your ranch in the sky?"

"God, no. I don't think Zee is, either."

"I think you owe it to the community to breed."

"How do you figure that? Is that a Tearn thing?"

"Yes. You have remarkable genetics."

"I'm not going to create a dynasty, if that's what you are saying."

"Not suggesting that you should. We would regard it as an abomination if one of our exceptional scientists refused to breed."

"You'd force them?"

"No. But there would be significant social pressure on them to breed."

"And what about the idiots in your society?"

"We don't have any. We've been careful about that for a long time now."

"Sounds a lot like eugenics to me."

"Nothing other than screening of the zygotes, my friend. Your Churchill was in favour of eugenics, so was Hitler and Stalin."

"Now there's a grouping of which I approve, a group of war criminals responsible for the most destructive war in Earth's history. I know on Tearn that you're the go-to guy on human history and it's interesting that you would group those three guys together. You've studied Earth for quite some time. So, how would you sum humans up."

"In a word: violent. Back in Churchill's day, Chamberlain favoured reconciliation; Churchill favoured war. Chamberlain, the peace maker was later ridiculed, whilst Churchill, the warmonger was revered. We know how that worked out. Churchill had the political instincts to present a different position to the English people so that he would get elected rather than him having any genuine concern for the populace. He hated the Germans, so war was a good idea for him. He was at his core, I believe, a politician, not a saviour. Unfortunately, that led, in part, to twenty million Europeans dying in that war."

"As always, political fearmongering worked out well for him, as it so often does on that planet, exploited by politicians to this day. Twenty million dead, in Europe alone. Most of Europe destroyed and yes Hitler did succeed in taking over Europe, but the English went to war with him to liberate Europe then handed it over to Stalin, the most homicidal maniac who ever lived. Fortunately for Stalin, he didn't have any interest in invading England."

"Not with the USA behind them. But let me say Hitler didn't want to invade England either. Otherwise, he would have done it when he had the chance. He just wanted them to shut up and stay out of the way."

"All wars are pointless in any case. Hundreds of million lives over several thousand years of human existence were lost to determine where the national boundaries in Europe should be drawn, and now they are all part of the European Union."

"I have to say that when I submitted my report of Earth's history to our Senior Scientific Council, they thought that I was making it up."

"Sadly, not."

"Are you going to ever step aside?"

"Interesting segue —comparing me to three of the worst leaders in Earth's past then asking if I'm going to step aside."

"No comparison intended; we were just talking about the history of human leaders. I'm interested. Will you?"

"There is too much to do is the answer to your question. Maybe retreat more into the background. As you know, there is no hurry, no natural end to my life."

"Any replacement President in mind."

"The whole current Board is full of capable and now experienced people."

"But they're not you."

"I'm thinking I'll be available for advice long-term."

"I think you should consider staying on permanently, to add stability—even if you fall back to just be a semi-titular head."

"I have been giving that some thought recently. I must say that I am very happy at *home on the range*."

"Think harder—the Federation needs you."

CHAPTER TWELVE

Then the Unthinkable

Tiberius had finally relented and built two starships in the traditional style of Earth's science fiction films. There was no need to carry globes designed to house people for years at a time, because the new warp technology made journeys between destinations so short. Even the globes—now mostly intended for colonisation—could be moved from place to place at warp speed.

On this particular day, Tiberius was showing off his latest Design-of which he was extremely proud-to Standart. He had nostalgically named the ship *Enterprise*. The ship was in orbit over Elysium and both men had just found their way to the bridge after a short tour.

"She's a beautiful-looking ship," Standart commented. "Your designers should be proud of her, particularly looking at her as I approached from the surface."

"Thank you, it's a design theme that I intend to continue throughout the fleet, so you'll be able to recognise us when we cross paths in flight. This is going to my flagship. We have two much larger star-cruisers nearing completion."

They were interrupted.

"Mr President, we have several ships dropping out of warp to starboard," the ship's captain came over to alert them both. "They look like the new Earth warp-capable starships. There's twelve of them in total." The captain went over to study his scanning consoles more closely and then continued. "And they are armed to the teeth. Twelve crew in each ship, all personally armed, and the ships are all carrying nuclear-tipped missiles. Wait, they are hailing us."

"Put it on speaker and put the ships up on the big screen, please."

"Elysium-based cruiser, this is Captain John Walker from the Earth starship *Velociraptor*. We intend to board you—by force, if necessary. Please heave to and drop your shields."

"I told you about these guys, Standart, didn't I? Don't they ever stop reaching for their guns? I'm not at all in the mood for this. Give me that communicator, Colonel."

Click. "Velociraptor, this is *Enterprise*. Go fuck yourself." Click.

"Succinctly put, Tiberius," Standart observed. "No time for diplomacy, then?"

"It obviously doesn't work with these people. This is the third attack by them, and I have no intention of tolerating this shit any longer."

"They have fired on us, Mr President."

Three nuclear missiles hit the shielding of the *Enterprise*.

"Any damage, Captain."

"They've upgraded their weaponry since the Martian attack."

"Are you saying the missiles had an effect on our shields?"

"God no, nothing. I'm just commenting that they have been hard at work on their weaponry."

"And their spacecraft design, from the look of it."

Just then, a massive Tracalonian battle cruiser dropped out of warp. It was the size of three football stadiums.

"Oh dear… they've drawn the attention of the wrong crowd," Standart said.

The Tracalonian ship immediately fired on eleven of the twelve Earth ships—a single blast of its green, laser-like beam for each—destroying them in a moment.

The Tracalonian captain appeared on the screen of the *Enterprise*, having cut into the communications feed that they had established with the Earth ships.

"Having a war without me, Standart?"

"Dackus, you prick, they weren't going to hurt anybody."

"All evidence to the contrary, Standart. In fact, I thought they were firing at us."

"Bullshit."

"I note your shields are much improved. We can't even scan through them. Are you armed?"

"No," Standart confirmed.

"I believe you; you guys were always squeamish about battle."

Tiberius expressing his outrage. "There were twelve crew members on each of those ships according to our scanners, and you just killed them all."

"Yeah, but we let one go," Dackus responded with what looked like a smirk on his reptilian face. "He's headed off to where he came from, to tell the tale, no doubt. I don't think they'll be back anytime soon. Who were they?"

There was no answer from either man.

"No matter—I've despatched one of our fighters to follow them. We'll find out soon enough. Did you see the rubbish that they were throwing at you? Made me laugh. I'd like to meet them even though they don't look like they would be much of an adversary. They don't seem to like you much."

"Shit," Tiberius said out loud. He began to pace; he knew the consequences of the Tracalonians *introducing* themselves to Earthlings. He concluded Earth governments won't be worrying about the Federation for much longer.

"You're looking old, Dackus. Still a captain, I see," Standart continued the conversation with Dackus.

"One of these days, Standart, we are going to crush the Tearn like the humanoid bugs that you are and then I'm going to jam one of those rejuvenation tanks right up your arse."

"Don't think you'll live long enough to see it, my old friend. Old age is a bitch, isn't it. Still haven't cracked that technology, then?"

"Who is your new friend? Another humanoid by the look of him." There was a pause whilst Dackus read a report handed to him. "We'll continue this another time. I have to fly."

In Tiberius's anteroom aboard the Enterprise, he and Standart discussed the encounter alone while defence authorities from both Tearn and the Federation were briefed.

"You know this guy… Dackus?"

"He's the one who shot me."

"Some history then?"

"Yeah, unfortunate, miserable history. He's a maniac, as he just demonstrated. He's typical of that species but even they are getting tired of these old warriors, which, I assume, is why they haven't promoted him."

Tiberius sat, deeply concerned, speaking in a low tone. "Bad news for Earth, I assume. I want to go after him."

"And do what? You're not armed. There is nothing anybody can do to stop them now. Earth is in free space."

"He's going to find an over-exploited, over-populated planet with three times as many people as it can sustain, a filthy atmosphere, and inhabitants who, for the most part, are just as trigger-happy as he is."

"If what you say about the planet's state is true, that might actually save them. In the end, the Tracalonians are pragmatic: if there's nothing worthwhile to exploit, they may not bother. They'll simply appoint Administrators and leave. But as you mentioned, if Earthlings do as they usually do—reach for a gun and attack the Tracalonians—the fight will be brief; once provoked, the lizards are ruthless."

"Administrators?"

"They wouldn't let separate governments remain, especially if they're corrupt. The sheer diversity of ruling bodies alone would force them to replace and centralise governance under a network of Tracalonian Administrators reporting to a central authority. Their Administrators won't tolerate overpopulation or lack of productivity. They'll want to recoup the costs of occupying the planet."

"What does that mean?"

"Well, if, as you say, there are two-thirds more people than the planet can feasibly support, then two-thirds will have to go. The Tracalonians see themselves as gardeners. Every planet they hold has to become productive—even if its people are downtrodden and devoid of personal freedoms. They believe in 'weeding the garden.'"

"Five billion Earthlings killed?"

"Earth chose its political parties, embraced self-serving leaders over real scientific development. We tried to intervene in small ways years back, but they couldn't rise above their politicians' agendas. Now they'll pay a steep price—reduced to a vassal world of an alien empire. On the plus side, there'll be a little cultural exchange."

"That being?"

"Your ex-friends will learn how to make—and eat—lizard stew."

Tiberius wasn't amused by Standart's well-worn flippancy. He put his head in his hands and started rubbing his face.

"But I could have helped them develop if I stayed, if I persisted… if they had approved."

"It's harder than you imagine, as we discovered ourselves. Besides, there are nearly two hundred and fifty million Earthlings already in the Federation who won't face the Tracalonians. But that also means your immigrant supply from Earth ends here. The Tracalonians won't allow evacuees. From now on, the Federation will have to grow on its own—including your cross-species endeavour on Hope."

They both paused, letting the grim reality settle.

"I know what you're thinking, Tiberius, but there's nothing you can do for Earth now. If the twelfth ship returned immediately, the Tracalonians will find them—probably already have."

"They'll definitely head straight home. What they witnessed must have rattled them, and they'll want to report back. They're probably blaming the Federation as we speak."

"By the look of it, the Earthlings will meet the true culprits soon enough. I figure the only thing that's stopped the Tracalonians from attacking Tearn again is our shielding, which was always a notch above theirs, and now—thanks to you—it's impenetrable. But even so, there's no chance our Council would take up arms against them to defend Earth."

"What about economic sanctions or embargoes?"

"Easier said than done. Besides, any of that would take time, and you're forgetting that Dackus is probably already in Earth orbit. This will be done and dusted in days. We couldn't mount a defence even if it got approved—which it wouldn't. And we have no weapons for it.

Dackus is probably bragging to his military leaders right now, telling them he's discovered a new, highly developed world just waiting to be subdued. He'll get the promotion he's always wanted. Then the question becomes what they do with the survivors—and maybe whether we have any role. All your family are off Earth, right?"

Tiberius said nothing, but he knew all his biological family had, at his urging, left the planet and were safe. Still, he was horrified.

"They'll likely appoint Dackus as Head Administrator, which he's always craved."

"They'll need ground forces, won't they? Everyone on Earth is armed—especially the Americans."

"The humans' weapons will be useless. Tracalonian ground troops will have shielding and more advanced firepower. They won't need many. Remember, the British once controlled nearly a billion Indians with only fifty thousand soldiers—it was part of a history unit I studied. It took a mere ascetic on a hunger strike to make the British back down."

"Mahatma Ghandi," Tiberius said mechanically, barely focused.

"In the British occupation of India, local people were elevated to positions of power—administrators controlling specific regions, propped up by the British. Those local chieftains depended on British support to keep their status and wealth. The Tracalonians will follow that model, appointing local leaders to keep the population in check— by 'local,' I mean humans, eventually. First, they'll subdue the planet from orbit, destroying any opposition. Our Intelligence Service tells us they have some new weapon that kills off a targeted genetic group without harming any other species or structures. They could wipe out as many humans as they like, from orbit."

Tiberius groaned.

"Look, if the planet is not already shielded, and judging by the shields on those ships that just attacked us, it won't matter if it is, there is no way you can protect them now. The Tracalonians are not going to stand by and let you assemble a planet-wide shielding system with their battle cruisers in orbit."

"I tried to sell Earth on the benefits of planetary shielding to protect them against global warming. But politics made it impossible—they couldn't agree on shit. I didn't have the technology at the time anyway; that's only become possible since you came along. But if I had persisted and developed it, then maybe I could have upgraded it now to protect them against your war buddies."

"It's not your fault my friend. The Tracalonians have not had an armed and aggressive planet with which to fight for quite some time. I think they will relish the opportunity. Dackus will be right in his element."

At the very same time that Tiberius and Standart were discussing the consequences of Tracalonian involvement, on Earth, citizen alerts were sounding in the streets and warnings to stay indoors were being broadcast by all networks. The reinforcements that Dackus had called for, once he realised the scale of the opportunity, had already arrived. There were thirteen Tracalonian war cruisers in orbit above Earth with about the same number being resourced on Tracalonia preparing for launch. The Tracalonians were already broadcasting warnings of their own to Earth, on all frequencies, asserting that an invasion was imminent in order to confuse and panic the Earth's militaries. They had started to use sound bombs, ear-piercing noise generators, to soften up and terrorise the populace below—a standard Tracalonian tactic.

Dackus had been joined by the Tracalonian Joint Chiefs of Staff, Vandort, who had brought his own formidable flagship with him. It carried the genetic weapons that Standart had just explained to Tiberius. In Vandort's war room on his ship, he and Dackus along with Vandort's senior staff were discussing the best way to proceed to subdue the planet. Dackus was being congratulated for finding a developed world in free unprotected space. There was already talk of him being the Administrator of it once the war was over. Just as their meeting was taking place, the Tracalonians came under attack from a fleet of Earth's starships, which were attacking in concert with nuclear missiles being launched from the surface. As the barrage hit, there was contained laughter amongst the assembled Tracalonian military leaders. Dackus stepped away from the planning table to issue the order to destroy anything and everything that was in the air or in orbit, including the missile launch sites from which the missiles had originated. He also ordered that all civilian aircraft be destroyed. Those tasks were accomplished in a matter of thirty minutes. Dackus was instructed by Vandort to add all satellites to the destruction order and all bases from which those planes and spacecraft were launched.

"We can replace what satellites we need later," Vandort said to his staff. "Destroying them all now will render them deaf, dumb and blind. Old technology in any case."

"We should scan the planet for any munitions manufacturers or stockpiles and destroy them as well," Dackus said.

"Agreed," Vandort confirmed, "and anywhere where they sell weapons."

"That may take some time to find them all, maybe a couple of days, maybe a week."

"Get it done, Captain. We have to discuss the hard stuff now."

Another of the Tracalonian military leaders took up the briefing. Dackus remained at the communication console.

"There are some obvious government buildings, I'm going to use the names that they have given these places as best that we can determine them to be from the communications we've picked up. Here in what they call Washington, Beijing, London." He was pointing to a map that he had pulled up on the planning table screen. "These cities are either the seat of their governments or have been built to facilitate government."

"Dackus," Vandort said without actually having to convey any order.

"Consider those buildings gone, General. Send me the coordinates from your map."

"Include any monuments or large statues you can find and any airport or station used for travel, transit hubs," Vandort added. "We'll need to contain them in order to educate them. Leave the bridges, and the power plants which interestingly are fusion reactors, somebody on that planet has some brains. We'll need all of that infrastructure going forward. The second fleet will be here tomorrow, so we'll have plenty of ammunition and support. They're bringing two squadrons of fighters with them; they'll be able to clean up anything we missed from orbit."

"Satellite dishes?" Dackus asked, trying to be as helpful as much as his limited intelligence would allow.

The Chief looked at him like he was an idiot. "With what exactly, Dackus, do you think those satellite dishes will communicate? The satellites that we just destroyed?"

"Yeah, right."

"Administrator, my arse," the Chief said under his breath.

"There are far too many inhabitants on this rock, anyway."

"We know," another senior staff member interjected. "I've read the scanning reports. Once our fighters finish their sweep—let's say day five—we'll use the new genetically targeted cluster bombs to cull the population. That way, the planet's flora, fauna, and infrastructure remain intact. Our Science Council will be thrilled to test these weapons on such a large population."

"What a mess that will create."

"They'll decompose. We'll assign local survivors to remove the dead once they're allowed back into the cities—where most of the cluster bombs will have been used, I imagine."

"That and areas which are populated by the wealthiest inhabitants," the lieutenant general added. "As best we can determine them, the size of the housing perhaps will be an indicator of prominent persons in any particular area. The last thing we want is a bunch of egos with money running around trying to fix things."

"Ah, yes," Vandort said. "Include the banks and churches as targets. They'll have to get their currency from us. I nearly forgot about the banks; we don't use them anymore. By my math, the initial cull should be around three billion."

"Do we really want to eliminate three billion inhabitants immediately? What if there are highly productive personnel included in that cull?"

"Fuck 'em," Dackus piped up from the communications console.

"There is no way," Vandort responded, "that the planet below can sustain that many indigenous. We can't afford the time it would take to sort through all of them, setting up camps, with the indigenous watching as we drag the rejects off to be killed. It would be a dreadful, debilitating spectacle and significantly delay the rehabilitation of the planet. Best to just get it done now, get it over with, then declare the peace. We'll cull day five, then leave them for a week to understand their resistance is futile. Do we have the communications sorted, Colonel?"

"Yes, Sire, mostly. There appears to be over seven thousand different languages, but I think we've got the key ones."

"No wonder they couldn't get along, they couldn't communicate with each other. I will expect you to have them all programmed into the communication system by the time we broadcast the *all clear*, Colonel."

"Don't you mean broadcast the *it's all over* message," Dackus said.

"Thank you for correcting me. Haven't you got work to do?"

"Yes, Sir."

"After a few days of respite, we'll drop leaflets and broadcast on as many frequencies as we can find telling them that *it is all over*. We'll ask them to assemble in specific locations for the allocation of tasks and to appoint team leaders. We'll eventually pick the best of those team leaders and make them local Administrators."

"We'll need at least ten thousand administratively competent personnel to do all of that in a reasonable time period, General."

"Probable twice that many. We'll need at least a hundred and fifty thousand troops on the ground to support the administrative personnel. Contact HQ and get them to assemble those people and to have them here within two weeks. The quicker we put the indigenous back to work and back to their families, the quicker we'll bring this under control. Then we'll see what we can make out of this place. It's a pity that they are not better equipped, make a decent fight out of it. There are so many of them, you'd think they would be further advanced."

"Too late," Dackus said.

"Indeed. If we get any organised uprising once we deploy our people, we'll just use the genetic weapons again, they won't affect our ground personnel."

"Our people will all be shielded in any case."

"I'm not sure what I would do without your insights, Dackus."

CHAPTER THIRTEEN

The Resistance Begins

It had been nearly four months since the Tracalonian invasion of Earth, and life on that planet had begun to settle—just as Standart predicted. The population largely accepted its fate. There had been various skirmishes, and one major organised uprising in America, but all were brutally quashed. Earth's fighters, lacking personal shielding and possessing weapons useless against Tracalonian shields, were outgunned from the start. Some had tried to steal Tracalonian equipment, but their weapons and shields were locked genetically to the soldiers, rendering them worthless to humans. Unsurprisingly, the locals capitulated.

True to form, the Tracalonian regime put people back to work. Most humans who'd escaped the cull could, four months after the ceasefire, support their families again, and some had even begun accumulating modest wealth—particularly the local Administrators. Not through corruption or extortion (the Tracalonian authorities forbade it), but because they were paid by the Tracalonians in proportion to the productivity of their districts. As with the English Raj in India, the Tracalonian occupation relied on local leaders to enforce compliance, rewarding them in turn. Meanwhile, ordinary citizens were also given some opportunities—Tracalonians were capitalists, after all. They had no use for a planet where everyone lived in fear, hiding, and refusing to work. There were few abuses; people weren't whipped or jailed. They were generally treated with a degree of respect—unless they picked up a weapon, which guaranteed a swift death.

The lack of any retaliation against the Tracalonians by the Federation was not sitting well with Tom Burke. Elizabeth had found him moody and disillusioned, and she was somewhat concerned about the increasing amount of time he was spending at the club with his army mates.

At the Services Personnel Club bar.

"I don't believe for a second that we can do nothing about it" Tom said to Seargent John Whitaker, a long-time friend of Tom's in the Defence Forces.

"The boss wants us to keep out of it," John replied. "The Federation and The Tearn have slapped them with trade sanctions and travel embargos. The lizards are not welcome anywhere in the known galaxy."

"Big deal," Tom growled. "Word is they wiped out three billion people—maybe more. Imagine if that included your family."

John groaned and waved for another round by pointing at both his and Tom's nearly empty glasses.

"Mate," Tom continued, "I'm crawling out of my skin thinking about it. I was starting to think Tiberius was right, that we shouldn't be armed. But I'd kill for a decent weapons stockpile right now—and the soldiers to use it."

"There are folks I know who feel the same."

Tom lifted his head slowly, newly interested in what John had just said.

"How many people?" Tom asked, emerging from his drunken haze.

"At least a dozen I can name."

Tom began to hatch a plan.

"There is a super-heavy tanker in orbit as we speak with a load of asteroid shit from the processing plants on Mars."

"No idea what you're talking about. What's a delivery of asteroid material got to do with it?"

"It's not what it's carrying, it's what's carrying it. I saw those things used as battering rams in the Russian attack on Tellurium."

"We'd need more than battering rams, mate."

"Not to get us in there we don't. The shielding on those things is a match for anything the lizards can throw at us." Tom had put down his drink and pushed away the new one. He was seriously thinking he might have a plan.

"Sure, we get onto the planet, then what?"

"We mount a rescue mission. Those tankers would carry, what, eight to ten thousand people once we dump the current payload."

"Just pick them up and fly away. And the lizards are doing what while we collect them? They'll know we're there, for sure."

"You know those shields are programmable, right? We can modify them to allow only humans through. So, we could stay shielded while we evacuate survivors."

John was starting to take him seriously and called over a couple of his fellow soldiers who were also drinking at the club, wanting them to listen and contribute to the conversation.

"So, I'll sort out the tanker pilot—he can either stand down or come along if he's willing. Then we load up volunteers from the Defence Force, anyone else who is keen and useful, and head off to say hello to the lizards."

Tom was satisfied with the plan; John was still thinking.

"Even if the ship could load ten thousand people, that's a drop in the ocean, Tom."

"Who said we are only going to make one trip?"

"Tiberius won't allow it."

"He's on Hope with his Tearn friends."

"He'll fire you."

"I'm not much good to him in the state of mind I'm in right now. Who's in?"

They all readily agreed, saying they knew others that would come.

"We don't need that many —this isn't going to be hand-to-hand. They've got us outgunned in a ground fight, but they can't shoot us down inside the tanker. That's our key advantage; we can use it to move from town to town, picking up citizens."

"When?"

"0600 tomorrow. No need to fuck around with it. Go get your gear. Let your families know what you're doing. Let anyone else know what we're doing who you think might be helpful and ask them to come along. I'll collect you all from the corn farm just north of here, Trucker's Farm. I'll bring the ship down close to the ground so we can board without a lander, which means we won't alert the local authorities until they see us leave, and by then we'll be at warp."

Tom was right: Tiberius was furious when word of the tanker hijacking came to his attention. Now back on Elysium to respond to the developments, he was tracking Tom's ship's progress with senior defence force personnel. It had already reached Earth and was breaching the atmosphere. Tom was ordered to immediately return but he ignored the communication.

Tom landed the craft outside a medium-sized town in South Carolina, figuring it best to start small, away from major Tracalonian bases, at least until he understood what was happening and how the Tracalonian forces would respond. The townspeople, still worried about the Tracalonian occupation—even though four months had passed since the "war" ended—welcomed them cautiously. The local Tracalonian Administrator had already reported the ship's arrival. By that time, orbital bombardment had begun, but Tom's crew and the new passengers settled in for the night after a long day spent gathering willing evacuees. Tom had brought blankets and some basic seating for the refugees.

Gathered in a circle after a meagre meal, the thudding of shells against the tanker's shields in the background, Tom and some Defence Force personnel listened as the locals described the current state of affairs.

"Don't worry about the knocking," Tom told them. "They can knock all they want but they can't get in. We would have left already but I just want to see how they will respond to us being here so that we can plan future flights."

"So far here, it hasn't been all that bad, if you survived the *cull*," one of the survivors piped up. "After the initial fighting stopped, which didn't take long, less than a month maybe, they blew up all the government buildings and the banks and churches, then it all got very quiet."

"We heard there was mass killing—the 'cull' you mentioned?"

"We believe so—the lizards openly called it a *cull*. Word is as many as three billion were killed by a weapon that only targeted humans, leaving everything else intact. We were spared. They only used it on big population centres in New York, California, Asia, Africa, Indonesia, India. The US got off relatively lightly apart from Washington, New York, LA. Washington's gone, apparently—completely. Didn't see any of it here. Our local Tracalonian Administrator confirmed it, said there were far too many people for this planet to support."

"Three billion," John said in despair.

"Then they let us get back to work. They have been confiscating a portion of all our produce but otherwise they have left us alone. Dissenters are dealt with brutally."

"We have to use their currency," another survivor took up the story, "and there is talk of a tax coming."

Suddenly, the shelling stopped.

"General," one of the on-duty crew came up to get Tom, "they've opened communications."

Tom hurried to the control room.

"Hailing the invading ship," the Tracalonian commander said.

"You're the invaders, not us, you arsehole," was Tom's terse response.

"My compliments on your shielding. Our scanners say our bombardment is having no effect."

"What do you want?"

"You are a Federation ship, I presume. The Tearn don't have anything that size. Have you come to rescue your relatives?"

Tom stayed silent, listening.

"Well, here's what is going to happen. You have ten minutes to release our citizens and leave."

"Or what?" Tom challenged. "What can you do?"

"Sure, you're safe in there, it seems—but there are still billions of humans outside."

"What's that supposed to mean?"

"Release our citizens, or we'll kill everyone within a twenty-mile radius."

Tom fell back into the command chair.

After a tense pause, he gave the order: "Get us out of here." It was a reflex, hoping to de-escalate. Within half an hour, they were on approach to Elysium's space port, where a furious Tiberius and the local police awaited.

"Arrest him," Tiberius commanded, pointing at Tom, "and the rest of the crew. And see the passengers are cared for."

He had paramedics and social workers on hand for the disembarking refugees.

"Have him in the Eastern Command Post in one hour, after you've processed him. I want a debriefing," Tiberius ordered before storming off.

An hour later.

"How could you be so stupid?" Tiberius started in on Tom. "The Tracalonians followed through on their threat. We were listening in. Everyone left in that town and its surrounds are dead—except for the farmers, I assume, since they need them producing. Didn't see that coming, I suppose. What the fuck did you think they were going to do once they realised they couldn't breach your shields? They'd already killed nearly three billion humans—what's a few more to them?"

"More than three billion, we think," Tom muttered under his breath.

"Don't pretend that you were *thinking*. Two point eight billion by our best estimates."

"Like the number makes a difference."

"And any number somehow justifies you getting what we think is another twenty seven thousand killed."

"Did they kill those people, though? Really? Or did they just say that's what happened? The area's barely populated, and I figured they'd need every bit of slave labour they could get for farming. Even if they did murder them—who's to say they wouldn't have done it anyway? They've already killed 2.8 billion. I was trying to get those folks out of danger."

"Yet, it appears twenty-seven thousand more are dead. Even if they weren't, you certainly put them at risk. I doubt the people you brought back will be thanking you for getting their neighbours slaughtered. Any plan that didn't involve airlifting everyone at once was always going to expose the ones left behind to retaliation… you idiot. It's physically impossible to lift them all at once—we'd have nowhere to put them, even if we could. Did you fail basic maths?"

Tiberius took a breath and sat down. Tom stood there, handcuffed and stunned.

"I… I—"

"Save it for your court-martial. Get him out of here. Wait…" Tiberius seemed about to add more but merely waved them off, remaining seated, despairing over Tom's actions and probable fate.

It took Tiberius two days to calm down. He was at home having dinner with Zee, both still very distressed.

"Elizabeth is inconsolable. I can't raise Tom's arrest with her without her bursting into tears, and she's one tough lady, I can tell you that."

Tiberius didn't reply. He simply chewed his vegetables with greater force.

"You're not seriously going to court-martial him, are you?"

The look Tiberius gave her said, *Watch me.*

"He's a good man, Tiberius. You know that—he's your grandson-in-law. He was enraged by what happened on Earth."

"We are all angry. That doesn't give him the right to pinch one of our tankers and go off on some ill-conceived mission, regardless of him being my *grandson*-in-law. I have actually treated him like my real son since his father died. He got people killed, you know."

"He was out of his mind with grief and frustration at the Board's inaction. There are a lot of people who feel the same way."

"Including you, I assume."

"Tiberius, you're the smartest guy I know, the smartest guy in the Federation. Is there really nothing we can do about the genocide?"

Tiberius stood up, grabbed his half-full plate, and dropped it into the sink with a clatter. Without a word, he headed to his study to find a cigar.

Zee followed him, now leaning against the study doorframe.

"You know I love you, right?" she said gently. "Stop thinking about the ones you didn't save and remember those you did— including me."

After a pause, Tiberius said, "I've been talking to Standart. We've done everything we can with sanctions, but nobody believes it'll make the Tracalonians leave Earth. They're dug in, and I think, given how they responded to Tom's misguided foray, only a full-scale counter-offensive would drive the lizards out." He hesitated. "I hate calling them 'lizards.' It's demeaning to a whole species."

"They deserve to be demeaned."

"Perhaps. But racism is racism."

"Tiberius, if you're blaming yourself for any of this, you shouldn't. You know that's bullshit. If you'd stayed on Earth, you and I might have been among the two point eight billion they killed. They prioritised wealthy regions—Hollywood Hills was razed. You'd have had no chance."

"Two point eight billion—rich or poor—it's crushing."

"You left because you were getting nowhere with Earth's corrupt politicians and clumsy bureaucracies. Millions of humans are safe and thriving now because you started anew."

Clearly, Tiberius was troubled, and his anger towards Tom likely stemmed from his own guilt. He said nothing, though he was listening.

"Besides," Zee continued, "if you hadn't left, you wouldn't have discovered Bessel, and our shields wouldn't be strong enough to stop the Tracalonians on Tearn or here. We might all be eating 'lizard soup.' And you did try to shield Earth—they rejected it."

She turned to leave, feeling she hadn't got through to him. But Tiberius spoke up.

"I'm thinking of trying to meet with their top leader—the head Tracalonian. Standart's against it, says it'd be pointless and dangerous."

"We can't lose you, Tiberius… I can't."

He got up and crossed the room, enfolded her in his arms, kissed her forehead, and rubbed her back comfortingly.

At the meeting convened to discuss their options regarding the Tracalonians, Tiberius and Standart sat in the large conference room in Elysium's Hall of Administration with the entire Federation Board present, while several Tearn Council members joined by video link. The Tearn council had minimal interest in their old enemy's utterly predictable behaviour, and most believed nothing could be done, so few Tearn bothered to attend.

Tiberius: "I want to meet with the Tracalonians' leader—the head guy."

Standart: "Their *Dewan*. I think that is not advisable."

The Tearn President, Chetwat: "They won't listen to you, they are bullies and have been since they first evolved."

Tiberius: "We can't sit here and do nothing."

Chetwat: "Your friends must have seen this coming, you warned them, you counselled them to prepare, to shield themselves."

Tiberius, in a raised voice: "So they deserved to be exterminated? Is that it?"

Standart: "My friend is understandably distressed, he meant no offense, Madam President."

Chetwat, now somewhat belligerently: "You have a solution then, Tiberius? One that doesn't include getting more of your compatriots killed?"

Tiberius: "No. I thought that was what we were doing here."

A tense silence fell, as everyone tried to gather their thoughts.

General Deborah Jarvice —formerly Colonel in the Expeditionary Fleet, once Captain of Denderah (the ship that discovered Bessel), and now interim Head of the Federation's Defence Force since Tom's arrest—spoke up:

"Then we build the weapons and bomb the shit out of them at home, on Tracalonia, until they agree to leave Earth."

Chetwat: "That is against our long-standing policy, and yours, of non-aggression."

Jarvice: "I think we are past that point surely. We have the technology and the smartest guy in the galaxy, I'll bet we could make something using Besselite that would hurt them… a lot. We have the industrial base to build new weapons quickly. What would a nuclear warhead primed with Besselite look like, Tiberius? You remember we stockpiled those Russian nuclear weapons on Titan, right?"

She had Tiberius's attention.

Tiberius: "With Besselite, a nuclear device would be massively destructive, as big a leap forward in weaponry as the atomic bomb was in Earth's World War Two. Besselite is a magnificent energy enhancer. I can see that, at the extreme, it could be enough to blow up an entire planet."

Chetwat: "So now it's *kill them all,* is it? We've gone from having no offensive weapons to building planet killers?"

Jarvice: "They can't stop us from parking our ships in orbit above Tracalonia. A bomb, of any type, itself coated with our current shielding would almost certainly penetrate their planetary defences. You've been at war with them in the past, are you saying we should allow them to continue to terrorise the neighbourhood? You must have some residual resentment about the costs of your war with them."

Standart: "We do, and I think I speak for all of us. In my case I still have the scars to prove it."

Tiberius: "Tracalonia has an uninhabited outer moon, right? I believe we could blow the whole thing to dust. The rubble wouldn't damage their planet because of their shields, but it would give them one hell of a scare."

Jarvice: "We'd need to send a bomb onto their planet surface as well, say a non-nuclear bomb, through their planetary shields to prove to them that any of our bombs could get through their planetary shielding. Then let them do the math."

Chetwat: "A non-lethal demonstration?"

Tiberius: "Yes, something that the then-President of the US, Truman, considered doing against the Japanese in Earth's World War Two but sadly rejected the idea before he dropped the atomic bomb on two largely civilian cities."

Chetwat: "Your people have a barbaric past."

Another of the Tearn Council Members, named Aat@#b**: "Our research on Earth's history tells us that humans have killed nearly as many people in all their own wars, or because of those wars, as the Tracalonians did five months ago. So why does this vex you so much?"

Tiberius: "Yes, humans have a barbaric past. It is truly a wonder that they didn't destroy themselves after they built tens of thousands of nuclear missiles in the late twentieth century. But it *vexes* me because we have come a long way since then, we all have. The Federation is clear proof of what we have become as a species. Can we truly allow, in good conscience, this barbarity to stand, even continue?"

A low hum of discussion spread through the room.

Chetwat: "Order."

Chetwat cleared her throat, somewhat dismayed at the ruling she was about to table.

Chetwat: "A demonstration then. No violence. Tiberius will build the weapon."

Jarvice: "It's no good to make the threat if you won't carry it through."

Chetwat: "Indeed, sadly true. What objective do we seek?"

Standart: "A treaty. Between the Federation, Tearn, Earth and Tracalonia. Not only mutual respect but the commitment to no aggression against all known species, including covering off on what happens when we find a new populated planet rather than potentially exposing that planet to the atrocities Earth has just endured. Of course, it's all conditional on the Tracalonian withdrawal from Earth. And, Tiberius, perhaps this time Earth might be open to joining the Federation."

Tiberius: "The treaty with the Tracalonians would have to have some face-saving benefits for them like trade with us and you, so they don't feel entirely defeated."

Chetwat: "Not trade in our technologies, that would be banned. Let's keep the upper hand to ensure the peace lasts."

Jarvice, under her breath: "Fuck 'em."

Chetwat: "A timeline?"

Tiberius: "The way Besselite reacts when combined with existing technologies, no more than six weeks. We can use the missiles and the fissile material the Russians used against us."

Chetwat: "It is settled then. Our defence personnel will coordinate about the practicalities, all confidential, senior levels only. I assume we're all thinking we won't ask for the meeting that Tiberius was contemplating until after the *demonstration*. We should let them come to us after they have fully grasped the extent of their vulnerability."

Standart: "Waiting for them to initiate the meeting would have the highest probability of a positive outcome."

Chetwat: "It is agreed as put. This meeting is closed."

Two months later, the newly built massive Federation starship *Endurance* was in orbit around Tracalonia's outer moon, Topsidious. The Federation had parked the *Enterprise* in orbit around Tracalonia as well, to observe proceedings. The *Enterprise* was receiving the standard Tracalonian "welcome"—a missile barrage. Given his history with the Tracalonian forces, Standart was given the honour of opening communications.

"Seems we have your attention. Thanks for the missiles—your scanners will tell you they're useless against our shields."

The missile barrage slowing dissipated.

"Please focus your observation telescopes on your moon, Topsidious."

In that instant, Topsidious was catastrophically pulverised, much of the debris soon raining down onto Tracalonia like a bereaved mother's tears. Harmlessly, the rubble struck the planet's own shields, The barrage of the falling moon-rock lasted about an hour. Tearn and the Federation waited until the majority of the debris had scattered or settled back into orbit.

Standart resumed communication with the Tracalonians.

"If you're wondering whether we can deliver the same ordnance that destroyed your moon through your planetary shielding, here are the coordinates of our next target—one of your deserts, where we'll detonate a smaller, mostly harmless device to demonstrate that your shields can't stop our weapons."

A bomb was launched, exploding in an unpopulated desert forty miles from their capital. It was a conventional explosive of one thousand TNT-equivalent tonnes.

"I can assure you we could place an equivalent device—like the one that just obliterated your moon—into that very same hole I just dug in your desert. We'll wait for your call, which we'll only accept if it's from your Dewan."

Click.

The *Endurance* and the *Enterprise* went to warp leaving the Tracalonians to have a think. *Endurance* headed straight to Earth to police Tracalonian reactions to the blast, *Enterprise* headed home to Elysium.

On the way back, Standart and Tiberius settled into the expansive lounge on the *Enterprise*, which included an open gas fireplace that set a homey mood putting the circumstances of the day into sharp relief. They were alone. Both men were exhausted from lack of sleep in the lead-up to the demonstration, but they felt a wave of release. Finally, they had done something about the barbarity. Both felt a measure of closure unaware of how intensely they'd internalised the trauma of the Earth invasion. They'd dismissed the steward, wanting to talk privately over a glass—perhaps prematurely—of the same Tearn wine Standart had served at their very first dinner together. He'd brought a bottle, anticipating success.

They had both sunk deeply into their plush leather wing-back armchairs, facing the fire, a small coffee table between the chairs accommodating their drinks.

"This wine seems to get better each time I try it," Tiberius said.

"It's better when it's fresh, unlike your Earth-based grape wines."

"Not just Earth-based wines. We've got a specialised globe just outside Copernicus, now producing magnificent Cabernets and Merlots. We've just built them a new huge globe for their white grapes."

"The grapes are growing well because you can totally control the climate and the soil, right?"

"Exactly."

They fell silent after that banal exchange, each contemplating the day's events. They both knew they were steering around the true gravity of what had just happened.

"Blew the shit out of that moon."

"We sure did."

"There was no one on it, right?" Tiberius asked.

"No one. We scanned it before we gave the *all-clear*. They'll probably make this day a public holiday on Tearn."

"Let's not get too far ahead of ourselves. Do you think they will buy it—a treaty, I mean, not the wine."

"Yes, if we give them a trade deal—enough to 'save face'—then they may stop terrorising the galaxy. I'm not sure they've any other option."

"You said you still have the scars from the battle with Dackus? I thought your rejuvenation chamber would have taken care of all of that."

"It did. I meant the emotional scars—if those count."

"They do, my friend. I've got a few I wish I could leave behind as well, but my tank won't help there either."

"Does General Jarvice really have relatives that were in the Tracalonian *cult*?"

"That was mostly hyperbole. We won't know until we get proper data on Earth—like a census—to confirm who died. Still, she's the right person for the job. Tough as nails."

They drank in silence for a while, the conversation drifting towards more philosophical matters.

"Do you believe in God, Standart? Do you think he'd approve of what we did today?"

"Now there's a question." After some consideration: "I keep looking for Him—or Her—in my travels. I get around the galaxy a fair bit, but no sign of Him or Her yet."

"It's a conceptual question, not a practical one."

"If a god created the Tracalonians, then perhaps he's not a god that I want to believe in. You?"

"Not so much, but I seem to have been blessed with more than sufficient gifts. These gifts mostly came all at once when I was in my sixties. Suddenly, the math that I had been struggling with for years all made sense. So, I'm reluctant to dismiss someone having a hand in it."

Standart knew where some of those gifts came from—they were, in fact, gifts of information, not intelligence. He was one of the two men that had visited Tiberius all those years ago. Neither he nor the Tearn were aware of the intellect that Tiberius carried when they gave him that assistance. Standart would never tell Tiberius about his help. To Standart, the information provided to Tiberius during that visit was inconsequential compared to what Tiberius had done with it and what he had become as a man and as a leader; the intellect that they had untethered. Now, they were on the precipice of civilising the known galaxy. To Standart, that achievement rested solely on Tiberius's shoulders.

Standart decided to compliment Tiberius, to reassure him that his success had not been that *sudden*.

"I suspect you always had that intellect—you just found a way to use it. Looking at Earth's history, it always bothered me that Earthlings put themselves in a box of their own making, restricting themselves to develop at a given pace, waiting for parental approval or the approval of their friends, constrained always by a system of schooling that keeps everyone moving at one pace and in one direction restricting thought and personal expression. *Good enough* is their catch cry instead of asking what could be possible from any given student. Your schools live by that *good enough* mantra, students are not allowed to evolve at their *God-given* pace. You would have thought Darwin might have triggered something more influential about how to bring up your children.

"I think there are many different-sized intellects on your planet of origin that, if unchained by their circumstances, would have been great leaders or scientists that would have changed the destiny of the planet. I'm trying to make sure we don't make that mistake again here in the new world."

After a pause from his musings, he returned to the conversation. "So, it's a yes on the God thing?"

"It is a *don't know* from me."

More silence.

"You produced that bomb quickly—and the armoury that the *Endurance* is carrying with her."

"It wasn't difficult. We had plenty of fissile material and the old-fashioned missiles the Russians used to carry them, courtesy of the Russian attack on Tellurium. The missiles needed a bit of an overhaul, but then they were good to go. If the Tracalonians get out of hand on Earth, it would only take one of those Besselite torpedoes to wipe out even a large Tracalonian warship. I guess you'd call them torpedoes—or is that just a Star Trek euphemism? I'm sure the Russians would be happy, given the circumstances, to see those weapons put to good use."

"How many is the *Endurance* carrying?"

"One hundred and fifty, with more in a stockpile on Elysium. Besselite is such a wonderful substance. I could do the math in my head at that meeting once the idea was put forward by Jarvice; I knew it would produce a weapon of the magnitude we just witnessed when combined with nuclear material. We have over five thousand missiles of various sizes that we took from the Russians, some with conventional warheads. That's from eight thousand that we collected, three thousand of which were irredeemable duds."

Standart wasn't really listening.

"Fuck, I enjoyed that, I must confess. Did you see a large chunk of that moon stayed intact, in orbit? Some of the rubble that resulted from the explosion—including that large chunk—will probably produce something of a permanent ring around their planet."

"Do you actually have a word for *fuck* in Tearn?"

"Not that you could pronounce."

After further introspection and a period of silence that can only be enjoyed without discomfort between close friends.

"That broken moon, Tiberius, is going to serve as a visual reminder—a monument, permanently in orbit around that accursed planet."

"A monument to what?"

"Villainy, and what it yields if you pursue that path."

"Amen."

"I thought you weren't religious."

"It's Latin. Do you expect them to respect the monument of that broken moon?"

"Their genetics say otherwise." After a pause Standart continued. "Are you ever going to tell me where you get the Besselite?"

"No."

"Are the Tracalonians ever going to find it?"

"No. But even if they do, or you do, it is so well protected now that no one will be able to get in."

On board the *Endurance*, General Travice had taken up station in orbit, circling Earth. They were there to watch what the Tracalonians were doing and to ensure that no further violence would be inflicted on the populace of the planet after that morning's demonstration.

On the bridge.

"How many Tracalonian warships are there in orbit?" General Travice enquired of the scanner operator.

"Twenty five."

"Are they all carrying that weapon—the one they used to do what they called *the cull* of the population below?"

"No, just one of them. That big black one straight ahead on your screen, General. It's just to starboard, looks like the command ship judging by the communications gear on top of it. I've been listening in, most of the commands are coming from a guy called Dackus and he keeps referring to who I assume is his boss, Vandort. Both are aboard that ship."

"Does it have those weapons loaded, ready for use?"

"Yes, General. It also has a squadron of fighters in its hangar on the lower level of the ship."

"Give me a communications channel to it, will you please."

Broadcasting.

"This is General Travice of the Federation Starship *Endurance*. As you are aware, we are awaiting news of a high-level meeting with your Council and our heads of government regarding your continued presence on this planet. We are on station here to ensure the peace whilst that meeting is convened, and its results published. Any aggressive act by you will be dealt with immediately. Please stand down until you receive orders from your Council."

The reply came from Dackus. "As if you can do anything. You are unarmed peace-loving sycophants like the Tearn."

"These guys," the console operator says to Jarvice not broadcasted. "They don't understand their current predicament."

Jarvice to the console commander. "This prick is giving me attitude, can you believe it? We can't risk them using those genetic weapons again. If they think they've been backed into a corner they could wipe out the entire population of the planet below out of pure petulance."

Jarvice began to pace, thinking whether she should risk an all-out war by taking out the ship carrying those weapons and removing the threat of their future use.

Then back on the communicator.

Click. "You obviously haven't been fully briefed on the demonstration this morning over your planet. Allow me to demonstrate it for you now, firsthand, so that you guys get an up-close look. Then your subordinates can make the relevant enquires about replacing you."

"My subordinates?"

Jarvice, now to the weapons Commander.

"Target that ship carrying those genetic-based weapons, please, Commander. Let's make sure that they don't use those weapons again."

"Locked, General."

"At your pleasure."

"Yes, Ma'am." The commander was only too happy to destroy the ship that had inflicted so much devastation on the planet below.

The torpedo was let loose and was soon attracting multiple strikes from the Tracalonian ship's green lasers. The laser attack had no effect on the Besselite shielded torpedo. The Tracalonia ship was blasted to smithereens.

"Let them suck on that for a while. A present from this ship full of peace-loving sycophants."

After a short while, broadcasting again, now to the whole Tracalonian fleet.

"We are carrying sufficient weapons to destroy every ship you have in orbit and every base you have on the planet surface. As you can see, your shields are of no consequence to us. I won't hesitate to do as I just demonstrated to all of you if you don't stand down. Please get an update from your leadership. You will, as it happens, also need to get them to appoint a new commander for your fleet. Out."

"I hope that doesn't start a war," Jarvice said to her second in command.

"As opposed to the war where they just killed three billion humans? I think that threshold has already been crossed, General."

"Copy that."

CHAPTER FOURTEEN

The Treaty

Over three weeks went by before the Tearn and the Federation, were asked to have a conference with the Tracalonian Dewan and his Council. There had been no other signs of aggression by the Tracalonians on Earth, because the fiercest starship in the galaxy, the *Endurance*, was on station there keeping guard. The destruction of their flagship, with their Chief of Staff Vandort on board, had ruffled feathers and there were calls for all-out war against the Tearn and the Federation. But the *demonstration* had given them pause and allowed cooler heads to prevail. Tiberius and his product development team had been hard at work developing and producing Besselite-based portable weapons that could be used in a ground offensive, a contingency against further Tracalonian offences and a long-drawn-out unproductive treaty negotiation.

At that meeting, the Tracalonians attended via video from their planet, while the Federation and the Tearn assembled in the meeting chambers of the Tearn Supreme Council. Standart, along with the Tearn President, Chetwat, and Tiberius, were in attendance, as well as all the Federation's Board members and, this time, the entirety of Tearn's Council. The demonstration had captured the Tearn's Council's undivided attention and emboldened them to consider the prospect of defeating the Tracalonians altogether.

None of the Federation or Tearn delegation were in the mood to negotiate any of the stringent terms in the draft treaty that had been circulated to all parties for review prior to the meeting. The Tearn were heartly sick of having to deal with Tracalonian warmongering and the Federation representatives were still appalled by the genocide on Earth.

The Treaty was the equivalent of five thousand pages, presented electronically, to cover off on the technical minutiae, including all conditions and trade tables. It did, however, have a very succinct summary page at the top of the document. It was that page that was currently open for discussion. It was thought that if the principles could be agreed, then the bureaucrats could deal with the wording of the rest of the document.

The summary of the Treaty proposed these determinations:

THIS TREATY, formed between the Tearn, Tracalonia, and the Federation, states and codifies herein the following actions and requirements:

1. *Tracalonia shall withdraw all its forces from Earth and forever leave them in peace without interference, and all aggressive actions between the Tearn, the Federation, and Tracalonia shall immediately cease.*

2. *Tracalonia shall not invade or coerce any developed planet newly discovered by the Parties to this Treaty and shall allow such planets, once contacted, to determine their own place in the community of developed worlds. As such, Tracalonia shall withdraw from the two planets as well as Earth currently occupied by them and allow them to determine their own future.*

3. *Tracalonia shall hand over all weapons capable of extinguishing life based on genetic coding and shall not produce any such weapons in the future. This measure will be subject to the verification procedures outlined herein.*

4. *A free trade agreement shall exist between the Parties to this Treaty with the objective of imposing no tariffs on such trade. Such trade will exclude technology of any kind.*

The Dewan: "This is outrageous. We are giving all the undertakings and getting nothing in return."

Chetwat: "What you get in return, Sir, is that your planet gets to stay in one piece under your feet."

The Dewan: "So, this is all about threats not treaties."

Chetwat: "Yes, it is. Many on this panel believe we should just exterminate you, now that we have that capacity, like the festering sore you have become in the galaxy. But we will start with trying to redeem you."

The Tracalonians were taken aback by the bluntness of the demands from the normally polite Tearn. There was discussion amongst themselves with the communicator switched off.

Chetwat, expanding on her previous answer and attempting to reopen the conversation: "What you did to Earth was unbelievably barbaric even for you."

Dewan: "We did them a favour. Over-populated, polluted, inefficient, poorly lead and corrupt. We fixed it for them."

The Tracalonian Minister of War, Dahak the Bellinorian, entered the discussion: "You are lucky that you didn't trigger an all-out war when you destroyed my warship in Earth orbit."

Tiberius: "It was loaded with the genocidal weapon that you used to *cull* that planet's population. You'd best tell your new fleet commander not to push General Jarvice too far, she is a mean one. She believes she had relatives in your *cull*, that's why we chose her to police your activities on Earth while we sort out this Treaty."

Dahak: "I don't believe that destroying our planet is in your nature. It is an empty threat."

Tiberius: "Our shields can't be defeated by your weapons so we can go wherever we wish to go, even to your personal residence, Dahak. Our missiles can penetrate your shielding at will. We have a weapon that can destroy your whole planet or any smaller target that takes our fancy. Consider those facts, believe that reality. There are many forms of the bomb you saw demonstrated on your moon, variants of smaller and larger destructive yields. If pressed here, we would start by destroying your entire fleet of warships and every military base you have anywhere in the galaxy, including those on your own planet. Allow me to be clear, when I say *start by*, I mean we will begin that task immediately if this meeting closes without resolution. How do you think the indigenous peoples you have under your boot, and indeed your own people, will respond to you being disarmed? After all of that was done, you would still have to come back to this table to begin these discussions again and at that point you would be holding fewer bargaining chips than you do now. Executing this Treaty is your only option."

Again, there was radio silence, but the video feed showed heated arguments occurring in the Tracalonian meeting room, culminating with Dahak storming out of the chamber. The discussions amongst the Tracalonians, unheard, went on for a further half-hour with most Council members at some point standing and gesticulating aggressively before reseating themselves, looking crestfallen. Then the communication was turned back on.

Dewan: "Complete the paperwork and send it over to our legal advisers. In principle, you have a deal."

Chetwat: "We would expect your immediate withdrawal from Earth."

After a pause.

Dewan: "I will give those orders once we've reviewed your paperwork. You're welcome to that stinking pile of rubbish. I have no idea why you want it back; its resources are depleted, its water and air are filthy, and the indigenous are unremarkable and prone to self-annihilation… even without us. Meeting closed."

Back in the Tearn Supreme Council chambers, after the meeting with the Tracalonians closed and the communications shut off, the mood was surprisingly subdued after what seemed to be a Tracalonian capitulation.

Tiberius: "Did anyone else find that disingenuous. I'll say what everyone here is thinking, the deal is not done yet and even if it were, are we going to allow them to just walk away from mass murder with a trade agreement and a slap on the wrist?"

Chetwat: "Who's to say that wasn't their endgame?"

Standart: "They had no idea we had, or could have developed, weapons of the power and sophistication we just demonstrated to them. They couldn't have anticipated this, they're not that smart."

Another Tearn Council Member: "Then let's use those weapons, now, whilst we have the justification to act. Let's finish this for good."

Tiberius: "That makes us no better than them."

Chetwat, musing: "What the hell does '*once we review the paperwork*' mean?"

Standart: "It means we don't have an agreement, yet, with no promise as to when we will have one, if ever. I am uncomfortable in the interim leaving them to do whatever they want on Earth."

Chetwat: "What if we let your General Jarvice find the Tracalonians invasion forces in breach of her instruction to them to *stand down*? It wouldn't be hard for her to find an excuse to wipe out the warships orbiting Earth."

Tiberius: "To what end?"

Standart: "To protect what's left of Earth whilst we deal with this administrative bullshit, this could go on for months. I agree with Madam President. Jarvice would simply be doing what she said she would do—that is destroy every warship in Earth orbit and blow up all the Tracalonian bases on the surface if they didn't stand down."

Chetwat: "If she was authorised to act in that manner, would that go some way to assuage the Earthling's desire for revenge?"

Tiberius: "You mean justice, not revenge. Destroying their Earth bases would be like stomping on a nest of cockroaches, they'd run everywhere. We can't use nuclear weapons to clear the bases for fear of collateral damage. Besides, that planet's ecosystem is too fragile to use nuclear weapons on the surface. What do their ground forces do after we destroy their bases? Regroup? Pillage?"

Chetwat: "A ground war would be messy and dangerous and would delay any finalisation of a treaty. Their troops are well-trained. Even if we did clean them out, we'd still have a treaty to negotiate."

Standart: "At least, we would have exacted some price for the genocide on Earth. They might just accept that their commanders on Earth crossed some line with Jarvice and she did what she said she'd do rather than see this as a reason for all-out war. It's not as if any one of them is going to be around to contradict her. But they may see that as a declaration of war by us and react accordingly."

Tiberius: "I doubt they would declare war; they fear our new weapons. But again, to what end?"

Standart: "As you rightly stated, justice, surely. They are probably beating the shit out of some indigenous as we speak. I'm telling you, Jarvice won't have any trouble finding a violation of her order to stand down, she could easily find an excuse to forcibly remove them from the planet."

Another Council Member: "Leaving them there, for however long, gives them the chance to rob the place blind and kill whomever they want."

Tiberius thought about what was said.

Tiberius: "I know, Standart, that your view of this is coloured by your hatred of Dackus, and the Tracalonians in general. But I hear what you say even if it sounds horribly like retribution, not justice."

Standart: "It's your ship, Tiberius, your weapons, Jarvice works for you. Your call."

Tiberius: "We have been preparing for the inevitability of a ground war. We have some new portable weapons in production as we speak. Let's put it to a vote here, now, and I'll accommodate the wishes of this Joint Council."

The vote was taken, all voted in favour of immediate action against the invading forces menacing Earth. Tiberius voted in favour of that proposal. It was agreed that the Tracalonians would be removed from Earth by force.

Within the hour, Tiberius was on the secure line to General Jarvice, explaining what had transpired at the Joint Council meeting and before that at the meeting with the Tracalonian High Council.

"So, you understand what we are asking of you, General?"

"Indeed, we have already received reports of Tracalonian actions on Earth that breach my order for them to stand down."

"Do you have any personal issues with what I'm asking you to do?"

"With all due respect, Mr President, fuck 'em. You're about to make a bunch of soldiers on the *Endurance,* and a bunch of our compatriots on the planet below us, very happy."

"Your order is to proceed immediately to destroy all orbiting Tracalonian war ships and fighters and the Tracalonian bases on Earth. Ensure that you broadcast a warning to the Tracalonians telling them that they are in breach of your order, then start shelling."

"Yes, Sir."

"I have more news for you, General. We will have three squadrons of armed fighters in orbit with you by this afternoon, and we've been working on the weaponry designed for ground man-to-man fighting anticipating delays with the Tracalonian Treaty negotiations. We are aggregating a ground force to do the clean-up on the surface once you've done all that you can do from the air. They'll be with you within the next forty-eight hours. It's going to get ugly. That force will include Tearn soldiers, so that's going to be interesting to see how they do in concert with our guys. They will be carrying conventional Tearn blasters and everyone will be wearing Tearn individual shielding and some will have the new weapon that we've designed. Once you bomb the bases, you'll need to clear out the remaining Tracalonian soldiers without delay; we can't have vengeful Tracalonians rampaging the populace. You are not authorised to use nuclear weapons on the surface, understand?"

"Understood."

"I have ordered two of our tankers to load up a resupply for you and your people. It will include a further one hundred and thirty nuclear Besselite torpedoes. They will be with you within the hour. We will also be dispatching several thousand Defence Force personnel, medics, councillors, and administrators once the surface war is over. They will only set down on the planet after you give the *all-clear*, but they will start arriving in Earth orbit once you confirm that the Tracalonian fleet has been destroyed and that the Tracalonians are not sending any further warships. Are we clear?"

"Yes, Sir."

"You will take operational command of the rescue mission—ground and air—until we have the opportunity to set up some semblance of administrative control on the planet."

"Yes, Sir."

"Then your order is to proceed now, General. You have the green light."

Just as Tiberius hung up on the call to Jarvice, Zee burst into Tiberius's office at FDF HQ.

"You're sending three squadrons of fighters to join Jarvice at the battle for Earth."

"Is that's what they're calling it? I must have a word to my adjutant about confidentiality."

"Tom still has a lot of friends around here, so I get all the gossip. Stop being evasive. I want in. I'm qualified to head up one of those squadrons."

"I knew you'd say that."

"Well, I said it. I'm not taking no for an answer simply because I'm your wife."

"I don't want you to go. It's going to get nasty, hand-to-hand on the planet to clean out that rats' nest. They are well dug in and getting even more fortified since *Endurance* arrived."

"I'm more qualified than any of your pilots. I flew half a dozen sorties for the US Air Force over that Russian trouble."

"No. You can't go."

"No!"

"I can't lose you either, Zee."

She came over and put her hand on his chest and patted.

"I'm reporting to the FDF fighter base. I'm going there now. There better be orders waiting for me when I get there, OK?"

Tiberius found himself at the FDF Detention Centre shortly after his *discussion* with Zee. He had capitulated and sent her orders to the FDF Fighter HQ, asking them to give her one of the three fighter squadrons. He was at the detention centre to see Tom Burke. Tom was brought out to the meeting room, handcuffed.

"That won't be necessary," Tiberius said. "Take those off him."

"Thanks," Tom said, rubbing his wrists.

"It seems like a holiday resort here."

"Sure, I'm late for volleyball. What do you want?"

"Don't get testy with me, Tom. You brought this on yourself."

"I know. Not happy about it, though. Sorry" Tom said as he sat on the bench opposite Tiberius.

"We're going back to Earth. It is going to mean a ground invasion to clean up the Tracalonian bases."

"About fucking time." Tom stood, excitedly realising why Tiberius might be here. "I want in. Is that why you're here? Give me a job—any job."

"I want you to head up the army we put down on the surface. You'll be reporting to General Jarvice, who is in operational command of the taskforce. We can't win this from the air alone. Jarvice is clearing out their warships and bases as we speak. But we'll need to get down there and clean up before their forces scatter. Once Jarvice is finished destroying their bases, they'll be on the move."

"Tiberius, I thought I had lost your trust forever. You have no idea what this means—"

"Sit down, shut up, and listen. Save it for your court-martial. For the time being, you are being reinstated with the rank of Colonel. We intend to drop twelve light five-hundred-person battalions onto the planet. All will report to you. Consider the rank temporary—your court-martial will determine what happens to you going forward. You can take your team of imbeciles with you. Consider yourself and them conscripted. The FDF is rounding up a team of volunteers to go with you—apparently including a battalion of Tearn. The Tearn are supplying their handheld blasters and the charging vests to go with them; those are at least as good as the weapons carried by the Tracalonians. The Tearn weapons will be coded for human or Tearn use only. We have also built a new handheld gun—the size and operational use of a shotgun, but loaded with self-propelled depleted uranium-tipped shells with a payload of traditional RX51-PETN explosive mixed with half a gram of Besselite. Those shells will blow the shit out of any shielded bunker—or soldier, for that matter. You'll have a limited supply to take with you initially. The rest will be ready for delivery in ten days. Until then, we'll use the Tearn blasters, and some of your men will carry the new Besselite shotguns. But we can't wait ten days to get started on the ground because we don't know what the hell the Tracalonians are doing down there. They'll be pissed as hell once Jarvice finishes shelling. Whatever they're up to, it won't be good. I have no idea how many soldiers you are going to end up with, but your group will be trained personnel only."

"Everyone will want to go, Boss. They all have been itching to do something."

"Yea, but I'm unhappy with the short preparation time. Mistakes are going to be made for sure—you'll have to deal with those issues as they arise. But we can't wait to extract those arseholes for fear of them doing something stupid once they realise that they are stranded on the surface. By now, Jarvice has already taken care of their warships and has started on their bases, so they'll shortly be out in the open. But they are extremely well-trained and a fierce opponent. It won't take them long to regroup."

"When?"

"Go get your gear. You're coming with me. Guard!"

CHAPTER FIFTEEN

The Ground War

Jarvice saw a small courier craft break warp dangerously close to Earth's atmosphere.

"Who the fuck is that?" she said to the scan operator.

"One occupant, Ma'am."

"Any idea who?"

"It's marked with the Tracalonian High Council seal on the fuselage."

"Ask HQ who they think that might be and tighten the blockade with some of those fighters that just arrived. I don't want anything else getting through."

Now Jarvice to the weapons commander.

"Send someone down there to welcome that ship to Earth will you, please."

One of the fighter planes interdicted the craft and blew it to smithereens on the ground, but the occupant had fled the ship. FDF Intelligence confirmed that it was the Tracalonian Minister of War, Dahak. He'd come to rally the troops having heard of the destruction of his fleet of warships. He had decided to take matters into his own hands, having failed to convince the Council to mount a counteroffensive. He'd brought four more warships with him as reinforcements and to serve as protection for his own craft. He could only muster four warships because the High Command was still conflicted about the

Treaty and fearing further use of the new weapon that they had just seen demonstrated.

Jarvice destroyed all four warships as soon as they broke warp. She had already destroyed all original Tracalonian warships and all airborne fighters so the Tracalonians on the surface were totally without air support.

Dahak had landed near what was left of the large Tracalonian command post just outside of Dallas, Texas. Jarvice had been busy destroying those bases but, as suspected, destroying the base didn't mean all occupants were killed. In fact, most of that base's soldiers had fled, hearing about what was happening to the fleet in orbit. Dahak had brought communications gear with him, and, using it, he ordered the scattered soldiers to regroup amongst the rubble of the burnt-out base. As they assembled, he began to brief them.

"We'll need men to go and communicate with our other bases. Let them know I've personally taken charge and that we are organising a counteroffensive." Jarvice had already destroyed their communications satellites, so they only had line-of-sight radio contact except for any of the bases that still had functioning subspace radios. "Did any of the vehicles survive?"

"Yes, Sir."

Dahak pulled out his map console and gave the coordinates where he wanted the men from the other bases to report, instructing the soldiers to continue to daisy-chain those instructions across the country until they were sure all had been contacted.

"Take two of those vehicles and go to the next nearest base. They'll be coming down to clean up for sure now that they have finished bombing."

He was still somewhat breathless from the adrenalin and from running away from his ship to escape being blown up with it, no longer the fit soldier he once was.

"I want us to be ready for them when they arrive."

Just then, three Federation fighter planes flew overhead and dropped munitions aimed at the assembled group who had hastily and ill-advisedly come together in the open to meet up with Dahak. He wouldn't repeat that mistake again. Jarvice had sent three fighters down for a look-see, having heard that the occupant of the recently arrived craft had gotten away and that he was a senior minister in the Tracalonian government. Several of the Tracalonian soldiers were killed by the strafing and one of the vehicles was destroyed. The rest scurried to cover.

One of the planes overhead was piloted by Zee.

"Have some of that shit, arseholes," she declared for the rest of her group to hear as she swung around for another pass. The soldiers had disappeared, but she put a missile into a nearby half-demolished Tracalonian warehouse just for good measure and then headed back to return to her squadron.

Just then, the left side of her fighter was blown off—a malfunction in one of the hastily assembled missiles.

Tiberius was right. Mistakes were going to be made in the rush.

Little did he know that prediction would directly affect Zee's safety.

Zee ejected, concussed by the blast but otherwise unharmed because of her personal shielding. She collapsed as she hit the ground, hard.

Having heard the explosion, Dahak watched her chute open.

"You three—go get me that pilot."

Twenty minutes later Zee awoke, chained to a chair in the cellar of one of the damaged but largely still standing Tracalonian buildings. Dahak was standing over her.

"Welcome back, little lady. Congrats on the personal shielding. I suppose this won't hurt, then."

Dahak struck her over the head with an iron pipe he'd picked up out of the rubble. It pushed her head sideways and didn't do her headache any good, but she was otherwise uninjured.

"I want to know how many are coming, where they will land, and what weaponry they are bringing with them."

No answer. He struck her again—to no effect.

"Your shielding won't protect you from being suffocated, girl."

"Ok," Zee said. "Ok, I'll tell you what you need to know. What you need to know is that it's going to hurt like hell when I stick that pipe up your arse."

"A comedian, eh?"

Dahak lifted his arm, preparing to strike her again with the pipe but hesitated.

"Wait a minute. I recognise you. You're that black humanoid from the wedding photo in the news—Tiberius's wife. My, my. This could be useful."

A soldier burst through the door.

"Minister, there is a large squad of enemy soldiers landing just to the south. Twenty vehicles leaving a carrier."

"Stay with her," he said to one of his men. "Lock the door behind me."

"Fuck off, prick," Zee yelled after him. "Go say hello to my friends."

Dahak left hurriedly to assess the situation for himself. Now at the surface behind a makeshift bollard.

"There are at least a hundred soldiers in twenty vehicles headed straight towards us," Dahak confirmed with his binoculars. "Fucking Federation troops… some Tearn. Open fire," he ordered.

Just as he put down his glasses, projectile fire from the Federation forces' RPGs began to hit the compound. They were Besselite-enhanced, so they were doing considerable damage to what was left of the buildings and to Dahak's men.

"You'd best get out of here, Minister."

Just then one of their remaining vehicles got hit.

"Take the last vehicle. Go now to the checkpoint."

Dahak hesitated, not wanting to leave the battle.

"Go and assemble our men from the other bases, Minister. Fight another day."

Dahak fled in the remaining functional vehicle.

"Stop using the RPGs," Tom yelled over the radio. He was in the lead vehicle. "The downed pilot is in there somewhere."

All Federation forces arrived almost in unison at the compound. Some were carrying the new shotguns with the Besselite rounds. The Tearn blasters were having little effect on the Tracalonian soldiers because of their shielding but the shotgun shells were blowing the Tracalonian soldiers to pieces.

The Tracalonian troops were quickly subdued, and Tom's squad was hunting out survivors whilst Tom went looking for the pilot. He spotted a partly demolished concrete guard post on the eastern edge of the compound and assumed that would be a likely spot to start looking. He cautiously found his way downstairs to a basement door locked from the inside, and kicked it in; with the assistance of his personal shielding, it only took one blow. He entered the room to see the pilot strapped to a chair.

"Look out!" Zee yelled.

Tom was struck by a blaster shot in his left shoulder blade, spinning him around just in time to see a Tracalonian soldier bearing down on him. He fired his shotgun. At that range, the soldier exploded into a mass of blood and viscera that coated the walls, Tom, and partially splattered Zee's face. The blast brought part of the roof down, blocking the door with a pile of rubble.

"Tom?"

"Zee?"

"What the fuck did you hit him with?"

"Tiberius's latest toy."

Tom pulled a rag from his pocket and wiped his face, trying to clear away the blood.

"How that shit got through my shields, I don't know—must be the Besselite residue."

He offered the rag to Zee and she gave him the requisite look that said *I'm bound up, you idiot.*

"Good weapon to use at close range, inside an unstable bunker, I see," Zee said sarcastically. "I can hardly hear."

"Oh. You want me to leave?"

"Get me out of these shackles, arsehole."

Tom dropped his backpack on the floor and started rummaging through it.

"I've got laser cutters in here somewhere… always be prepared."

"Listen, boy scout, don't even think about using that gun to blast away the rubble. You'll bring the rest of the building down on top of us."

"You think?"

Tom found his cutters and went behind Zee's chair to work on the shackles. He sat on the floor with his legs extended straight out either side of the chair; he looked like a child who had just unexpectedly been given their favourite lolly and had sat down to enjoy it.

"When do I get one of those guns?" Zee asked.

"We don't have that many of them. More coming, though, so at the moment they're only being given to the men."

Zee's arm jolted, rattling the chains as she instinctively tried to smack him. "You know you and Tiberius have a lot in common."

"How's that?"

"You both know exactly how to push my buttons."

Tom stopped what he was doing, thinking he had best get some help. He unclipped his radio from his belt.

"Not sure I should let you out of these if you're going to beat me up."

Now on the radio: "Mac, there is a concrete guard post on the eastern end of the base. The pilot and I are in the basement, trapped by a cave-in."

"Roger that, Colonel."

"Can you get a digger out of the carrier please and get us out of here? Be gentle—the building is unstable."

"Since he blew the shit out of it," Zee added loudly.

Now to the *Endurance*. "General Travice, there was a vehicle that fled the scene down here—headed south. Did you see where it went?"

"The Besselite dust plays havoc with our scanners, Tom, we're blind up here."

"Get me loose, will 'ya?" Zee insisted, growing frustrated.

"Alright, alright. I'll just cut the binding chains, we'll have to get you back to the ship to remove the wrist and ankle braces. I wouldn't want to cut anything off that you might need later."

"Thoughtful."

"Thanks. Did they question you?" He continued to work on the chains.

"Sure. I told them everything they needed to know."

"Did it involve the guy's rectum?"

"Yeah, and the iron bar he was beating me with."

Tom had her free in a couple of minutes. Zee stood, rubbing her wrists underneath the still-attached metal cuffs.

"Did you find out who the guy was that landed here?" Tom asked.

"Some big wig minister. Dahak, I think."

Tom relayed that information to Jarvice and underlined the urgency of finding him quickly, but central intelligence had already identified the occupant of the craft that landed.

"So, Colonel, eh?" Zee said.

"Yeah, that's right, Lieutenant."

"I thought you were in jail?"

"Looks like I still am."

The quizzical look on Zee's face caused him to elaborate.

"Tiberius needed some well-trained help, and so…"

"Well-trained, eh?"

"Fuck off."

There was a pause where they both put away the bravado.

"Good to see you're back at it, Tom."

"Good to see you too, Zee."

They came together and embraced. Then still holding each other, Zee continued, "I've looked better, and I have a stinking headache."

"Always beautiful, Zee, and the headache means you're concussed. We'll have to get you up to the *Endurance* and sickbay."

"Fuck that, I just need another plane."

"You won't be flying again for at least a week. By then, judging by what we just did to their troops outside, I'll have this all wrapped up. Besides, we don't have enough planes for you to keep busting…"

"Finish that sentence and you'll be concussed."

There were momentary thoughts of what might have eventuated between them, quickly dismissed, but residual feelings came to the surface as they held the embrace longer than colleagues should.

A light appeared as a hole broke through the rubble, and a Federation soldier's face appeared on the outside of the small breach.

"Hang on, Colonel." The face disappeared, followed by a shout: "Bring it over here." The soldier's face reappeared. "We're going to reinforce the doorway before we clear the rubble."

Back on the surface, having been extricated from the basement, Tom and Zee stood in the open, dusting themselves off. Tom called over Sergeant John Whitaker, his friend from the ill-fated rescue mission, and introduced him to Zee.

"Mate, can you get a shuttle down from the *Endurance* please to take Zee back up and into sickbay?"

"No problem." The sergeant got on his communicator and relayed the request, then noticed a large cloud of dust rolling up from the south.

"What the fuck is that?" John called over four of his people who were within earshot. "Are the lizards back for more?"

Tom got out his binoculars.

"It seems to be a dozen pickup trucks. They look like they are carrying humans. Stand down, guys." The four soldiers went back to their assigned duties. John remained with Tom and Zee, gun in hand.

Ten trucks were soon in the compound. They rolled up in a cloud of dust and noise. Around twenty Texans got out, armed with shotguns and rifles. They came over to where Tom, Zee, and John were standing. As what appeared to be the main guy walked towards them, Tom thought he had been transported back into an old-style Western movie.

The man looked to Tom like the spitting image of actor Sam Elliott—Mexican-heel cowboy boots, jeans, a scruffy yellow-and-red checked shirt with the sleeves rolled up to his elbows, and grey hair escaping from the undone top buttons of his shirt.

As he opened his mouth to speak, he even sounded like Sam Elliot.

"We saw you guys land," the cowboy-hatted visitor said. "Figured we'd lend a hand. About fucking time you guys showed up."

He had one hand on the butt of his shotgun, which was broken open resting over his shoulder, and a six-shooter strapped to his leg. Unkempt grey hair, what Tom could see of it, unshaven with a huge moustache, and a belt full of shotgun cartridges and ammunition for his Colt.

They shook hands.

"The last thing we need," Tom started out, "is a bunch of pissed-off, poorly armed Texans getting in the way. No offence."

"None taken. But maybe we could get some of your blasters and help out."

"Not enough weaponry to go around, sorry."

The cowboy appeared disappointed. "It looks like you cleaned this lot up pretty damn quick."

There were three Tracalonian soldiers being marched off to detention, shackled, passing behind Tom.

"Don't 'spose we could have a word with your lizard friends over there, I assume you've taken their shielding."

"What did you want to say."

"I want to tell them a little bit about the consequences of trespassin' on someone's property in these parts."

"They're POWs now. I can't let you hurt them."

The cowboy paused, took his hat off and scratched his head. "Never mind, then."

"Look, it would be best if you guys went home. You could let your friends and neighbours know that we're here and that we intend to tidy this thing up. Hang on."

Tom yelled out to one of his soldiers near the carrier, which had been moved up into the compound to load equipment and prisoners.

"McGee, do we have any spare communicators?"

McGee disappeared into the carrier for a couple of minutes, then ran over with five communicators, which she gave to Tom.

"Here, use these," Tom said, passing them to the cowboy. "If you come across any displaced Tracalonian soldiers, let us know. We've already destroyed all their bases, so there may be a few wandering around. Don't try to take them on yourselves. Shielded and armed, these fuckers are dangerous."

"Well aware. Didn't stop us from tryin', though. 300-grain Sabit shotgun slugs set 'em back a pace or two, but other than that, it doesn't have much effect. You're carrying a shotgun."

"Yeah, we're using these." Tom cracked his gun open and pulled out one of the Besselite shells that they were using and tossed it to the cowboy. "Less propellant than your shells, 227gs, but the payload is what does the damage. The slug is shelf-propelled, but not guided, you still have to aim it, and the payload is a mixture of powder and Besselite, which explodes on contact. Depleted uranium tips—help get it through their shields."

The cowboy examined the shell. "Makes a mess of 'em, judging by the fact that you seem to be wearin' one of them. I assume that's lizard guts all over you."

Tom tried to brush off the mess with his hand, only making it worse.

"You don't want to be close when one of those shells goes off. It was close quarters—I didn't have a choice."

"He brought part of the building down as well as the lizard," Zee added for colour. Tom gave her a look that said *will you ever leave that alone.*

The cowboy slipped the shell into his shotgun without closing the breach. "Fits like a glove. Don't suppose—"

"McGee, get a case of the Besselite shotgun slugs out of the carrier, will you?" Tom cut in.

He turned back to the cowboy. "Keep that one. Be careful with these things—they could bring down a tank. They've got a tiny depleted uranium tip, so keep them in the box I'm giving you until you're ready to use them. When you do, wear gloves. Not much of a charge, just enough to get it going—no kick."

McGee jogged back, carrying a portable ammo case about the size of a bread box, with a handle. It contained 150 slugs. Tom gestured for her to hand it over.

"This is all we can spare at the moment."

"Much obliged. We'll put them to good use."

"Call us if you need us."

The Texan looked satisfied and waved his friends back to their trucks.

"Sorry for your loss," Tom shouted after him.

The Texan stopped and turned back.

"These will help assuage some hurt feelings."

The loss was too great to articulate, and nothing sufficient could be done to redeem it, but the ammo was appreciated.

"Good luck with the rest of those critters—they're nasty fuckers," he said as he climbed back into his truck.

"I understand the sentiment, Tom," John said as they both watched the Texans get back in their trucks and leave, "but are you sure you should be handing out that ammo?"

"They're on our side. We need all the help we can get."

"You know they're going to go hunting, right? That's a hundred and fifty-one dead lizards, right there."

Tom thought for a second. "Fuckin' hope so," he said, slapping John on the shoulder before turning to walk back to the carrier.

"They'll probably get hurt doin' it" John called after him.

"I don't think they give a shit" Tom said as he kept walking. "It's Texan payback time."

Just then, Zee's shuttle arrived.

In sick bay on the *Endurance* a couple of days later.

"How are you feeling?"

Tom had come up from the planet briefly to see how Zee was doing. She was sitting in one of the visitors chairs next to her bed, totally sick of being couped up.

"Fine, going out of my mind with boredom."

"They just want to be sure you're okay… because you're, you know, a princess."

Zee smirked, deflecting his smart-arse remark.

"I thought you'd be hunting bad guys."

"I am. It's going well. We've just finished a third dust-up with them at a base north-east of where you were in Missouri—it ended quickly, just like the first two. The other units are doing just as well as we are cleaning up. We'll need more of those shotguns, but they are no match for us with our shielding and those new weapons. It seems to me it's getting a bit senseless, frankly. They should just chuck it in. They're outgunned and outmatched. We've now got twelve light battalions on the surface—about six thousand soldiers—cleaning up across the planet with little effective resistance."

"Have you spoken to Tiberius?"

"No. I think he and I still have a problem."

"You should tell him how you rescued his wife. I'll embellish it if you want—you know, you found me crying, beaten. That should do the trick."

"As if he'd believe you. He knows how tough you are. But thanks anyway."

"What are friends for."

"He's such a principled son of a bitch. I don't think he'll ever let me back in. It wasn't the walls in that detention centre that distressed me—it was the wall I created between me and Tiberius."

Just then, Tiberius walked into the sick bay, his third visit in as many days.

"Son of a bitch, eh? You got the principled part right."

He went over and gave Zee a hug and a kiss.

"How are you doing, sweetheart? You look fine."

"Still got a headache, but otherwise okay."

"You need to rest up. I'll give you a go in my tank when we get you home."

"Fuck that, I'm not going anywhere. There's still work to do here to finish this."

Tiberius turned to Tom, his expression one of distain.

"Why are you here? Shouldn't you be hunting bad guys? Isn't that what you were itching to do?" Then he paused. "I hear you've been enlisting vigilantes."

"Whatever it takes, Boss. A dead lizard is a dead lizard. If you don't like the way—"

"Stop there. I've always admired your single-mindedness, Colonel."

A nurse interrupted. "You're both wanted on the bridge."

"It can wait," Tiberius responded, turning back to Zee.

"It's urgent, apparently."

Then, on the bridge.

"What is it, General? I want to spend some time with my wife."

"They've surrendered, Mr President. Standart is just briefing me." She gestured towards the communications monitor with Standart on it. "Apparently, Minister Dahak has been communicating with the Tracalonian Council by subspace radio. He's ready to give it up after seeing what Tom did to his crew."

Tiberius turned to the screen. "Standart, they've had enough?"

"Yes. Their Council has agreed to the treaty as drafted, effective as soon as they receive confirmation of a ceasefire—conditional on us evacuating their remaining troops without further harm and returning them to their home planet."

"They're hardly in a position to be demanding conditions."

Tom jumped in. "Not Dahak or Dackus, they will need to stand trial on Earth. Make them both surrender to me in Dallas."

"Why Dallas?"

"Because as far as we're concerned, the regional laws on Earth still apply and Texas has the death penalty."

"Good reasoning, but it's going to be difficult to get Dackus to surrender," Tiberius said.

"Why the hell not?" Tom said indignantly.

General Jarvice stepped in. "Because I blew the shit out of his warship at the kick-off to this little soiree—with him and his boss, Vandort, in it. Plus half a dozen of their other top brass. Judging by the comms, it was their flagship, and it was carrying those genetic cluster bombs—locked and loaded, according to our scanners. I thought it was important to take those weapons out of play."

"Good enough. Quicker than a trial, I guess. But we need someone to face justice."

"Nobody is questioning your judgment on that matter, General," Tiberius said, sensing that she felt the need to justify her actions. "Your decisiveness probably shortened the war dramatically and protected the populace below from further attack. Their surrender today confirms that fact."

Then, turning to Standart, he added, "I know you wanted to have a word with Dackus, but you're not going to get that chance."

"He's where he belongs."

Tom looked at Standart. "Why don't you come with me—to Dallas, I mean, for the surrender."

Standart thought only briefly before responding "I'll be on the *Endurance* in an hour." He hung up.

Tiberius turned back to Jarvice and Tom, spelling out the next steps.

"General, confirm with their High Council that we require Dahak to stay on Earth to stand trial. Have them communicate with their men still on the planet to ensure they know it's over. Give them the location of our twelve carriers currently on station down there, where they'll be required to report for deportation."

"They have to surrender their weapons and shields at the muster stations," Tom added.

"Yes, confirm that as well. Colonel, ask your men to stand down but to remain vigilant, and tell them what is happening, so we don't have any mishaps as the Tracalonian soldiers start to arrive at our carriers. Organise some of our large bulk carriers to be at the relevant locations to transport their troops back to Tracalonia. Treat them with respect, make sure your men get that instruction. We're going to have to build a new relationship with these people, starting now."

Tom started to leave to attend to his orders, then stopped and turned back to Tiberius.

"They're not getting Dahak's body back either—assuming he gets the needle. We don't want them erecting monuments to their lost *hero* back on Tracalonia."

"Yes, good point. Perhaps we can have a monument of our own with him buried, unnamed, beneath it surrounded by the names of the two point eight billion people he killed. The ones we can identify, at least."

"That will be a fucking big monument," Tom muttered under his breath as he walked away.

CHAPTER SIXTEEN

The Return to Earth

Tiberius stood on the site of his old warehouse property in Dallas, the one that had once been converted into a GMS engine production facility—now nothing but rubble.

The Federation's Dallas defence base, Camp Burke, was just down the road. Long since abandoned, it also had been completely destroyed in the Tracalonian occupation. The invaders had viewed both sites as threats to their pursuit of total control over the hearts and minds of the indigenous population.

Stepping over the smashed remnants of the production facility, Tiberius made his way to where he thought his original workshop and office had been nearly forty years earlier.

"Memories?" Zee's voice came from behind him, soft and familiar. She had accompanied him back down to the planet after being discharged from sickbay.

"Indeed. It's sad to see it as a pile of twisted metal."

"I used to train down the road at Camp Burke."

Tiberius went over and picked up part of one of his old whiteboards.

"That's wrong," he murmured as he saw some of his old musings still visible on the board. He rubbed out one of the variables in the incomplete mathematical equation with his thumb.

"You don't have a whiteboard marker on you, do you?"

Zee came over and took his arm with both hands and gently said, "No."

It wasn't the time for maths.

Tiberius spotted a couple of upturned chairs, dug them out of the rubble, and banged them on the ground to shake off the dust. Zee took his silent invitation to sit.

"My computer room was there, my office over there. I remember I had the weirdest visit just before things picked up for me. Two guys—I can't quite picture their faces—came by. They were very complimentary about my work and told me I should do something about climate change. Funny the things you remember. I got a call the next night from Elizabeth on the same subject. She was only ten then. I guess that's what got me moving."

"Good thing it did, or you'd be buried here in this rubble somewhere, assuming you hadn't already died of old age."

Tiberius looked at her, knowing she was right but resenting the crack about his age. The thought of being killed in the bombing sent a shiver up his spine.

"I should never have abandoned this place or Camp Burke... or Earth."

"So, you'd prefer to be a token lizard, or a dead human in the wreckage of your old warehouse?"

Tiberius had never shaken his sense of responsibility for what had happened on Earth.

"I guess not."

He patted her on the knee, acquiescing to the obviousness of her observation, leaving his hand resting on her leg.

"We beat those murderous arseholes because of you, Tiberius. Earth is free again because of you."

"I seem to remember a ferocious fighter pilot who took them on single-handedly."

"Hardly. But I certainly would be dead now too if not for you. I wouldn't have knuckled under if I'd been here when they invaded. If the cull didn't get me, they would have killed me for resisting. I owe my life to you, Tiberius." Then putting her hand on top of his, still on her knee. "I'm glad you're not under that rubble, husband. I love you."

"Me too… to both sentiments."

That same day, Tom and Standart were standing together at the site where Tom had originally landed to take on the Tracalonians.

The captured Tracalonian soldiers in the area had been rounded up and were standing in line, awaiting processing. There were going to be holdouts, though—both men knew it. Hardheads unwilling to accept their defeat by humanoids.

"In World War Two on Earth," Tom began, reminiscing, explaining to Standart, "remaining Japanese soldiers of the Imperial Japanese Army, the IJA, and the Imperial Japanese Navy, the IJN, in the Pacific Theatre continued fighting after the surrender of Japan at the end of the war. Japanese holdouts either doubted the veracity of the formal surrender or were not aware that it had happened. There were thousands of them, at least initially. Most didn't *hold out* for long, though—they succumbed to plummeting morale, disease, and starvation. Hiroo Onoda, an IJA officer, hid in the Philippine jungle for thirty years after WWII. He was the last one to surrender."

"You have a fine knowledge of Earth's military history, Tom. We can't let that happen here—any of it—ever again. We need to get them all back to their home planet and give Earth a fresh start. We also need to keep in mind that many of the surrendering Japanese were killed in the confusion as they tried to surrender. We can't let that happen here either."

"No, I guess not. You know a fair bit about our history too."

Behind them the surrendering Tracalonian combatants slowly made their way into the makeshift, tented facility set up by coalition forces for processing.

Everything was going smoothly—except for the occasional scuffle when the Tracalonian soldiers were ordered to surrender their weapons and shields.

Two of Tom's men approached, each holding an arm of a handcuffed Dahak.

Both Tom and Standart smiled—partly out of relief that they had found him, partly because they knew what he was now facing.

Tom broke the silence.

"There you are, Minister. I thought we'd lost you. Last time I saw you, you were deserting the battle here—fleeing with your tail between your legs."

Dahak attempted to free himself from the soldiers' grasp to strike Tom.

"A reference to some accursed Earth animal, I assume."

"He has always been a closet coward, Tom," Standart said, pretending to brief Tom seriously. "All bombast—but always from the comfort of his office."

Tom nodded as if in agreement, "I see."

They both looked at Dahak disparagingly.

"You're going to stand trial for genocide, Dahak—right here in Dallas," Tom continued. "They have designed fast lanes in this State for processing criminals sentenced to death. So, you ain't going anywhere, and you won't have long to wait. In fact, neither you nor your remains will ever leave this planet."

"That sounds like fun," Dahak replied. "Your Earth courts are weak as piss from what we've heard. That's part of why your planet went to shit. They'll probably just deport me."

"This is Dallas, baby. I'm sure they'll figure out the right mixture to inject into your lizard arm."

"Now, Tom," Standart said, "you were told to be respectful."

Tom looked at him surprised—this from a guy who had suffered directly at Dahak's hands.

"This cunt is going to fry for sure. Much more painful."

The smartarse look disappeared from Dahak's face. "The High Council won't allow you to try me."

"Ah," Standart responded, "but they have already agreed to it, that was part of the surrender arrangement. You will be tried here, and I don't fancy your chances."

"You forgot to blow up the prisons, arsehole." Tom said, then instructed the men. "Take him to Polunsky."

"Polunsky?" Standart asked politely.

"Yeah, the Allan B. Polunsky Unit is a prison in West Livingston. The most notorious prison in Texas used for prisoners on death row. Once they go in there, they never come out... alive, anyway."

"I see," Standart said casually.

"It's only about thirty miles from here."

"Off you go then." Standart could not hide his personal satisfaction on giving those instructions. "And, fuck you and the horse you rode in on. Although the *horse you rode in on,* Dahak, is that blown-up pile of shit lying over there."

Dahak was dragged off and Standart and Tom walked over to the processing tent to assess progress.

"Very good choice of the local vernacular, Standart."

"I try to stay relevant."

"Now we just have to round up some judges to preside over his trial," Tom said.

"Can you find enough judges?"

"Sure, there has got to be a few around here somewhere. Not out-of-state judges, I hope, they'd probably order the Tracalonian deportees to be returned to Earth."

"He'll probably claim he was just following orders."

"Didn't work at Nuremburg."

"Nazis on trial, your Second World War, right?"

"Yeah."

"You won't be able to get a jury of his peers, though, the lizards on this planet can't talk... some of them do have genocidal tendencies, though."

Laughter.

"I think it will probably just be three to five judges, more of a tribunal than a trial, no jury, a military-style court. Hopefully, the judges will be from the Supreme Court, if they can find any. If they can't, the locals will do, and they'll probably do the job quicker. Supreme Court judiciary would be more seemly, I think."

"Washington is a ghost town, Tom. They got everyone."

"That can't be such a bad thing, considering the circumstances."

They both laughed again—this time, the laughter was truncated by a sense of guilt at making such a joke.

Dahak's trial was indeed a speedy affair as Tom had predicted. There was a great deal of hatred piled up against the Tracalonians and Dahak's head helped quell those feelings.

Within six months, he had been tried and executed, and, as Tiberius had promised, a memorial was under construction. Dahak's body was buried at its centre, beneath an ever-expanding array of semicircular marble panels.

Each panel—one foot thick, six feet wide, and standing ten feet tall—radiated outward from his unmarked grave, which had been topped, disrespectfully, with the head of a gargoyle.

Every granite panel was inscribed with the names of the humans who had died in the conflict—names that were still being progressively identified. It was expected that the semicircular panels, set up with spaces every thirty feet to allow foot traffic through the monument, would eventually stretch out to a diameter of several kilometres.

It was as if the dead were watching Dahak, blaming him for eternity for the horrific slaughter he had inflicted on the planet.

In that same timeframe, much of the administrative work related to the setup of the replacement government on Earth had been done or was nearing completion.

Each American state and each autonomous country had been assigned an Administrator, with staff and mechanisms put in place to allow them to govern effectively.

A census was to be conducted, asking citizens in each region what form of local government they wanted. It would be left to each independent state or country to decide whether to join the Federation—continuing under the Administrator system used in Federation Colonies—or to return to the governmental structure they had before the Tracalonian invasion.

This applied to all countries, which had been reinstated within the same geographical borders that existed before the invasion.

Only half of the former US states chose to join the Federation and keep the Administrators. The rest reverted to their old system—the same one that had served them so ineffectively in the past.

The result was a divided United States—one part forming a new federal entity, where several states agreed to a democratic election system, and the other part becoming a collection of independent states—or Colonies, as they were now called, aligning with Federation nomenclature. Those independent colonies each had membership in the Federation and were governed by Administrators appointed by the Federation selected from the local citizenry and, as per Federation policy, regularly changed with their performance myopically scrutinised.

An administrative and trade capital was established in Dallas for the Federation Colonies on the American mainland.

Ironically, to Tiberius, the division between old-style states and Federation Colonies closely mirrored the split that had occurred at the beginning of the American Civil War.

Additionally, around half of the smaller independent countries had joined the Federation, with Russia and China reverting almost immediately to their various forms of dictatorship.

The Federation entities gained access to free trade with the rest of the Federation Colonies, whereas the non-Federation entities were subjected to a tariff regime. The proceeds from these tariffs were allocated to rebuilding Earth's infrastructure.

Most importantly, Tiberius had finally succeeded in installing a planet-wide protective shield.

Close to Tiberius's heart was the implementation of a Federation-style education system in the newly established Earth-based Federation entities. No university could operate without adopting the Federation's curriculum and agreeing to scrutiny regarding the elimination from their curriculum of propagandised social issues.

Additionally, Tiberius had reinstated a defence and police base on the site of his old warehouses, incorporating consulate and trading offices for use by the American Colonies engaged in commerce with the Federation. Seeing the site of his original workplace renewed was a source of considerable satisfaction for him.

None of Washington had survived—including almost its entire population. The destruction of Washington had been a priority for the Tracalonians due to its status as the seat of American power and its deep symbolic significance for the American people.

What remained of the District of Columbia was absorbed into Virginia, while Virginia and West Virginia combined to form the independent Federation Colony of Virginia.

The term Colony had evolved into a revered designation, representing an independent, self-governing entity that participated in the well-being of the Federation as a whole. It had become synonymous with personal liberty, self-determination, and low taxes. Many of the Federation's Colonies were now larger than some of Earth's former nations.

Aside from the tragic loss of life, Tiberius found himself somewhat pleased that the pit of snakes that was Washington had been excluded from the New World Order. While the city had been founded on well-meaning principles, its fate served as a reminder of how far America had strayed from those ideals.

Tiberius felt that the Declaration of Independence was as relevant as ever in the planet's current circumstances:

We hold these truths to be self-evident, that all men are created equal, that they are endowed, by their Creator, with certain unalienable rights, that among these are life, liberty, and the pursuit of happiness.

That to secure these rights, governments are instituted among men, deriving their just powers from the consent of the governed.

That whenever any form of government becomes destructive of these ends, it is the right of the people to alter or to abolish it, and to institute new government, laying its foundation on such principles, and organising its powers in such form, as to them shall seem most likely to effect their safety and happiness.

Shortly after the US War of Independence against the English, the taxation that had initially sparked that uprising had ultimately returned as politicians consolidated power. Those founding principles were gradually subjugated to self-interest. A 2.5% tax levied by the British on tea—the catalyst for the Boston Tea Party— so despised by the American people that they took up arms against the British, was, over time, replaced with an average 44% tax on all income earned by the citizenry, collected by various levels of American government. This was in addition to sales tax and a myriad of other levies invented by politicians.

Authoritarianism had swiftly crept back in to enslave the newly liberated population after the war with the English, though through a different system of government than the one imposed by the Imperialists. The outcome, however, was the same as before the revolution: a privileged elite ruling class ran the government while benefiting from a compliant working population.

Tiberius believed Washington had become a nest of bureaucrats, existing solely to feed themselves rather than serve the people. The right of the people to *alter or abolish* such a system of government had never been more appropriate but never realised before the invasion. Political corruption—the pursuit of self-interest over duty—had fuelled that bureaucracy. It had created a symbiotic relationship between wealthy elites and self-serving politicians. The select few within the system gained what they desired—power and wealth—while the rest were left to work themselves to exhaustion.

The appointment of Administrators, chosen based on qualification and character, educated in public administration, and drilled on ethical and public responsibility—all under strict citizen oversight—was, in Tiberius's view, a vastly superior system. It was certainly preferable to Joe or Jane Blogs getting elected solely because they had a nice smile and the backing of corporate media or party interests.

That system had failed to work partly because the scrutiny, supposedly provided by the *free press,* had disappeared, if indeed the *free media* ever undertook that task effectively. There was the need for audits, approval mechanisms, electronic consensus gathering, visibility and measures of performance, some of which was a function that was supposed to be performed by the *independent press.* But the press simply became part of the club. The old *democratic* system became a well-oiled machine whose participants took what they wanted and paid only cursory attention to the citizenry they were supposed to serve. In such a system what newly *elected* representative, even if initially well-intentioned, could resist accessing the wishing well for their own benefit.

The old system became a charade of public administration unexamined by a *free press.*

To Tiberius, democracy was no better than a dictatorship—at least in a dictatorship, there was no pretence about the destruction of individual rights. He believed that governance oversight should never have been entrusted to commercial media organisations, which, by their very nature under capitalism, had their own agendas.

By all means, a free press should exist—to broaden perspectives and provide a variety of information sources—but allowing it to serve as the primary auditor of government power was, in Tiberius's view, insanity. Americans often talked about reclaiming the fourth estate, but genuine, ethics-based journalism had long since been lost to commercial interests.

These entities had a duty to their shareholders, not the public. And without true oversight, democracy had been doomed to inevitable surrender.

Alongside that reality, the lack of public visibility surrounding secret covert operations conducted in the name of national security was, in Tiberius's view, a recipe for waste and corruption. It encouraged the pursuit of personal agendas, whether by the operatives themselves or their political overlords.

Those agencies spent taxpayer money—vast amounts of it—yet were largely exempt from public review. If spy movies were to be believed, some of them even killed people.

How many billions of dollars were funnelled into these black-op programs by various nations, when total transparency in all global operations would render them irrelevant?

They should show their cards, expose the threats, allow solutions to be publicly debated.

Why would any well-meaning society allow this vast waste of money all in the name of *national security*?

These same agencies would argue that the general public "couldn't handle the truth"—perhaps one of the most self-aggrandising and unproductive justifications ever conceived.

It was a rationale designed solely to protect bureaucracies that leeched funds from an otherwise productive society.

Who, on Earth, decides what the public is capable of understanding?

Would they riot? Would they panic?

If politicians had been hiding contact with alien species before the Tracalonian invasion, then that deception had directly contributed to Earth's lack of preparedness.

For now, Washington's iconic buildings would not be rebuilt.

Before any reconstruction took place, all Federation Colonies—including the newly incorporated District of Columbia—would have to decide their collective future.

The ruins of Washington would remain standing—perhaps as a monument to the failure of the old system, or perhaps as a historical site for a new generation of more informed citizens.

These Colonies included New Virginia, the Carolinas, Alabama, Georgia, Florida, Arkansas, Mississippi, Texas, Louisiana, Kentucky, Tennessee, Oklahoma, and New Mexico—with several others still deliberating on whether to break from the old system.

Tiberius was concerned that he was leaving a substantial part of his home planet technically in the dark but consoled himself with the fact that, as always, they were given the choice to move forward or continue to wallow in the same political bullshit. It was understood that the roots of control ran deep in Russia and China and several other communist states, so expectations of them joining were low. Their underperformance compared to Federation states would perhaps in the long run be sufficient impetus for them to change.

Tiberius was also uneasy about the fact that, by default, the Federation had become the galaxy's new police force. He was uncomfortable accepting that level of responsibility.

Discussions had already begun with the Tearn leadership regarding the creation of a Central Council—an entity that would oversee interplanetary governance and security, preventing the Federation from becoming the sole enforcer of galactic law.

For the moment, Standart had stepped away from public life. After the victory against the Tracalonian forces, he felt he had earned a sabbatical.

There would be many retirements ahead for him, but for now, he and Zara had chosen to start a family. They had moved next door to Tom and Elizabeth on Hope, the Federation's utopian colony, to build a new life. By the pool in their backyard, Tom and Elizabeth's two children—Sunny and April—splashed and played, enjoying a perfect summer's day.

The events of the Tracalonian invasion of Earth, and Tom's eventual court-martial, had finally begun to fade into the past.

Tom's court-martial had resulted in nothing more than confirmation of his demotion to Colonel. He had been treated leniently, largely due to his distinguished service to the Federation.

With their extended life expectancy, Tom and Elizabeth had time to pursue new careers—perhaps in defence, public administration, or something entirely new.

A galaxy now lay at their feet, waiting to be explored.

There had been talk of allowing Tracalonian families to settle on Hope. But it was generally agreed that the wounds were still too raw. Even among the Tearn, resentment toward the Tracalonians ran deep.

The trauma of war had not yet healed, and their hatred for the species that had tormented them for generations remained strong. Yet, among the more enlightened minds, there was a recognition that excluding them entirely could be a grave mistake—one that might, in time, bring dire consequences.

The two planets previously occupied by the Tracalonians, now independent colonies, had already been welcomed to Hope. Both were humanoid species, and both were grateful to be free of Tracalonian rule. Several families from these liberated worlds had already eagerly settled on Hope.

It seemed that humanoid form was Mother Nature's preferred template for sentient species—at least within the known universe.

Both of the newly liberated species were strikingly similar to humans and the Tearn. At a glance, when fully clothed, it was difficult to tell them apart. However, they were taller, owing to the lower gravity of their home planets.

One species had a vestigial set of two small additional arms, reminiscent of a tyrannosaurus rex. The other had the remnants of a shortened tail.

Both exhibited a wide variety of skin colours.

As Earth's own evolutionary history had demonstrated, Mother Nature was a comedian.

Still, among both the Tearn and Federation leadership, there was a growing consensus: Hope was destined to be a melting pot. And that, perhaps, was the true future of the galaxy.

An advocacy group had emerged on Hope with the goal of encouraging genetic integration among all species on the planet—excluding the Tracalonians, due to the genetic incompatibilities between them and humanoid species. These unions were entirely voluntary, and assistance with reproduction would only be granted if a secure home environment could be provided for the offspring throughout their maturation.

While non-viable zygotes would not be reimplanted, and no implantation would occur if the mother was medically unfit to carry the child to term, there was growing momentum to experiment with all possible genetic combinations—as long as the child's well-being and the mother's health could be ensured.

Even if surrogate or adoptive parents were required, the advocacy group believed that the future of a peaceful galaxy lay in the amalgamation of all species.

CHAPTER SEVENTEEN

The Ugly Truth

Tiberius and Zee had purchased a small ranch in the hills outside Hopeton, the new capital of Hope. Tom and Elizabeth were now permanent residents of Hope, meaning that Tiberius was near his granddaughter and two great-grandchildren. Tiberius had also taken a well-earned sabbatical from his role as President of the Federation. For the time being, no one was willing to assume his position—it was widely expected that the role would remain vacant until he chose to return.

The previous owner of their ranch was one of Hope's original settlers—a Texan rancher who had immigrated to the planet. The rancher and his wife had moved to a larger property to focus on cattle breeding—a crossbreed of Newcon and Tearn livestock developed with the assistance of the in-vitro specialists at the Hope Medical Centre. His hybrid meat had garnered universal interest and was now in high demand, not only on Hope but across the Federation and the Tearn home world. With his business expanding rapidly, he required a much larger ranch, so he sold his original farm to Tiberius and Zee.

Life on the ranch had settled into a comfortable rhythm.

Tiberius and Zee spent their days working the farm, visiting family, and cooking, experimenting with the wide range of produce now available in the Hopeton markets. Occasionally, they even supplied their own excess produce to the markets. Tiberius recalled the travelling cooking shows from Earth's past, where the host would marvel at local open markets and their exotic offerings. He imagined how overwhelmed such a host would be at a market featuring produce from multiple planets, supplied by several different species.

Tiberius was not yet missing being a central part of the Federation. He was enjoying his time on the ranch with his family centric new life.

That is until a meeting that he had with Standart. Tiberius had only intended to take six weeks off after the Tracalonian War, but it had been drawn out to nearly four months directly because of that conversation. Standart had decided to come clean with Tiberius about his original visit to Earth all those years ago. Standart had finally confessed the details of his visit to Dallas and how they had provided Tiberius with certain mathematical solutions along with the basic designs for the gravity management equipment, nuclear fusion, and shielding.

The revelation shook Tiberius to his core.

The disorienting realisation that he had not truly developed his groundbreaking work sent him into a deep malaise.

Now, two months after their heart-to-heart, Standart had returned to the ranch to check on him. He found Tiberius in his garden, painting—something he had never known him to do. Tiberius felt disappearing into the minutiae of painting might clear his head.

"I didn't know you painted" Standart said as he approached Tiberius in a slow walk.

"Neither did I. Something you stuck in my brain, perhaps?"

"Not over it yet, I see." Standart stood there with his hands on his hips, then gesturing with his finger "I told you the extent of our help. It had nothing to do with you painting. Your mother was an artist, right?"

"You know more about my family than I do."

"You're still bitter."

Standart found a folding chair that he opened and sat on, then continued.

"What did you expect us to do? We needed to get that planet out of the death spiral that it was in, and yes, we did check you and your family out thoroughly. We were determined to get it right; we believed it to be critical for the survival of your planet."

That didn't seem to be influencing Tiberius's mood. Perhaps a diversion.

"You weren't our first try, you know."

"What does that mean?" Tiberius stopped painting and turned to look at Standart.

"There were two before you, many years prior. It wasn't me who visited them, it was my predecessors. It didn't do much good."

"Let me guess who."

"I'd prefer you didn't."

"Nobody religious, because you guys aren't into that stuff. Copernicus and Galileo."

"Yes, to the former, no to the latter."

"It wasn't you guys who did that pyramid bullshit was it?"

"No, that was all you; the pyramids were pure narcissism, the people on your planet know no bounds to egotistical endeavour."

"It's not my planet."

"Most developed civilisations look to progress the group as a whole not just deify themselves."

Tiberius nodded in agreement. "Sure, one would hope." He returned to his painting.

"The other person we contacted was Da Vinci."

"Ah, also a painter. Did you teach him to paint as well?"

Standart rolled his eyes. "Will you stop with the painting crap? I told you what we provided you—nothing more." Then he softened. "Da Vinci was not just a painter—he was many things. And he had a great mind—like you."

Tiberius was not overly enthused by being compared to someone like Leonardo Da Vinci.

"We were too early in Earth's development for Da Vinci to have the effect we were after; he didn't have the basic tools or the right technological environment to turn things around as we had hoped. He became a world-wide influence in later years after his death, but his effect during his lifetime was largely provincial. So, we decided to let your people grow up a bit before we tried again."

Tiberius had lost interest. "Da Vinci did OK."

"Look, Tiberius, you are totally underestimating the role you played in all of this. You were already working with the math that we helped you with, you already had the basic concept of the GMS in your head and on your whiteboards, and the same was true with nuclear fusion. You were well on your way with fusion. The rejuvenation tank was just us protecting our investment in you."

No response.

"You were going to be our last try, our last hope of making a difference there. The Council had instructed that we let it be whatever it was going to be regardless of whether it worked out with you or not. That's why we went a bit heavy-handed on giving you a big start for the designs of the GMS and the fusion technology, but I think you would have worked it out yourself even if we had given you less information. Can you imagine where you and your family would be if you hadn't done everything that you achieved? You'd all be dead and long gone."

Tiberius stopped again.

"You've made it impossible for me to know what was truly mine and what was put in here." He pointed to his head. Then, with a sudden flash of suspicion: "What about the piano-playing shit?"

Standart chuckled. "That was all you. You figured out how to use the rejuvenation technology for something it wasn't designed for—managing muscle memory. That was totally your breakthrough. Now we've incorporated it into our own tanks. Originally, the tanks were designed to eliminate toxins, infections, and rejuvenate cells—nothing more. You turned them into tools that could manipulate muscle memory and hunt down cancers."

"I'll have to take your word for it." He went back to his painting.

"Look, you are being ridiculous. Can't you see what you've built? The Tearn didn't rid the galaxy of those warmongering arseholes— you did. You saved Earth, not us. You did the exploring. You did the building. That was all you."

"So, you went from god-like manipulators to appreciative students, is that it?" Then, more dryly: "I assume there are people on your Science Council who take full credit for what I've done."

"Sure, but that view is misplaced. They don't have your intellect."

"Next thing you'll tell me is that you were probing humans." Then, suddenly, his expression darkened. "You didn't stick anything in my arse, did you?"

Standart burst out laughing.

"Of course not. We had scanners to study human physiology—no probing necessary. That's an Earth-based science fiction myth."

Then, after composing himself: "Anyway, back to my point. We gave you a leg up on shielding—which you then improved to be the best in the galaxy. We gave you a start on cell manipulation, but you turned it into a life-saving technology we now copy from you. Gravity management?"

Tiberius raised an eyebrow. "Yes, gravity management?"

Standart sighed. "Okay… that was basically a Tearn design but you had the structure for it drawn on your whiteboards, you were stuck on the design for the electromagnetic fluid."

Tiberius smirked. "Thought so. And fusion technology?"

"Well, fusion is fusion. Once you have the basic maths and understand the chamber structure, there's not much more to do."

Standart leaned forward.

"But can't you see? Everything else—that was all you. Including the magnificent leadership you've provided to the Federation."

Tiberius shook his head. "And the two maths problems?"

"For god's sake, Tiberius. You basically had them both solved—it was frustrating seeing them unfinished on your whiteboards. One was stuck on a stupid denominator issue. The other had the wrong variables. We gave you very little help. It was just a timing issue—we needed you to finish that and move forward instead of going around in circles. How long did it take you to figure them out after we left?"

Tiberius thought for a moment. "About a day."

Standart nodded. "Exactly. We knew the answers. But we didn't give them to you. In the end, you figured them out."

Tiberius looked thoughtful. "Why did you choose me?"

Standart smiled.

"After all that's happened… after everything you and the Federation have achieved… do you really think we chose badly? The Federation, by the way—that's all you."

Standart stood up, ready to leave. It was clear that he wasn't getting through to Tiberius. But just as he turned to go, Tiberius said somewhat consolingly.

"I don't mean to sound unappreciative, Standart. A lot of good came from your interference." He thought for a moment. "But I have to find myself in all of this. What was truly me and what was… you? And that—that's maddening."

He exhaled sharply.

"Standart, you've become a dear friend. But you should have asked my permission before downloading all that information into my head."

Standart shook his head. "And risk sending you insane? The stakes were too high. You're struggling with it even now—imagine how you would have reacted back then, with two aliens turning up on your doorstep."

He gestured toward the horizon.

"Look at what you've built, Tiberius. Look down at that city—at all of it. This isn't over, you're not done yet."

"I appreciate you telling me all of this. But now I have to decide whether to tell my family."

Standart studied him.

"Why wouldn't they understand? After everything you did for them—for the Federated Colonies? Does it even matter now?"

Standart turned and walked away, straight past Zee, who had just arrived with a tray of refreshments. He nodded in farewell saying nothing as he climbed into his vehicle.

Zee frowned as she approached Tiberius. "Why did you upset him? He's your friend."

Tiberius exhaled slowly blowing out his cheeks.

"It's… complicated."

A week later, Tiberius still hadn't told his family about Standart's visit back in Dallas nearly forty years prior. It was weighing on him—but he needed to make sense of it himself first.

That's how he found himself on his favourite ridge—eighteen hundred feet up in the mountains overlooking Hopeton. He had lugged his painting gear up the hill, setting it up on a flat section of rock that jutted out from the cliff face. He intended to paint the vista.

As he sat before the easel, he murmured to himself:

"I wonder how my mother would paint this scene."

Then, after a pause: "Probably watercolours."

He picked up his charcoal to start drawing.

Then muttered: "I hate fucking watercolours."

Another pause.

"In fact… I hate fucking painting."

Frustrated, he shoved the easel over onto its back.

The deep melancholy that had been plaguing him suddenly surfaced. It overtook him as he threw the drawing charcoal as hard as he could over the edge of the cliff. He began to contemplate dark and unwelcome thoughts. He stood and began to pace, hands on hips.

Then realising where he was, "you know, I could trip," he said out load, continuing to talk to himself, now serious, distressed, he walked over to the edge of the cliff and looked over. "No one would know. The fall would no doubt kill me." Tiberius had not been wearing his personal shielding device since his conversation with Standart about their visit to Dallas because of the personal self-loathing that had buried him; he didn't deserve to have such a device he believed even though he invented it. Zee was aware that he was physically exposed but didn't want to push the subject, not fully understanding the depth of his depression, instead accepting the façade of normality that Tiberius was projecting. His inability to determine the line between his own endeavours and that installed in him by the Tearn all those years ago had deeply affected his sense of being. He had begun to think of himself as a fraud and a poser.

He looked down over the cliff. It would definitely kill me, he thought, and ever the analyst: "You wouldn't want it to just cripple you and then bleed to death in pain. There would be nothing to indicate that it was suicide. The easel is here with my painting gear. Clearly, it must have been an accident."

He edged a little closer to the precipice. For some reason, one of his favourite Shakespearean lines from *Hamlet* came to mind courtesy of his eidetic memory. He recited it out loud.

"To die, to sleep—
No more—and by a sleep to say we end
The heartache, and the thousand natural shocks
That flesh is heir to. 'tis a consummation
Devoutly to be wish'd. To die, to sleep—
To sleep—perchance to dream. Ay, there's the rub!
For in that sleep of death what dreams may come,
When we have shuffled off this mortal coil,
Must give us pause—there's the respect
That makes calamity of so long life."

"Yes… such a long life, such a long time for anyone to stay sane living in the same head for so long," he mused talking to himself. "What dreams may indeed come," he repeated for only his troubled subconscious to hear.

"The dream of a loving wife, mourning.

"The dream of an unexplored galaxy, waiting.

"The dream of that township down there, blossoming…" Then after a pause:

"The dream of a destiny, unfulfilled."

He stepped back one pace, then after settling himself, went back to his chair and sat. He attempted to summarise what Standart had said to him when he was attempting to explain their intervention. If it was just an assist with fusion, gravity management, and shielding, was that as big a deal as his confused psyche was making it out to be? He was certain that he had been toying with those concepts for years, sometimes very seriously, and that he was well advanced on the math, before he met Standart. Or was his mind playing tricks on him?

"NO!" he asserted loudly; he was certain he had been struggling with those designs for years and with the two math problems. "Some of that work goes back to when I was at university. I have paperwork and drawings going back thirty years before Standart arrived."

That was enough to cause him to reconsider his state of mind.

"FUCK… THIS."

He went over and packed up his painting gear and headed back down the hill. As he made his way home, his stride lengthened as he neared the house. Arriving at home, he dumped his painting gear in the foyer and hunted down Zee, eventually finding her in the kitchen.

"Zee, it's time for you to get off your arse and go and do something productive," he said to her excitedly.

"What? You're the one…"

"Enough of your excuses, enough holiday, it's time for you to get back to work."

He hurriedly went over to his computer.

"We have to find a manager for this place. Might not be easy, given the state of the jobs market."

Zee came up behind him and put her hand on his shoulder as he typed.

"And you," he twisted his head around to face her, "you need to get over your aversion to having kids."

"What the hell. What does that mean?"

"You know little versions of you and me running around, breaking things and shitting everywhere."

"Sounds delightful, but, again, it was you…"

He stood and took her by the shoulders, lovingly.

"What do you say babe, one of each?"

"Did you take something?" she replied, sceptical of his mood change.

"Yes, a serous dose of reality." He pulled her over by her hand to sit next to him on the lounge. He calmed down, seeing that he was worrying her.

"Look, I've wallowed enough. I was struck by self-doubt given the responsibility of being some kind of galactic policeman." This is not the story about Standart's interference that he had decided he would tell her as he walked down the mountain, but he continued with it anyway. "I wasn't sure that I could continue to do it, or if I even wanted to continue to do it. But I've changed my mind. I want to get back into it."

She looked at him with obvious concern about his sudden change of heart. He continued to explain.

"I'm sorry I didn't talk that through with you. I've been dragging myself around here like a pouting child. I'm over it but I'll only go back to it if you want to come."

Zee didn't respond, then: "You locked me out, Tiberius. I knew you were keeping something from me. This—" waving her finger back and forth between him and her— "this doesn't work like that. We need to be open with each other." After studying his countenance, "and there is still something you're not telling." She saw his head drop. "There is, isn't there?"

Tiberius stood and began to pace.

"That argument with Standart the other day…" he didn't want to tell her but thought for the sake of the relationship that he must. "Standart and I had met before, or so he tells me, years ago when I was by myself in Dallas."

"You didn't think to mention this to me."

"That's just the thing. I didn't remember it."

She looked at him in disbelief. "You have an eidetic memory; you didn't remember it?"

"Yeah, they took steps to ensure that I didn't remember it."

"They?"

"He had a colleague with him… they… the Tearn. They came to my shed and talked to me about how much shit the planet was in. I agreed with them, of course, but I thought they were pranking me, but they weren't. I asked them to leave, but they came back that night whilst I was sleeping. They *downloaded* some information into my brain—that's how Standart described it. To assist in my work, he said, and they didn't want me to remember that they had assisted me."

Still not believing him.

"Remember that recurring dream I was telling you about years ago?"

"You still have those."

"Yeah, the two guys in my bedroom late at night with needles. Apparently, that was real. It was them. They gave me something to stop me from remembering it."

"Why would they do that… why?"

"They wanted me to think that I had come up with the solutions to certain key problems myself. They thought that if they told me who they really were, that they were aliens from another planet wanting to stick things in my brain, that it would send me mad. They were probably right. It's driven me crazy even now… and I actually know who they are. They were desperate to help in Earth's development, he said."

"So, all those things you came up with was all them?"

"Standart says no, not all. He says they just gave me a few prompts to help me get over the line with issues that I was already working on."

"Sure… but…"

"That is what I have been struggling with, and asking myself how much help did they give me. He says they never came back, that they simply let me get on with it."

"It was all you, then… the last forty years of it anyway. They just gave you a kick in the arse and sent you on your way, is that it? You're panicking because Standart gave you some cliff notes and woke you up. By the sound of it, you needed it. You certainly got on with it. You could have solved a few mathematical problems, got your Noble Prize and gone back to sleep like the rest of the planet. But you didn't. Instead—look what happened."

"I guess, but as you can understand, I hope, it has been hard for me to get my head around it."

Zee stood. "You should have told me what was going on."

"Never again, Zee." He took both of her hands. "I'll never keep you out of my life ever again. You are my life, baby, and I want to get on with it."

"Here, sit back down with me," she said and drew him back to the couch, "and calm down. You know that I love you, right?"

He didn't answer, he thought he didn't have to.

"Does any of what Standart said really matter?" she continued. "So what? They gave you some information, hoping you'd run with it. And you certainly did run with it. I would say they got a lot more than they were hoping for."

"Sure… but…"

"No *but*. You did all of that yourself, Tee. It was you, not them. What did you expect them to do, sit on their hands and watch the Earth go to shit? The community is safe now because of you, not just because of the shielding, but because you neutralised those accursed lizards."

"Maybe..."

"Shut up and get over it."

He didn't expect her to dismiss it so easily, but he was willing to go with her judgment on the matter.

"It was a kick in the arse," she summarised her thoughts, "that's all? Them telling you now, you already knowing that aliens exist, is probably a good thing, rather than springing it on you at the time."

"So, it's time to say thanks mate and move on."

It all seemed so simple and predictable to her.

"Now," she moved closer to him, "we need to talk about something more serious. What were you saying about having kids?"

Tiberius returned to real life. "Yes, I think we should have kids. I've been thinking about it for some time now, before all this shit with Standart distracted me. All of this has straightened out my priorities, I think. I guess."

"Sweetheart, I was meaning to talk to you about this too, but you seemed so preoccupied. I want the same thing."

"One of each, then?"

She kissed him. The deal had been sealed. "But you'll have to give me a go in your tank afterwards to put everything back where it belongs."

"Certainly, I like it right where it is now."

"And a six-pack... and piano."

"Deal."

Tom had survived any punitive action at his court-martial because of his service to the Federation but had to accept his demotion to Colonel. He and Elizabeth had both been posted to Hope—her as Head Administrator for the planet because of her wealth of experience in that role, him as Defence and Police Head. It meant Tom wouldn't fly, but that suited them both for the moment as they raised their two precocious youngsters. Hope had become a planet preferred by many families because of the open clean sky and mixture of cultures. After all, with access to Tiberius's cell regeneration tank, they both had new lives to pursue in the future if the desire to do so struck them.

Tom and Elizabeth had set up a dinner party to which Tiberius and Zee had been invited. Tom had also invited his army buddy, the sergeant that went with him to Earth on their ill-fated raid, John Whitaker, who had also been released without charge after his initial arrest. John had migrated to Hope and Tom had given him a position in the Hope Defence Force.

That night, John had brought along his Tearn girlfriend. As it happened, John's girlfriend was the lieutenant who had accompanied Standart to make first contact—the one Tiberius had once commented on regarding her obvious femininity. She had since been posted to the Hope Defence Station as the Tearn Liaison Officer, which was where she and John had met.

Standart and his wife Zara also attended.

"You two make a fine-looking couple," Standart commented, referring to John and the lieutenant. "John, have you come up with a name for the lieutenant that's pronounceable in English, or are we going to keep referring to her as 'the lieutenant'?"

English was the language spoken at the table, but the lieutenant was using her translator.

"Joy," the lieutenant responded.

"Good choice, Joy," Zee said. "How appropriate to this planet. We have some news too—Tiberius and I have decided to have children."

"Only because the planet is underpopulated," Tiberius added, into a spattering of friendly applause demonstrating his dry sense of humour. Zee gave him a look of disapproval—her usual response to his jokes. "We felt we needed to do our bit for the community."

"About time, Tiberius." Tom said, "we were hoping you would have kids so our kids would have someone to play with."

On Hope, and in the Federation more broadly, there was no need to hold back on such an announcement out of any uncertainty regarding whether the pregnancy would occur and be successful. Once a couple committed to procreation, the medical services could make the pregnancy happen and ensure it made it to full term as a healthy baby.

"Okay," John said. "Given that we're playing 'Top That', I've got another one for you—Joy and I have decided to marry and have kids too. So that playgroup just got bigger."

A round of genuine congratulations followed.

"I have so many questions," Zara said. "Is reproduction even possible between species?"

"Yes, most definitely," Standart jumped in to confirm. "Our medical teams have conducted tests since we've been here on this planet, and yes—it's definitely possible. We're all fascinated to see the outcome. We can guarantee it will be viable and healthy, but beyond that, there are too many variables to determine what the child will look like—other than the fact that it will most certainly be humanoid. They're also sure they can manage the gender outcome. So, you'll need to start thinking about the sex of your first baby. You too, Tiberius."

"We haven't discussed it in detail, but I'm thinking boy, then girl, in that order," Tiberius said. Zee agreed.

Interest returned to the mixed-race couple.

"I'm reluctant to ask," Zara continued, greeted by an audible groan around the table, the guests knowing where Zara was going with her questions. Zara's frankness was now socially well known, so everyone was expecting a very personal question. "How are things going for you both, sexually, I mean?"

"Dear God, Zara," Standart said.

But Joy answered with the forthrightness installed in her by her military training. "The bits fit together very nicely, if that's what you're asking."

"You can say that again," John confirmed, "very nicely."

Joy couldn't stop a cheeky grin coming across her face.

"I am extremely happy with the way that works," John elaborated.

On a more serious note, Tiberius asked, "And your emotional compatibility?"

"We are both ex-military, so we know each other's priorities. We also have a similar sense of humour," Joy answered.

"Socially, any push back from the general community?" Standart asked, interested to know if the social experiment was working out.

"None," John replied. "I guess it is somewhat expected on this planet to see mix-species couples."

"We have a number of mixed-species couples as friends," Joy expanded, "many of whom are also seriously thinking about marriage and some of whom have already moved in together. So, you are not going to have to wait long to see how things turn out, Standart, with the product of interracial breeding."

"And the language gap?" Zee asked.

"John's given up on learning Tearn, I think. English is the simpler language so I'm giving it go. The communicators, as you can tell, are not an inconvenience at all, and getting better as we speak, which is a deliberate pun. You see, the translator software is also conversant in the various slangs or nuances in each language, and it learns as it goes along." That struck a chord with many at the table. "But we'll teach the kids both languages," Joy reached out and put her hand on John's leg affectionately, expecting him to join her in that commitment. "Perhaps one or two other languages as well. It amazes me that the translator can always find an English word or phrase that conveys to John any emotion I am feeling, and that the translation of that feeling has the same resonance in both Tearn and English. To me, what that means is that our development as a species shares a universal subset of experiences, emotions, and desires."

"God, you should write that down somewhere."

"Yeah," Standart said, "we could put it in our migration advertising."

"I think speaking another language is a sign of great intelligence," Tiberius said, "but the advent of the translators took away the incentive."

"Have you set a date for the wedding?" Zee asked.

"Yes, we'll send you all an invite shortly."

The enjoyable conversation at the table helped Tiberius completely shed the remnants of his depression. The possibility of interracial marriage on Hope had once again ignited his enthusiasm for planetary exploration and reminded him of the initiatives that he and Standart had implemented so successfully.

CHAPTER EIGHTEEN

The Supreme Interplanetary Council

Eighteen months had passed since John and Joy had married. She had given birth to a healthy male child within a six-month gestation, the normal full term for a Tearn pregnancy. The child had been named Tobulian by Joy, who loved the way the name came off the tongue of either a Tearn or Newcon speaker. As it happened, Tobulian had a mathematical data conversation connotation, though spelt differently as "ToBoolean," which pleased Tiberius. Inevitably, the boy would get his name shortened to "Toby" at school.

Toby was now a precocious one-year-old. He was already exhibiting attributes in advance of either a Newcon or Tearn child of the same age. He could walk, even run, and had a basic, but childish, grasp of both Tearn and English. It appeared that he had greater strength and speed compared to other children, but that was yet to be fully determined. He was slightly taller than the norm for either species at that age, but John was quite tall.

Tobulian had olive skin—something John welcomed, having suffered several serious bouts of sunburn as a child. He had large eyes, no bigger than those of a Tearn child, but they were deep brown, almost black, like a Tearn's eyes. His hair, however, was the colour of John's rather than the distinctive white of Joy's. Inevitably, he would be subjected to numerous tests to determine precisely how the genes of his two parents had interacted. All in all, he was a good-looking and healthy boy—without Spock ears.

There were fourteen other interracial pregnancies currently in progress on Hope, plus four other births after the birth of Tobulian, all progeny having similar characteristics. There was talk, momentarily, of educating them separately with the objective of clearly identifying intellectual disparities between them and either Tearn or Newcon children, but the education system already accommodated a vast range of developmental progressions, and it was thought that excluding such children from a mainstream educational environment would be prejudicial and would constrain the development of their social skills. These children were the future of Hope, and perhaps even beyond that planet, so isolating them in any way from the rest of the population was considered counterproductive.

On this day, Tiberius found himself at the headquarters of the newly formed Supreme Interplanetary Council (SIC), which was housed in purpose-built council chambers on Tearn. Tiberius's whole family had come with him; he was to receive an award and be welcomed as the inaugural Chairman of the Council.

Tiberius had returned to his position as President of the Federation, but by this time, the Federation's operations and administration were so well-oiled and efficient that it allowed him the flexibility to take on this additional role. His new position as Chairman of the SIC was largely titular, with the President of the Council, a Tearn, handling most of the administrative duties. Neither role carried executive powers beyond the execution of tasks assigned and approved by the Council.

As part of today's proceedings, the Council was also set to announce a large-scale, twelve-starship expedition into deep space. The destination was the centre of the known galaxy, nearly eight kiloparsecs (twenty-five thousand light-years) from Tearn. The fleet would head in the direction of the constellations Sagittarius, Ophiuchus, and Scorpius, where the Milky Way appeared brightest—visually close to the M6 Butterfly Cluster and the star Shaula, just above the Pipe Nebula.

It would be a long journey, even at warp speed, particularly with the need to stop regularly to expand the star maps. Most of the fleet consisted of Tiberius's large-sized globes connected into long-stringed, warp-capable starships. Each of these daisy-chained starships carried three additional, fully self-sufficient globes that would be placed on habitable planets for colonisation. Each colony would be given a squad of three armed Defence Force personnel—both as protectors in the event of unforeseen threats but would also act as a domestic police force. Their performance would be closely monitored, and they would be rotated every three months—measures designed to ensure fairness in their dealings with colonists.

All involved were certain that with the Besselite shielding, they would be immune to any attacks—whether from natural events like meteorite clusters or from rogue, Tracalonian-like civilisations. They considered it inevitable that they would encounter intelligent life.

Reluctantly, they had jointly agreed to send the *Endurance* with the Expeditionary Fleet, and one of the other new battle cruiser, the *Vanguard*, being one of three new Endurance Class battle cruisers currently in service. The new cruisers, including the *Vanguard*, were larger than *Endurance* because of the addition of an enclosed flight deck under the craft, which carried six of the new Defence Force fighters and the same number of shuttle craft. Those cruisers and fighters were well armed with Besselite torpedoes of various outputs and both ships had an armoury of Besselite shotguns and traditional blasters. Each battle cruiser had twenty Defence Force personnel to carry those weapons should the need arise.

However, it was believed that the fleet's impenetrable shielding—which prevented detection by any known scanning technology—meant their armed status would remain undetectable to any advanced civilisation scanning them. Thus, new contacts would not be alarmed about the expedition's intentions.

The Tracalonian War had left a lasting impression on many SIC members, fostering a mindset of caution rather than blind optimism.

To document this historic mission, the Council had also approved a film crew to accompany the fleet, including a director and a writer. They would produce a documentary series chronicling the expedition in real-time—something akin to Star Trek boldly going where no one had gone before, except this time, for real.

The documentary would be broadcast as a series across the Federation Colonies and a translated version would air on Tearn. It would also be featured on Tiberius's reinstated media networks on Earth.

The Federation had recently resumed advertising on Earth, encouraging migration—both to relieve still present population pressures and to ensure that if new colonies were established during the expedition, they would have a supply of willing settlers.

General Jarvice, appointed as Head of the Expedition, and her crew were about to become household superstars.

The Supreme Interplanetary Council (SIC) was composed of a representative from every colonised world, including each of the fourteen planets of the Federation, as well as Earth's new Colonies. Typically, the Head Administrator of each of these entities also served as the SIC Representative, meaning Elizabeth had her own seat at the table.

The SIC convened monthly, unless urgent matters required an emergency session. This limited schedule ensured that the role of each Representative was light enough not to interfere with their other responsibilities.

In addition to its Members, the Federation and the Tearn each had ten full-time representatives dedicated to handling the Council's administrative duties, all of whom had voting rights. The Tracalonians, while permitted to participate, were only allowed to send one non-voting representative.

As Tiberius entered the Council chamber, all Members of the SIC rose to their feet, erupting into applause. He had earned widespread appreciation for his leadership in defeating the Tracalonian threat, and there was a shared sentiment that the award he was about to receive was an insufficient tribute to his role in the War and his efforts in peacefully populating the near galaxy.

Making his way to the podium, Tiberius prepared to deliver his speech, marking the official opening of the Council and his acceptance of the award. The speech was being broadcast live across the entire Federation and Tearn, translated into all known languages. He spoke without notes.

Distinguished Members, guests, and friends.

It has been quite the journey for us all, a journey that continues today with the launch of the Expeditionary Fleet seeking out new life and new opportunities between here and the centre of our galaxy. General Jarvice, who will be leading that expedition, is with us here today.

[Jarvice stands to generous applause in appreciation of her role in the War, then sits.]

What we have already achieved is not the product of one person's effort—we have achieved our hard-fought gains together and we have united to present the universe with a better way to live and with a community, committed to equity, which is both curious to learn and observant of moral principles.

Aggression defeated…

[Uproarious cheers erupt, with Members rising to their feet in a standing ovation that lasts several minutes despite Tiberius's efforts to quell it. Once the noise settles, he continues.]

…With aggression defeated, our comradeship affirmed, and a lasting peace achieved, we can all look back with satisfaction and forward with hope in our hearts. The villainy of violence and the yoke of oppression have been subsumed by the strength of acceptance and inclusion. With validated judgement and the knowledge that unification equates to prosperity and happiness, we set forth anew into the unexplored galaxy unafraid and well prepared.

With thanks to my family, I accept this award on behalf of all of you, those assembled here today and all those brave souls watching who have taken that step into the unknown with us. The establishment of this Council is a tribute to the achievement of those people willing to share and to grow together. This Chamber represents the pinnacle of civilisation in the known universe. Its objectives are pure-minded, its focus is on the safe and prosperous development of all worlds, and it is committed to peace and individual liberties. I accept the honour of being the inaugural Chair of the CIS with gratitude and well-founded hope for our future.

www.ingramcontent.com/pod-product-compliance
Lightning Source LLC
Chambersburg PA
CBHW040525170726
48295CB00012B/341